Resort to Murder

*Also by Carolyn Hart
in Large Print:*

Death in Paradise
Sugarplum Dead
White Elephant Dead

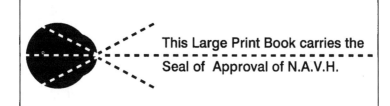

Resort to Murder

A Henrie O Mystery

Carolyn Hart

Thorndike Press • Waterville, Maine

This is a work of fiction. Names, characters, places, and incidents either are the product of the author's imagination or are used fictiously. Any resemblance to actual events, locales, organizations, or persons, living or dead, is entirely coincidental and beyond the intent of either the author or the publisher.

Published in 2001 by arrangement with William Morrow, an imprint of HarperCollins Publishers, Inc.

Thorndike Press Large Print Basic Series.

The tree indicium is a trademark of Thorndike Press.

The text of this Large Print edition is unabridged. Other aspects of the book may vary from the original edition.

Set in 16 pt. Plantin by Myrna S. Raven.

Printed in the United States on permanent paper.

Library of Congress Cataloging-in-Publication Data

Hart, Carolyn G.
    Resort to murder : a Henrie O mystery / Carolyn Hart.
      p. cm.
    ISBN 0-7862-3490-3 (lg. print : hc : alk. paper)
    1. Henrie O (Fictitious character) — Fiction. 2. Women journalists — Fiction. 3. Bermuda Islands — Fiction.
4. Large type books. I. Title.
PS3558.A676 R47 2001b
  813′.54—dc21
                                      2001034762

Resort to Murder

one

The honeycomb-weathered limestone, prickly as tiny needles, poked into my hands. I edged my sneakered feet on the narrow trail and pressed against the outward-bowing boulder. A wave crashed on the rock pinnacles beneath me, the water swishing with a thousand eager fingers into the crannies of the cliff, relentlessly sculpting the ancient fissures.

The grainy rock, the thunderous crash of the waves, the fine mist beading my face and hands, the scent of seaweed and salt water enveloped me, creating an embryonic world confined to this place, this moment, these sensations. Slowly, carefully, knowing a false step could tumble me onto the rock pinnacles below, I moved ahead, easing around the bulge.

I felt a moment of triumph when I saw a widening shelf, a three-foot indentation invisible from the rocky headland above, cupped on either side by jutting boulders. Trails lead somewhere. I'd followed the faint ridge in the rock and my gamble had paid off.

Breathing hard, I dropped shakily to the mist-slick ledge, drew my knees up under my chin and looked out at the dark surging ocean. I watched as the pink tendrils of sunrise turned the water from the blackness of night to vivid color. I don't know how long I sat, long enough for the sky to move from a milky opalescence, streaked with red and gold, to a pale cloudless blue. I looked south at the distant horizon and knew there was nothing beyond that meeting of sky and sea but hundreds of miles of water. Ships were out there, of course, and birds and ocean flotsam, but at this moment nothing moved on that endless horizon and I had this spectacular marine world to myself.

My lips quirked in a wry smile. That was always the problem, wasn't it? Wherever you go, the old saying points out, there you are. Here I was, recuperating from pneumonia, a guest at Tower Ridge House, one of Bermuda's lovelier small hotels, and yet I was not at peace. Instead, I was trying to empty my mind of fleeting images jostling and tumbling as unpleasantly as modern television's witless flip-flip-flip of pictures. I'd pushed those images away, submerged them in the moment of struggle on the rock face, savoring the challenge, glorying in the feel of sun and mist on my skin and the sensation — one I'd not had in many years — of sheer adventure.

I cocked my head, watched a flock of terns diving for fish. I'd had an instant of fun, the kind of fun you know when you are ten and the limbs of a tree beckon you high above a garden or the roller-coaster crests the rise and plunges down the slope. But I wasn't ten. I was seventy-odd and, truth to tell, had no damn business clinging to slick rock with waves crashing beneath me. Besides, now that I was alone in my retreat, the images could not be denied:

Diana slumped in the window seat, staring determinedly out of the airplane at the expanse of ocean, her young jaw set, a tear trickling down her cheek. She had her mother's delicate, almost sharp, features, her father's fair complexion and reddish-gold hair. Lovely Diana, my cherished granddaughter, facing a future she could not alter and was unwilling to accept.

Dark-haired Neal astride the bright red scooter, remembering to stay left on the steep hill, shouting, "Hey, Grandma, hold tight," his voice exuberant, but his sideways glance at his sister somber and concerned. Chunky, blunt-faced, direct, uncompromising, my adored grandson. Neal, though, was always pragmatic. What would be, would be.

And the others:

Lloyd Drake, my former son-in-law, raising his champagne glass, earnest face flushed: "To Connor, the loveliest woman I know." Lloyd had looked across the dinner table last night with doglike devotion, uncritical, impervious to the waves of dismay and hostility and anger rising from the other guests, his attention focused solely upon Connor. Lloyd was enjoying late-come love with the enthusiasm of a basketball fan at the Final Four, pumped up, eager and oblivious to criticism.

Connor Bailey fingering the quite perfect pearl choker at her slender throat, her coral nails bright as the bougainvillea spilling over the yellow stucco walls of the hotel. Connor was almost beautiful — sleek black hair cupping a Dresden-china face, flashing eyes shiny as amethyst, a lithe yet voluptuous body. What kept her from true beauty? The restless movement of her hands? The glance that demanded too much, gave too little? The unceasing hunger for admiration in her bright, beseeching eyes?

Marlow Bailey pushing up too-heavy, unfeminine tortoiseshell glasses, her dark brows drawn in a worried frown. She was near in age to Diana, but they might have sprung from different planets — Diana

10

graceful and vibrant, Marlow subdued and understated. Odd to see them in such agreement, both opposed to the wedding scheduled for Saturday afternoon.

Aaron Reed smiling ruefully at his future mother-in-law — Connor — and future stepfather-in-law — Lloyd. Last night Aaron had looked perplexed and sad when Marlow stormed from the bar, angry because Lloyd had dismissed Marlow's suggestion that they plan a ski trip in March to the Bailey family's lodge in Vail. "Not this year," Connor said firmly. "Lloyd wants to go to Barcelona." Aaron tried to patch over the moment. "Things sort themselves out." His voice was husky, pleasant and vacuous, but his eyes were sharp and thoughtful.

Jasmine Bailey, perhaps the most cheerful member of the Bailey family, staring adoringly at Lloyd, her ten-year-old face wreathed in a sunrise smile when she and Lloyd tossed a beach ball back and forth. "Lloyd, I'll bet I can catch it a hundred times," and Lloyd's good-humored laughter. "Hey, if you do, I'll go up to the pool and get you a Shirley Temple." But Marlow's glance at her little sister held a touch of pity.

Steve Jennings, the Bailey family lawyer and old friend, sipping a Dark 'n Stormy and listening attentively as Lloyd described one more time the first day he ever saw Connor: ". . . it was right there" — Lloyd pointed to the moongate at the top of the limestone steps that curved down from the first terrace to the second — "and there she was and everybody knows moongates are all about love and she had a kind of blue dress and it made me think of that song, you know the one, 'Alice Blue Gown' . . ." I looked at the moongate, knowing the common semicircles of limestone often serve as a frame for newlyweds in Bermuda — what was a wedding without a picture of the happy couple standing beneath the stone arch of a moongate? — and I wasn't sure which astounded me the most: Lloyd responding to the old tradition, or Lloyd dredging from somewhere deep in his mind a song that had been old when I was a child, or his lack of poetry in re-creating a moment that obviously meant much to him, or the unfaltering geniality of Connor Bailey's old friend. Of course, Jennings was drinking the national drink of Bermuda, a mixture of Black Seal rum and ginger beer, which argued automatic conformity or a total lack of imagination. Yet the lawyer's light eyes — tan flecked with green — were bright and shrewd and, when he looked at Lloyd, cold.

Those images were worrisome. There were other, darker moments from the bar last night. I was tired and didn't want to join the group there after dinner, but I was disturbed by the pinched look on Diana's face, so I'd forced myself to join them. I'd gained a different picture of Connor, realized that Lloyd certainly wasn't the only man in the room aware of her presence. The bartender was a darkly handsome man in his forties. His demeanor was polite, deferential, but his eyes returned again and again to Connor. Steve Jennings sat close enough to Connor that their shoulders touched. Another hotel guest, drinking at the bar by himself, half turned to watch her. He was a big man with a shock of red hair, and when he spoke, a flat Texas drawl. He moved toward our table. "Did I hear you folks mention Dallas?" He stuck out a rawboned hand. "Curt Patterson. Fort Worth." He'd even taken the trouble to repeat my name. "Henrie Collins? I have an Aunt Henrietta, but nobody would ever have called her Henrie. Her loss, ma'am." His tone was admiring. Soon he had joined us. Before long, Connor's face was flushed and her voice gay. She absorbed the attention of the men as hungrily as a sponge soaking up water. Lloyd's smile was strained. He tried twice to close the evening down and each time Connor resisted, turning to Jennings or the Texan with an eager laugh and glowing eyes.

I'd stayed until Diana pushed back her chair, said flatly, "Good night, Dad." Lloyd had scarcely noticed her departure. As we walked to our rooms, I wanted to tell Diana that some women, often without conscious effort, exert an incalculable magnetism upon men. But I wasn't sure that observation would be helpful to Diana. I doubted it would be helpful to Lloyd either. Diana and I bade each other good night, neither of us saying what was in our hearts.

This morning I'd left the hotel, but I had not left behind my concern over this wedding journey so freighted with undercurrents of unhappiness. I wished the fresh mist spraying up from the water could wash those images from my mind. Below me, a bigger wave crashed against the headland. The tide was coming in. I'd better start back. It would be trickier now, the rough rocks shining with wetness. I felt suddenly exhausted and wondered if I'd pushed too far in making the climb. It takes a long time to recover from pneumonia. I took a leaden step, pausing to rest.

I hoped it was the aftermath from pneumonia that made me feel dull and old, apprehensive and weary. Surely this lassitude was coloring my perceptions of Lloyd and Connor and their entourage even though it was reasonable that a second marriage could create enormous tension for all involved, especially the extended family.

A quick grin touched my face. Connor Bailey had taken the addition of her husband-to-be's former mother-in-law to the wedding party with grace. Or was it simply disinterest? Moreover, Connor scarcely seemed to notice when either Diana or Neal appeared. Her glance swept right over them, a negligent nod her only greeting. She'd merely given me a cool glance when we'd met at the airport in Atlanta.

I'd mightily resisted the idea of accompanying Diana and Neal to Bermuda for their father's wedding. It certainly had nothing to do with the fact of the impending marriage. Lloyd and Emily had been divorced for almost ten years. Emily had remarried two years ago and was, I believed, quite happy. It would surely be churlish to wish less for Lloyd. As for Emily and Lloyd's marriage, as with any and all marriages, I would never presume to judge why one marriage succeeds and another fails. I'd had misgivings for them from the first — Emily mercurial and passionate in her enthusiasms, Lloyd conventional to an extreme and terribly sensitive to the opinions of others. I'd never felt they understood each other. When they began to draw apart, Emily plunging into the children's world and into the community, and sometimes sponsoring unpopular causes, such as the battle against teaching creationism in the schools, and Lloyd working longer and longer hours, but always finding time for golf and eager for the approval of his conservative friends, I'd wondered if their common love for the children would be enough. It wasn't. As with all broken marriages, there was pain enough for everyone.

I'm always puzzled by society's casual attitude toward divorce. The very word is harsh and discordant, signaling breakage. But in a world where one of every two marriages ends by decree, perhaps dismissive acceptance is a kind of balm. In any event, today's world accommodates all kinds of marital and nonmarital arrangements, so perhaps my attendance at my ex-son-in-law's wedding was not that unusual.

Still, I wasn't particularly comfortable in this role and wondered again at Emily's entreaty that I come with Neal and Diana. After all, they were certainly old enough —

Neal a high school senior, Diana in her second year of college — to make the trip unaccompanied.

As I carefully began to ease around the bulging boulder, my feet toeing hard against the trail, I remembered Emily's voice, husky with strain, "Mother, please. Go with them. It's fine with Lloyd. You know he's always liked you" — I'd quirked a skeptical brow at that. Lloyd was alert and cautious around me, like a lawyer handed a contract with a codicil in Urdu. Of course, he always exercised a lawyer's caution, since that was his training. At least, he had until he saw Connor Bailey framed by a limestone arch, the soft breeze of Bermuda stirring the folds of her blue gown.

"— and the trip will be good for you since you've been so sick. A week of sun and sea and sand . . ."

I hadn't been tempted. I loved Bermuda, had spent several wonderful holidays there with Richard, my late husband, staying at lovely old Rosedon, built as a private residence in 1906 and at one time the only house in Bermuda with gaslights: walking on the pale pink sand of Elbow Beach, snorkeling in Church Bay, fishing for amberjack off Argus Bank, bicycling on the Railway Trail, playing tennis on a beautiful court above Whale Bay, climbing to the wind-swept top of Gibbs Hill Lighthouse. Yes, Bermuda was an isle for lovers, young or old, just beginning or nearing the end, first time around or tattered at the edges but clinging to hope.

"I'm too tired to travel —" I'd begun.

Emily had interrupted. "Mother, Diana needs you. Please."

I'd held the telephone, frowning. There was more than concern in Emily's voice. There was fear.

Now I clung to rock with arms that suddenly ached and wondered anew what Emily had meant. She'd given me no chance to probe, talked fast about travel dates and tickets and clothes. I didn't yet understand why Emily wanted me here. Yes, I could see clearly that Diana was unhappy about her father's remarriage, but my presence couldn't change that fact. I hoped, whatever I said or did, to encourage Diana and Neal to accept Connor. It was important for the children to be a part of their father's life. Or, to turn it around, it was important for Lloyd to be both their father and Connor's husband, just as Emily was their mother and now Warren's wife. I wanted that to happen and would do my best to help it happen. Perhaps everything would go fairly smoothly. Certainly every effort was being made to make this a happy holiday for everyone. Connor had planned a full week of entertainment for the guests.

We'd each received a small photo album. Gold letters on the red leather cover read: BERMUDA. Within the outline of a heart, Connor and Lloyd's names were intertwined in silver script. The inside front cover held a map of the coral archipelago, from Paget Island in the east to Ireland Island North in the west. On the facing page, in bright red print, was a "Programme."

First on the schedule, this morning, was an outing to the old village of St. George's. It was the nearest an American would ever come to seeing a reflection of Jamestown. St. George's was founded in 1612, five years after the earliest colony and three years after the *Sea Venture*, en route to Jamestown, was wrecked on Bermuda's reefs. I looked forward to seeing some parts of the old village again, especially the Featherbed Alley Print Shop where Bermuda's first newspaper, the *Bermuda Gazette*, was printed in 1784. And I always visited St. Peter's on Duke of York Street, the oldest continuously used Anglican church in the world. I wasn't interested in noting the blue channel where trussed victims of witch-hunts were thrown in the late sixteen hundreds. If they floated, it surely meant the Devil held them up, so they were quickly dragged out of the water and hanged. The original no-win situation.

I was a little hesitant to plunge into the activities for the wedding party. Even though I definitely was an invited guest, I felt that perhaps Connor's creativity actually hadn't been intended to include the mother of Lloyd's former wife. Although it would be fun to see St. George's again, there was almost a full week ahead of us, with plenty of free time. Excursions were planned for either morning or afternoon and the rest of the day devoted to the beach or napping or shopping or cards or golf or fishing, or whatever the guest desired. It would be easiest to take part in planned outings in the hotel minivan. But I could walk down the steep hill to the South Shore Road and catch the bus into Hamilton and transfer to a bus to St. George's. Perhaps at breakfast there might be a moment to exchange some pleasantry with Connor and I would feel less an interloper. I would decide after breakfast.

Everything, of course, comes down to attitude. Right now it was clear that some of the members of the wedding party were determined not to have a good time, no matter how beautiful the surroundings, no matter how important the occasion for Lloyd and Connor. I would do my part to encourage good humor. I edged forward. One step, two, and I would be safely back —

Tiny stones rattled over the edge of the cliff above.

"Wait up, Dinny." Neal's shout was loud.

Startled, I looked up, but I could see only the outward curve of black rock. My grandchildren were above me, on the narrow headland that overlooked the bay, a high and private place with a spectacular view of the shore and sea. Over the sounds of the water surging and gurgling among the rocks below and the caw of seabirds and the *whop-whop* of a helicopter, Diana's passionate, angry voice rang out. "I had to get out of there. If I'd looked at her one more minute, I'd have thrown something or bashed her in the face. I hate her, Neal, I hate her!"

"Oh, come on, Dinny." Neal wasn't quite the impatient male dealing with the irrational female. But close. I could have told him that his response was the equivalent of heaping gas on an open flame. But I was female.

"Neal" — her voice was an open wound — "don't you even care?"

A silence. I wondered if he shrugged. Or

stared out at the sea with puzzled eyes.

"Neal, she's awful." Diana's voice oozed disgust. "You saw how she acted last night. Like a bitch in heat. She'll ruin his life —"

"Dinny, get over it." A rock arced above me, to splash in the water, Neal venting his irritation in action. "It's going to happen." Another rock, another splash. "Dad's going to marry her and we've got to put up with it and —"

"Do we? I'm not going to the wedding. I don't have to." Her young voice was implacable. "I wish I hadn't come. I shouldn't have. I hate missing a week of classes. If she had any sense at all, she'd have set the wedding earlier, before the semester started."

"Come on, Dinny. Her kids are missing school, too. And you'll survive." His voice was dry. "Two cuts in every class? Big deal. Besides, it was that closing of Dad's that pushed the wedding into late January. And you sure wouldn't have liked it if she'd had it over Christmas."

"He spent Christmas with her anyway." The words were freighted with pain.

Neal didn't answer.

"I wish she'd die." Diana's voice was almost unrecognizable, deep and guttural like a seal's bark. "I wish —"

"Dinny, shut up." He sounded young and

22

anxious, bewildered and scared.

Diana's laugh rang out, discordant and chilling. "That would solve everything, wouldn't it? If only she'd die . . . Maybe she will. Maybe she'll swim out too far. Or fall out of the tower. Let's ask her if she'd like to go to the top. If she steps —"

"Dinny, Dinny, stop it!" His voice was now both scared and angry.

"Let go. You're hurting me. Oh, I hate you too." There was a clatter of running steps.

"Dinny . . ." A heavy sigh. "Oh, hell."

I waited until the sound of his heavy steps faded away, then resumed my cautious progress on the path, but I was scarcely aware of the bulging rock and the slapping of the waves below. I knew now why Emily had begged me to come. She should have told me . . . But I understood her silence. Sometimes, too often, perhaps, we refuse to put our fears into words because the words will make them concrete, inescapable, overwhelming.

Emily knew that her daughter's pain was deeper, wilder, than it should be. Emily was afraid of what Diana might do.

And so was I.

two

I stood beside a huge azure pot brimming with lace-white stephanotis, the sweet-smelling, trumpet-shaped wedding flower, and looked down a shallow flight of steps at the drive where a gleaming blue minivan waited, door ajar. From this vantage point, I could see the main part of the hotel, the wall marking the upper terrace, the steps leading down to the pool on the lower terrace, and look down the hillside to the tumbled blackish gray rocks and the rich sheen of turquoise water.

In the drive, a tall, slump-shouldered woman with frizzy orange hair polished a side mirror. The van glistened with care, the paint glittering with wax. On the side was the legend TOWER RIDGE HOUSE and the outline in white paint of a crenellated tower. A van and driver were available by special arrangement with the hotel. All tourists travel by taxi, van, bus, moped or on foot on Bermuda, as there are no rental cars. In fact, each Bermudian family is limited to one car, an attempt to control the number of vehicles on the narrow curving roads which are treacherously slick during rains.

The woman gave a final energetic swipe, swung toward the steps, saw me. She tucked the cloth in the pocket of her drooping brown cardigan and raised a thin hand in greeting. "Good morning, Mrs. Collins. We have another perfect day." She spoke with the cheery firmness of a nursery-school teacher, but her eyes were somber.

"Good morning, Mrs. Worrell." I smiled and started down the steps. I'd met the hotel manager upon our arrival. This morning I realized that she was older than I'd gauged, probably in her fifties, her freckled face lined and gaunt.

I reached the drive, walked toward the van. Mrs. Worrell nodded at me, then stood quite still, staring up the steps. For an instant, her blue eyes glinted, shiny and impenetrable as sunstruck metal. I felt a wave of malignancy. The feeling was gone as quickly as it came and I heard her cultivated voice raised in greeting: "Good morning, Mrs. Bailey, Mr. Drake. Everything is ready for the outing."

I stared at the manager, but now she was smiling, and though the smile didn't reach her eyes, her manner was that of a genial, impersonal hostess. Surely I had imagined that instant of hostility. I turned to look up at Connor and Lloyd. They stood by the front door: Connor, her dark hair panther-sleek, her finely sculpted features glowing with health, and, it seemed to me, uncharacteristic eagerness and hope; and Lloyd, his squarish, ruddy face burnished by the sun, his pale green eyes squinting against the brightness. Connor wore a blue chambray dress, a pale rose cashmere cardigan over her shoulders. Lloyd's bright green blazer was so crisp it shouted its newness, and his gray wool slacks had a knife-edge crease. New clothes to begin new lives.

I pushed away the thought and the sadness that swept me. Damnit, I was getting morbid. Of course everything is transitory. I knew that this day would roll into the next and the next and the next, and that Diana and Neal, coming up the stairs from the lower terrace, their movements confident and easy, would someday lose the swiftness of youth. But not right now. Right now they were young and I could take pleasure in their youth. Right now Connor and Lloyd, who were not young, had another chance to find life's most elusive prize and I wished them success.

Diana hurried up the stairs. "Dad, you've got to come down to the beach with us when we get back. Neal and I found the coolest place. You can see forever. It's way out on the headland. We thought maybe everybody — you and Connor and Marlow and Aaron and Jasmine and Steve and Grandma — could come and we could get a picture of all of us together." Her smile was enamel-bright. She looked swiftly toward Connor. Captured in the golden pool of sunlight atop the steps, Diana stood with her head flung up, graceful and invincible as her huntress namesake.

Neal, hands jammed in his pockets, gave his sister an uneasy glance. Then he pulled free a hand, raised it in an easy salute. "Hi, Dad. Connor."

Lloyd beamed. He reached out, pulled his daughter close, gave her shoulders a brisk squeeze. "That's a great idea."

Connor's porcelain-cool face softened, looked suddenly vulnerable. The beginnings of a smile lifted the corners of her coral mouth. "All of us?" She usually spoke in a tired drawl, as if the words were almost too much trouble to utter. Now the tone was wondering and pleased.

Marlow's shoes scraped on the tiles. "Won't we get enough pictures before the week's over, Mother?" Her voice was dry. "Pictures are such —" She broke off as Aaron slid his arm around her, nuzzled his face against her hair.

They were an unusual couple — Aaron remarkably handsome with curly brown hair, blue eyes, a blunt chin and merry smile; Marlow determinedly plain with her dark hair drawn sharply back, no makeup, but with arresting silver-flecked hazel eyes behind the unstylish glasses.

Aaron grinned at her. "There's no such thing as too many pictures. I want a bunch of us out on the headland. I hiked up there last night. Diana's right" — he nodded at my granddaughter — "you feel like you're on the edge of the world. I'll take a bunch. Of course," and he glanced ruefully toward Diana, "I don't have a fancy camera like Diana's" — her Leica hung from a leather strap around her neck — "but my handy little disposable will do pretty good."

Jasmine bounced up to her big sister and Aaron. She tugged on Aaron's sleeve. "Will you take my picture, Aaron? Out on the rocks? Me and Lloyd?" She swung toward her stepfather-to-be.

Connor's smile was pleased. "All of us together, Jasmine."

Aaron tousled Jasmine's short hair. "Sure, kid. I'll be chief photographer, me and my disposable." He slipped one arm through Jasmine's and the other through Marlow's and started down the steps.

The main door opened. Steve Jennings shaded his eyes from the sun. He saw Connor and his angular face creased in a lopsided smile. Jennings, though near in age to me, moved like a young Gary Cooper, confident, unhurried, commanding.

Lloyd suddenly stood straighter, but he looked small compared to Jennings.

Jennings's lazy drawl was casual. "Am I the last?" There was no apology in his tone, merely mild inquiry. "Almost skipped but thought it would be fun to see *Deliverance* again. Makes you grateful for creature comforts. I'm afraid I'd have stayed on the island." His smile was self-deprecating.

Deliverance is a replica of the ship built with the timbers from the wrecked *Sea Venture* and from planks from the island's luxuriant cedars. The tiny ship, forty feet long and nineteen feet wide, carried 132 people, crew and passengers, on its voyage from Bermuda to Jamestown in 1610. There was scarcely room to stand in its cramped interior and the cook had to manage with one big pot. But the little ship safely reached its goal.

"We're all here now." Lloyd was just a little impatient. Impatience was one of his traits. He was always on time and expected punctuality from others. "All right, everyone. Connor thought we should start with St. George's —"

Brisk steps clattered around the corner from the upper terrace.

"— because it's the oldest —"

Curt Patterson saw their group on the stairs, threw his arms wide. "People! Hey, I thought this place was dead, then I heard you folks." He had a salesman's sunny smile, an unsquashable here-I-am, I'm-your-buddy, laissez les bon temps rouler. "Hey, looks like you've got some action going. What's up?" He shoved his hand through his curly red hair, beamed at Connor.

There wasn't a woman alive who wouldn't have responded to that frank stare of admiration. Certainly not a woman like Connor. Her vivid blue eyes sparkled. Her richly red lips curved in delight. "We're on our way to St. George's." Connor gestured toward the hotel van.

The big Texan clapped his hands together. "Good deal. I've been here a half dozen times and never seen the place. But if you're going there —"

Mrs. Worrell cleared her throat. "Certainly, Mr. Patterson, if you wish to plan ahead for your party — your sister, Mrs. Elliot, and her husband, I believe — I will be happy to convey you there. Today the van is engaged by Mr. Drake." Her crisp Bermudian accent, to American ears so very British, was quite pleasant but firm.

"Oh hey, sorry. I wouldn't want to horn in." Patterson strode up the steps, stood looking down at Connor, stood perhaps an infinitesimal space too near. "Maybe some other time I'll —"

Connor reached out, touched his arm. "Oh, do come with us." Her voice was eager. "There's plenty of room." She looked down at Mrs. Worrell. "We've room, haven't we?"

"Connor." Lloyd's tone was stiff.

"Why, Lloyd, it will be fun to have Curt with us. You said yourself — the more, the merrier." She slipped her arm through Patterson's and started down the steps.

Diana gestured from below. "Hey, Dad, Neal and I will save you a seat."

In the general movement toward the van, I followed Lloyd. I wished I could tell him to grin and catch up with Connor and slip his arm around her shoulders and tell Patterson about the plans for the wedding.

But Connor would probably invite Patterson and his sister and her husband to the wedding and I didn't think that would make Lloyd happy either. At the door to the van, the big Texan took Connor's elbow.

"Here you go, little lady." And he swung up beside her. He looked over his shoulder, "Coming, Lloyd?"

Diana grabbed her dad's hand. "We're taking the back row. Those are the best seats."

A tiny frown touched Connor's face, then she shrugged and patted the seat beside her for Patterson. "I can't believe you've never been to St. George's . . ."

I ended up in a seat by myself two rows in front of Neal and Diana and Lloyd. Marlow and Jasmine and Aaron sat behind me. I looked out at the masses of green shrubbery and occasional spots of color as the van curved on the twisting narrow road. Hibiscus blooms even in January, but the riot of color that I always remember of Bermuda would begin in March, especially the bougainvillea with blooms of purple, magenta and salmon. As I took pleasure in the lovely pastel houses, I wondered at the human capacity for stupidity. And boorishness. Patterson's booming laugh was exuberant. Connor giggled like a schoolgirl.

As the van veered from Collectors Hill Road into Middle Road, I half-turned, wondering about Lloyd and the children. Diana was talking to her father, her voice light and cheery, her face far too satisfied. I wanted to catch a moment alone with Diana. There was no way — no good way — to reconcile Diana's outburst on the headland and her apparently friendly overture to Connor on the hotel steps. One had to be false and I had no doubt which. What did Diana intend? What was her objective? Why corral everyone in our group for a photo session on the headland? That was the very place where this morning Diana had wished for Connor to die. I didn't like remembering that moment, but I knew I had to talk to Diana. The sooner, the better.

If I hadn't been uneasy about Diana and concerned for Lloyd, I would have enjoyed the drive, the incredible vistas of the sea, the cottages in pastels softer than summer sunsets, and Mrs. Worrell's brisk commentary. She recommended future day trips to Spittal Pond and the Bermuda Aquarium, regretted that the Leamington Caves were closed but suggested a visit to the Crystal Caves, and pointed out a majestic old tamarind tree, a favorite lounging spot of Mark Twain, who thought Bermuda might well be preferable to heaven. And I listened to the snatches of conversation swirling within the van:

Connor: ". . . early Saturday afternoon and I hope the weather . . ."

Patterson: ". . . perfect spot to get married . . ."

Marlow: ". . . the last time we went down, there was a huge squid . . ."

Aaron: ". . . like to fish for barracuda . . ."

Jasmine: ". . . said there would be trifle tonight. I love . . ."

Neal: ". . . look at that catamaran . . ."

Diana: ". . . remember the time we . . ."

But not a word from Lloyd.

The van reached the causeway and I knew we were almost to St. George's. Mrs. Worrell pointed out Mullet Bay, where boats seized by privateers were held in the eighteen hundreds. At the entrance to the old town, we passed a pink-walled flower bed chock-full of purple pansies. The tourist area would be jammed in summer, but on this cool January day, there was plenty of parking available in the Town Square. January didn't offer fabulous blooms. It did offer quiet and peace. As we climbed off the van, Mrs. Worrell pointed toward the Globe Hotel. "We'll start there. It's now the Bermuda National Trust Museum. Actually, it was built in 1699 to serve as the Governor's House and . . ."

I lagged behind the group moving toward the softly pink building. I had no wish to watch Lloyd's grim face. I wanted to grab his arm and say, "Laugh, Lloyd. Connor doesn't mean any harm and this is going to be the pattern of your lives." I was equally ready to grab Diana's arm and give her a good shake and say, "Don't gloat, Dinny." I couldn't at this moment do either. Moreover, Lloyd, hurt and angry, would neither listen nor understand. As for Diana, I'd get only a toss of her head and a bland expression.

I stopped. Neal and Diana had already disappeared into the building. I reached out a hand to brace myself against the rose-pink wall.

"Mrs. Collins, are you all right?" Steve Jennings was beside me, a firm hand on my elbow.

I blinked. I was dizzy, likely the result of worry combined with fatigue and too little breakfast and the lingering malaise from the pneumonia. I'd not had any appetite when I came in from my early rocky excursion. I was still hearing the ugly tone in Diana's voice, "I wish she'd die."

Jennings and I were alone on the quiet street. "Would you like to rest for a moment? There's a café in the next block. We can get some tea."

He kept a firm hand on my elbow as we walked up the cobbled street. When we settled at an outside table overlooking the harbor, I ordered coffee and a sweet roll. Jennings chose tea.

As the waitress served us, Jennings gave me a rueful smile. "Did you have a bad night's sleep, too?"

I'd slept the heavy, weighted sleep of one recently ill. I shook my head. "No. Actually, I slept deeply." I'd still felt tired upon awakening. "Is your room not comfortable?" I was surprised. The block of rooms reserved for the Drake-Bailey party was contiguous and I assumed all the rooms were as lovely as mine. The appointments were charming: white wicker furniture, rose walls, paintings of Bermudian scenes including the steep, stepped, brilliantly white roofs, Gombey dancers, and the ever-changing sea. The paintings could only dimly reflect the beauty of the tiny country. I had only to step onto my balcony for a dramatic view — the white tower on the ridge to my right which gave the hotel its name, the dazzling gardens below, the terraces and pool, and then, always, the rugged black rocks and sapphire sea.

"Oh, the room's fine." He rubbed his cheek, looked at me sharply. "So you weren't awakened? I thought you might have been. I believe our rooms are next to

36

each other. I'm in room twenty-six."

"No. I'm in room twenty-two." Diana was in room 24 and Neal in room 20. I sipped the strong, hot invigorating coffee, relished the spurt of energy from the sugary roll, and wondered what excitement I'd missed. I spent almost fifty years as a reporter, so I'm not shy about asking questions. "What happened? Loud guests?" That seemed unlikely. The small hotel was genteel, and none of the guests I had seen appeared to be the sort likely to erupt with late-night festivities.

Jennings frowned. "Somebody knocked on my door. About two A.M. I thought you might have heard it."

"No." If I heard the knocking, the noise had merged into my dreams — dreary, tiring dreams of locked doors and blocked hallways, the subconscious signaling fatigue and frustration.

"It was quite loud. And sustained." Jennings no longer looked genial. "It took me a moment to wake up."

I understood. Two A.M. is not an hour when most of us awaken easily.

"When I got to the door, there was no one there." He frowned. "I thought I heard running steps. I slipped on some clothes and came out to the upper terrace."

"Was that wise?" I asked mildly.

He shrugged. "Oh, it's very safe here. Besides, if anyone meant harm, they'd scarcely knock on the door and disappear. Anyway, it made me mad. Like a kid's trick, you know, knocking on the door and running. But at two o'clock in the morning . . ."

No, that wasn't an hour when kids were likely to be out playing pranks.

"When I reached the terrace, I looked toward the garden —" He broke off, his silvery brows drawn in a puzzled frown.

I waited, but he seemed to have come to a full stop. "You saw something odd."

His head jerked up. "How did you know?"

I don't claim psychic abilities, but I've read a lot of faces. "You'd just been awakened. You were half mad, half worried. You didn't see a person or animal. But you saw something that puzzled you." And worries you.

"Oh, it was late. I was half asleep." He almost seemed to be talking to himself, persuading himself. Abruptly, he forced a smile. "Nothing worth mentioning. Now, tell me, Mrs. Collins, is this your first trip to Bermuda?"

If Steve Jennings hadn't resisted describing what he had seen, I might not have been concerned. But I didn't like the possi-

38

bility, which occurred to me at once, that the rousing knock on the door might have been intended for Diana's room. Surely she would not open the door without checking the peephole. But she might assume that her brother was in the hall . . .

I definitely wanted to know what Steve Jennings saw in the deserted garden late last night. I ignored his question. "Perhaps you should inform Mrs. Worrell —"

His interruption was sharp and final. "I couldn't do that. Absolutely not."

How odd. Wasn't the manager the first person who should be informed if someone played a malicious prank on a guest? And "malicious" seemed apt. Being awakened late at night to find no one at the door is disturbing. But Jennings's response to my suggestion was immediate and I thought its sharpness and finality out of proportion. Why would it be unacceptable to inform the manager? I was dealing with nuances I didn't understand.

Jennings shrugged. "Sorry I brought it up." His tone was brisk. "Believe me, it doesn't matter —"

Didn't it? What had he seen in the garden? Why wouldn't he tell me? After all, my grandchildren were staying in the hotel. I intended to be certain no danger threatened them. But clearly I would not find out anything from Jennings. However, I had no compunction about speaking to Mrs. Worrell.

"— and I'm sure it won't happen again. Is this your first visit to Bermuda?"

This time I answered his question. "No." I remembered the warmth of the sand beneath our feet as Richard and I walked hand in hand on Windsor Beach, alone together with only the crash of the surf and the cry of the seabirds and the sand that shimmered a delicate, elegant pink in the late-afternoon sunlight.

Perhaps it was a result of my recent illness, perhaps it came from the turmoil of emotions accompanying this journey, but sudden tears burned my eyes. I do know that grief ambushes the heart without warning, triggered by a scent, a sound, a memory.

Jennings looked at me kindly.

I blinked and managed a smile. "My late husband, Richard, and I came here several times. We always stayed at the Rosedon. The garden . . ." The Rosedon's garden is extraordinarily beautiful. Richard and I often walked just after dawn to watch the sun spill over the horizon and touch the gorgeous plants with glory.

Jennings looked away. It was a moment before he spoke. "I've never known whether memories help or hurt."

I drank my coffee. "Both."

We looked at each other with understanding.

He stared toward the water, but I knew his gaze went far beyond St. George's Harbour. "This is the first time I've been back since . . ." He stopped, took a sip of his tea. "My wife, Ellen, died last April. Ellen and I started coming here almost thirty years ago with R.T. and Margaret. Margaret was R.T.'s first wife. They were only married a few years when she died. R.T. worked like a madman but I was always able to persuade him to come to Bermuda with Ellen and me. When he married Connor —"

I attached the identities to the names. Ellen had been Steve Jennings's wife. R.T. must have been R. T. Bailey, Connor's husband. R.T. had been married previously to Margaret, who predeceased him.

"— we picked up the old habit, Ellen and I and R.T. and Connor. We didn't come the year that R.T. died, but the next year Ellen and I encouraged Connor to come with us. We continued to come every January. I suppose we took Connor under our wing. She was much younger than R.T. and was left a widow very early. Actually" — his eyes narrowed — "I was surprised when Connor and Lloyd decided to get married here."

We were silent. I was curious whether he would explain what he meant, but he simply continued to look out at the glittering blue water. Jennings had piqued my curiosity. I didn't have faces for Ellen or R.T. or Margaret, but they pressed against the edge of my consciousness. I'd given no thought at all to Connor Bailey's past when I agreed to attend the wedding. I knew only that she was a widow with two daughters. I'd had no idea that she and Lloyd had met here, nor had I known that this was a favorite resort of her first marriage.

"Did Connor and her first husband stay at Tower Ridge House?" I finished my coffee, shaded my eyes against the sun.

"Always." His tone was casual.

"Are there children from R.T.'s first marriage?" I was guessing there were not, or surely they would be in attendance.

Jennings confirmed my guess. "No. R.T. and Margaret were married such a short time before her death. And he didn't meet Connor until he was almost fifty. It came as quite a surprise to everyone when he remarried." Jennings looked amused. "R.T. was a tough old bird, but Connor bowled him over. She was just out of college and had her first job with an ad agency that was doing a corporate promotion featuring R.T. and she was assigned to follow him around for a couple of weeks. By the end of a month, he'd decided to marry her."

I wondered at Jennings's bemused tone. Had he opposed that long-ago marriage?

Perhaps the lawyer sensed my question or perhaps he wanted to keep talking about anything other than what he'd seen last night in the garden. He cleared his throat. "I thought it would be a disaster. But R.T. knew what he was doing. Connor thought he was wonderful. And he decided Connor needed looking after and he was the man for the job. She took to his protective manner like a duck to water. And the greatest happiness, of course, was the children. R.T. loved his kids. He thought Marlow was the neatest person he ever met and he was proud of Jasmine being a towhead the way he'd been as a kid. And he loved bringing them here. I think that's why Connor decided to keep coming back, even after he was gone."

"And this is where Lloyd and Connor met?"

"Last year." The words were clipped, his face impassive. Was he remembering that meeting or was he thinking of his wife's last visit here and her death only a few months later? Suddenly, he lifted a hand, his face breaking into an easy smile. "Here they come." He stood.

Jasmine Bailey ran toward us, her hand outstretched. "Uncle Steve, look what I got!" She raced up to us and opened pudgy fingers to reveal a silver charm of the *Sea Venture*. "Lloyd got it for me."

"That's wonderful, honey." He patted her head.

We were swept up by the others. Connor was gesturing energetically to Lloyd, but the big Texan was close at hand, still booming. I felt sorry for Lloyd, wished my granddaughter would stop frowning, and continued to battle occasional waves of dizziness. Yet these were swift, surface thoughts. During the rest of our visit in the narrow streets of old St. George's, despite the pleasure of seeing an altar in St. Peter's and knowing that human hands lovingly fashioned it more than 376 years ago, and my disappointment that the Featherbed Alley Print Shop wasn't open, I was preoccupied by my talk with Steve Jennings. I kept wondering about a knock in the dead of night and something glimpsed in the silent garden.

three

Low-hanging metallic-looking clouds had turned the sky a pale gray. The wind was picking up, whipping whitecaps as far as the eye could see and roiling the water over the reef. I steadied myself against the breeze, strong enough to pluck at my hair, tug at my clothes.

Connor's dress flattened against her. "Oh, it's too windy. Let's go back." She lifted her hands to press against her wind-ruffled hair.

"Oh, Mom, it's fun!" Jasmine exclaimed.

We bunched at the beginning of the headland, everyone except Aaron. He strode exuberantly toward the narrow point, moving through a moongate to stand at the farthest edge. He peered over the side. "Hey." He turned toward us, gestured with his arm. The wind lifted his brown curls, ballooned his jacket, flared his trousers. "The waves are huge!" He shouted to be heard over the crash of the surf.

"Come on, Dad." Diana urged everyone forward. "It won't take long. And this will be a picture no one will ever forget." The breeze tangled her strawberry curls, touched her cheeks with pink.

Neal laughed. "We can title it 'Waiting for Rain.'"

Jasmine pointed out to sea. "Look at the waves coming over the reef." She darted to Lloyd. "How close can we go to the edge?"

Connor reached out. "Stay close, Jasmine."

Lloyd laughed, took Jasmine's hand. "Let's take a look." He called over his shoulder, "It's okay, Connor, I'll keep her safe." He and Jasmine stepped through the moongate, went almost to the edge.

Steve Jennings grinned at Connor. "The sooner we get it done, the sooner we can retreat with dignity." But his voice was good-humored.

Connor looked out at the darkening water. "All right, all right." She was suddenly amused, an impish smile lighting her face. "It's a good thing I'm going to the beauty shop Friday."

For the first time I had an inkling of Connor Bailey's charm. I was glad I'd decided to make the climb and be part of the picture even though I'd almost stayed behind to rest. But I hadn't wanted to disappoint Diana and I hoped to catch her for a quiet chat after the picture taking was done. Diana had announced her plan at lunch. "I have it all arranged. George will come up with us and take the pictures." George was a lanky young Canadian who worked at the hotel as a waiter. He had a mop of light brown hair, a peeling, sunburned nose and an agreeable smile. Now he held Diana's Leica comfortably in one big, rawboned hand and looked expectantly toward her.

Diana waved her hand. "We'll stand in a semicircle looking out to the ocean. Dad, you and Connor in the center. Mr. Jennings next to Connor —"

Lloyd's face was rigid for an instant.

"— Marlow next to him, then Aaron and Jasmine. Neal, you can be next to Dad, then Grandma and me. George, why don't you go to the moongate and look toward us."

As we sorted ourselves out, stepping carefully because the rocky surface fell away sharply on both sides, George edged past us, stood with his back to the moongate. When George lifted the camera, Diana called out, "What's in the background? Does the hotel show?"

George peered through the viewfinder. "Some of it. Mostly you see the tower . . . Hey." He lowered the camera, squinted toward the hotel. "There's something on the platform of the tower . . . no, no, I'm wrong.

I thought I saw something white —"

Steve Jennings's head jerked around to look up the hill at the tower. He wasn't alone. Connor, too, her face stiff, swung to look. She remained half-turned, face taut, intent on the tower.

"Okay, everybody. Look this way," George instructed. "Now come a little closer together . . ." He lifted the camera.

I slipped my arms around my grandchildren, felt their arms around me, and looked toward George.

George took one step nearer, another. "Smile . . ."

Obediently, we smiled.

The camera clicked. "One more for luck." George snapped another picture.

As we moved apart, Connor gripped Lloyd's arm. Head down, she was tugging him along the narrow path.

Steve Jennings looked after Connor and Lloyd, his face creased in concern. But it wasn't Jennings's expression that disturbed me. I could see Diana clearly. Her green eyes flashed; her lips curved in triumph. She gave her brother a swift, utterly satisfied glance, then moved quickly along the path. Neal frowned.

Jasmine tugged at her sister's arm. "Did you hear George? He said —"

"Hush, Jasmine." Marlow's voice was sharp.

I was the last one off the headland. I followed the others slowly down the craggy path to the sand. We picked our way across the boulder-strewn beach to a gridded cement walkway, avoiding the mounds of sargassum seaweed that smelled of rot and drew tiny flies in whirling clouds. The walkway was steep. It led from the beach to a hard dirt path that sloped up toward the hotel beneath the interlocking branches of leathery-leaved bay grapes that created a tunnel of greenery. The pathway was always dim. Now the clouds had turned the sky pewter-gray, and the tunnel was almost dark.

I stopped to rest midway up the long slope, perhaps a city block in length. I heard the others far ahead. I felt cut off from their cheerful holiday chatter. I wasn't cheerful. I was disturbed. That picture-taking session on the headland had been planned by my granddaughter and I was afraid the object had been to distress Connor. When George claimed to have seen something white near the tower, Connor was startled. Perhaps even frightened. I wanted to know why. I wanted to know what George thought he saw. I wanted to know why Connor Bailey and Steve Jennings stared at the tower. And these questions reminded me of Steve's refusal to tell me what he saw last night in the garden. The tower dominated the ridge beyond the garden. Most of all, I wanted to know whether my granddaughter had engineered a family photograph on the wind-swept headland solely because the tower loomed in the background.

I had the hotel hallway to myself. It didn't matter, of course, whether anyone saw me, but I wanted to be alone to make a quiet survey. The others had scattered after the picture session. Lloyd, Connor, and Steve had taken a cab into the capital city of Hamilton to shop at Trimingham's. The large old department store had the same fusty charm as Woodward and Lathrop's in Washington, D.C., in the 1950s. The young people had sped off on their mopeds. I would try to find Diana upon their return. Jasmine had refused to go shopping, insisting she'd be fine at the hotel and wanted to play in the pool until the rain came. It rains often in Bermuda, sometimes with force and fury, more often a gentle, steady downpour that lasts a little while and then the day brightens again.

I studied the silent corridor. There were entrances at either end of the hallway. This two-story building sat atop a ridge, separate from the smaller main house. Our rooms were on the second floor facing the ocean. I was in room 22, Neal in room 20, Diana in room 24, Steve Jennings in room 26, and the rest of the party on down the hall: Aaron in room 28, Marlow and Jasmine in room 30, Connor in room 32, Lloyd in room 34. I'd been a little surprised that Connor and Lloyd were in separate, although adjoining, rooms. I wondered who made that decision and thought it displayed remarkable delicacy, considering today's mores. I guessed that the Drake-Bailey party were the only guests on this floor and that the opposite rooms were empty. There were perhaps a dozen or so other guests at the hotel and I thought most of them were in the main building. January was, of course, the off-season.

Jennings said he'd dressed last night after the knock on his door awakened him, and hurried out to the upper terrace. I walked down the hall. A push bar opened the door. Outside, I stopped on the step and noted the small placard which informed that the doors were locked after 9 P.M. but would open to a room key. That indicated access to the building after 9 P.M. was restricted to guests or hotel employees. Of course, an in-

51

truder might enter through the balcony of an unoccupied room although the sliding door should be locked.

I walked slowly down the steps. I had a choice at the bottom. One walkway led west to the main house past a wall covered with bougainvillea. A second walkway led south to the upper terrace. I took the south walk. The terrace was a broad grassy expanse between the hotel and another rock wall that marked a drop-off. I looked over the wall at the swimming pool on the lower terrace. No one was in the water. Despite the gray skies and freshening wind, two leathery-skinned middle-aged women in swimsuits rested on deck chairs, one knitting, the other immersed in a book. I welcomed the warmth of a cashmere cardigan and wool slacks. No doubt they were Canadians.

Jennings said he came to the main terrace, then looked toward the garden. It was there that he broke off, refused to say more.

The garden sloped to the east, beds of flowers and shrubs running downhill, then up. The poinsettias blazed a vivid coral and blue petunias wavered in the wind. My gaze rose to the tower that stood at the crest of the ridge, overlooking the garden. Despite the sweep of flowers and shrubs, the eye was drawn immediately to the thirty-foot-tall, shining white tower. The parapet at the top was crenellated, so the tower had the appearance of a battlement on an English castle.

I walked through the garden, down and up the hillsides, past orange blossoms of an African tulip tree, poinsettias and lacy green ferns, always keeping the tower in view. I paused to rest midway up the far slope. Moist air pressed against me. Rain could not be far distant. I started on, picking up my pace. The wind was brisk when I reached the base of the tower. I circled, looking for an entrance.

I don't know whether there was a sound or whether I simply sensed movement above me. I looked up and jerked back as a white shape fell toward me. A round face poked over the side of the parapet, then quickly disappeared. I looked down. A big bed pillow in a smudged white case lay on the flagstones. I left it there and moved on. The door to the tower, on the far side, was ajar. I pulled it wider, stepped onto a stone floor. Uneven circular steps curled upward.

I didn't relish climbing the steep stairs. There was utter silence above. I wished for a flashlight, but there was a patch of lighter gray far above where daylight streamed into the tower from the openings to the platform.

I started up. I made no effort to be quiet. "Hello!" I called out.

I was midway to the top when a young voice responded warily, "Hello."

I was out of breath when I reached the platform. The wind made an eerie sound in the rafters, rustled the shrubbery far below, stirred Jasmine Bailey's short blond curls as she leaned against the parapet.

She cut her eyes toward me when I stepped out onto the platform.

I doubted it would get us very far for me to admonish her about the pillow or question whether her mother would want her to be in the tower dropping pillows or suggest she was rather a distance from the hotel. Instead, after catching my breath, I said quizzically, "An experiment?"

Her round face creased in a pleased smile. "Oh, yes. That's where Mr. Worrell landed, you know."

"I didn't know." I came up beside her, looked over the edge of the stone wall at the pillow far below. Mr. Worrell. Steve Jennings had insisted he couldn't mention what he had seen in the garden to Mrs. Worrell. "Down there?"

Jasmine wriggled with eagerness. "Right there. And now he's a ghost. George says he came last night. At least, George thinks it was him because there was something white and Mr. Worrell always wore white."

"Really." I kept my tone casual, but I was surprised. It seemed apparent that the young waiter was quite willing to provide information to hotel guests, even young ones. "Did you know Mr. Worrell?"

Jasmine said importantly, "He sang songs in the bar. He was married to Mrs. Worrell, but she's the one who takes care of the hotel. And he fell out of the tower and killed himself."

I doubted that Mrs. Worrell would be pleased to hear that an employee had been telling a very young guest that her dead husband appeared as a ghost at the tower. And now I understood Steve Jennings's reluctance to discuss disturbances in the garden with Mrs. Worrell. And I was afraid I now knew why Diana planned the picture session out on the point.

Jasmine peered over the edge at the pillow. "George says ghosts come back to the place where they died if they have unfinished business." She glanced at me, her eyes bright with inquiry. "Why do you suppose Mr. Worrell's come back?"

"I don't know." The first fine drops of rain spattered on us. "Maybe we'd better go down and get the pillow. You don't want to sleep on a wet pillow tonight."

She giggled. "I'd just trade with Marlow. Wouldn't that surprise her!" The little girl whirled and plunged for the steps. I hoped she'd hold on to the railing, but the hurried scuff of her sneakers indicated a rapid descent.

I followed more slowly, chilled not by the wet wind on the parapet but by the child's casual announcement: "That's where Mr. Worrell landed, you know."

Jasmine stood in the doorway, clutching the pillow, looking out at the steady sweep of rain. I hoped the moped riders were safe and dry and would seek shelter until the rain passed.

Jasmine plopped the pillow on the bottom step of the staircase. "Would you like to sit down?"

The pillow was long and oversized and must have been a challenge for her to wrestle all the way to the tower. I grinned. "Thanks." I patted the pillow beside me. "We can share."

She plopped down beside me, regarded me curiously. "You know," she confided, "you don't look like a skeleton."

I'd lost some weight from the pneumonia and was a bit bonier than usual. I knew I seemed very old to Jasmine, my dark hair streaked with silver and my eyes deep-socketed in a lined face. But I had an inkling she'd overheard someone else's comment. "The skeleton at the feast," I murmured.

"That's what Mom said." She peered at me.

So Connor had indeed taken note of the presence of her husband-to-be's former mother-in-law. That was surely more normal than her apparently casual acceptance. I smiled and said easily, "Oh, that's just an expression, Jasmine." But, of course, it was Death who was the unseen companion at merry feasts. "Now tell me about your experiment. Did Mr. Worrell die a long time ago?"

"Oh, no." She hunched forward eagerly. "It was last year. We were here. Mr. Worrell fell out of the tower late one night." Her face screwed up in disgust. "I didn't hear a thing! I was asleep. Aaron said he'd had too much to drink. Anyway, Mr. Worrell fell over the edge. They said it was an accident. The police came and everything. All of the guests went over to the Southampton Princess the day of the funeral, so Mrs. Worrell could have everybody here. Have you ever been to that hotel? It's huge. There were Gombey dancers and it was so loud I thought my ears were going to burst. We left two days later."

"Did you like Mr. Worrell?" I looked at

her curiously. Her report had all been delivered in the same tone, Mr. Worrell's fall given the same emphasis as the loud Gombey dancers.

The excitement fled. "I did like him." She spoke assertively and I gathered there were those who had not. "He was nice to the kids and he had a big laugh. Not like Mrs. Worrell. She frowns all the time. I don't think she likes kids. And she always seemed mad at him. She was always frowning" — Jasmine turned her lips down into a scowl — "when he talked to my mom. Of course," and she spoke proudly, "he was in love with my mother. Everybody always is."

I doubted Jasmine was quite yet into an adolescent girl's preoccupation with sex. There was no hint of adult understanding in her pronouncement. I guessed she'd heard someone else comment on her mother's attractiveness. Steve Jennings?

The rain pattered softly. I pictured the water sluicing down the steep-stepped roofs to swirl down pipes to the catchment, lifeblood for a remote island without springs or streams. "I'm sure everyone finds your mother very charming."

She cocked her head at me. "Uncle Steve doesn't like Lloyd." She scuffed her toe on the stone floor, her face suddenly forlorn.

"Marlow doesn't either. But Lloyd's really nice. He plays Monopoly with me." Her eyes were suddenly shrewd. "I think he lets me win. Of course, he isn't funny like Mr. Worrell —"

No, serious, striving Lloyd was not the least bit funny.

"— but Mr. Worrell could be kind of mean. I heard him tell his wife she was about as much fun as a wooden leg. She turned away and I think she was trying not to cry." Her face crinkled into puzzlement. "But when he died, she cried and cried." Jasmine stared out at the curtain of rain.

"And George says he's come back?"

Jasmine twisted to look up the curving stairway. "Yes. Maybe if I stay up real late I can see him."

I almost told Jasmine ghosts didn't exist. But she wouldn't have believed me. No, I didn't believe in ghosts, but that was unimportant. What mattered was the effort being made to create the ghost of Mr. Worrell. Who was doing it, and why? I had no idea. I only knew that something dark and ugly and devious was near at hand. Moreover, my granddaughter had involved herself and was apparently trying to exploit the unhappy history of the tower.

Oh, Diana. It was time we talked.

four

I carried a beach towel up the steps from the pool area to the upper terrace and dried a rain-wet wooden chair. Water still gurgled softly down drain spouts, but the rain had ended, one of Bermuda's quick, gentle showers. The sun felt warm. It might be winter in Bermuda, too cool for the chirp of the tree frogs and the blooms paltry compared to those of spring and summer, but it was definitely summery compared to the weather in my small-town Missouri home in January. My spirits lightened as the pale yellow walls of the hotel glowed from sunlight. I settled in the chair, listening to the splashes in the swimming pool on the lower terrace. From here, I would also be able to hear the mopeds curling uphill to the parking area near the entrance to the hotel.

I pulled a paperback from my pocket. I'd found an old copy of *Around the World in Eighty Days* in the book cabinet in the hotel drawing room. I was midway through. I began to read, but closed the book in a few minutes. The charm of the familiar story was lost on me today.

A motor chugged. I rose, dropped the book into my pocket and strolled toward the curve in the wall that overlooked the drive. As I looked down, Lloyd and Connor stepped out of an elegant old-fashioned, London-style cab. Lloyd reached into the backseat and lifted out four cardboard cylinders.

Connor smiled and held out her arms. "I'll take them up."

"Are you sure?" He was eager to help, his good humor obviously restored by a sojourn alone with Connor. I hoped Curt Patterson wasn't anywhere near.

"Yes. I'll rest a bit, then meet you for tea." She gave him a swift, sweet smile.

Lloyd looked after her as she moved gracefully up the main stairs, his square face softened by love.

I backed away from the wall, returned to my chair, thinking idly that Steve had apparently stayed in Hamilton, that the kids weren't back yet, that Lloyd and Connor had likely bought prints of Bermuda scenes to take home as keepsakes of their wedding journey, and most of all, that Lloyd was very much in love.

I sank into a reverie, my mind a collage of memories: Emily's wedding day; my first glimpse of Diana as a tiny, wispy-haired baby; Richard and I one perfect October day in Mexico City; Neal running into his grandfather's arms. The common thread was faces full of love. I was far away in time and place.

"Henrie." Lloyd's voice was cheerful.

I jolted to the reality of place.

"I'm sorry. I didn't mean to startle you." Lloyd dropped into the chair beside me. "Are you enjoying the trip?" His glance was hopeful but tentative.

This was likely the first time in more than a decade that we'd been alone together. It had taken some courage for him to approach me. Also, of course, Lloyd was one of those persons who always want to be around people. Perhaps an ex-mother-in-law was preferable to solitude. "Absolutely." I spoke warmly. "I'm so glad I was able to come. It was very kind of you to invite me to accompany the children."

"My pleasure." His tone was expansive. And pleased.

"It's truly lovely here." I spread my hand to encompass the hotel and the terrace and the garden. "I hadn't realized this was where you and Connor met."

Once again, happiness transformed his face. The slight puffiness under his eyes, the heaviness of his jowls, all the telltale traces of middle age disappeared in the eagerness of his gaze, the joyous curve of his lips. "Right there." He pointed to the moongate and the steps leading down to the lower terrace. "That's where I saw her."

"Was it love at first sight?" My tone was gently gibing.

Serious, intense Lloyd simply nodded. "Yes. Yes, it was. That's the way it should be, you know. One day you walk along and suddenly you see someone and you know nothing will ever be the same, that the future's going to be different and wonderful. It happened for us." His light green eyes glowed. "And the neat thing is, the same thing happened for Marlow and Aaron on Elbow Beach the year before. They just happened to be on the beach at the same time. Both of them came here for spring break and they'd never met on the campus even though they both were in school at Emory. It's fate, you see."

I was long past belief in fate or karma, but I was glad Lloyd had a romantic illusion that pleased him. He was so open, his love there for everyone to see. There are none so vulnerable as those who love. I reached out, patted his hand.

He turned his fingers, held mine. "That's nice of you. You're a very nice person. To wish me well."

I was not at all sure how nice I was. But I was too old to be critical. One of the surprising by-products of age is empathy for everyone — the right, the wrong, the good, the bad, the best, the worst, the kind, the cruel, never approving evil or ugliness or selfishness but recognizing the corrosive cost to those in the grip of darkness. "I hope everyone will wish you and Connor happiness."

His grasp slackened. He lifted his hand, brushed his fingers against his face as if smoothing away a cobweb. "Yeah."

The single word told me that serious, intense Lloyd was well aware of the unhappiness swirling around them.

I saw no point in talking about the resistance Lloyd and Connor faced and I doubted he wanted to discuss that with me. I said briskly, "What prompted you to come to Bermuda last year?"

"Golf." Happily, he described his foursome and some of their previous journeys. "One of the guys had stayed here before. The hotel has privileges at some of the best courses. Even the Mid Ocean Golf Course." There was awe in his voice. "Actually, I'd wanted to stay at the Southampton Princess. That's a great course, too. But thank

God, we didn't. The very first night we got here I saw Connor. By the third night, I knew I wasn't going to let her get away from me." He spoke in a possessive-caveman tone, but it was more endearing than over-bearing.

"That must have posed a logistics problem." My tone was light.

Lloyd never met a joke he recognized. "I flew to Atlanta every weekend. It's a direct flight from Dallas."

I'd not given any thought to the aftermath of Lloyd and Connor's marriage. Lloyd was a partner in a small law firm in Dallas, his specialty corporate mergers. Connor and her daughters lived in Buckhead, a posh Atlanta suburb. I'd known she was a widow. Since my talk with Steve Jennings, I realized R. T. Bailey must have been very successful. I didn't know what kind of company he had owned. It wasn't, as a matter of fact, any of my business.

"Will Connor and the children move to Dallas?" It was a casual question.

For an instant, the brightness left Lloyd's face and he looked more than middle-aged. He looked lost. He cleared his throat. "Connor's lived in Atlanta all her life. Jasmine's in school and Connor doesn't want to upset her. And Marlow said they couldn't ever move from their house."

Instead, Lloyd could close down his law practice and lose his golf foursome. What price love?

Lloyd said loudly, a man reassuring himself, "I'll have plenty to do. Connor says there's lots to look after with her properties and the business. Steve's been handling all of that, but I can give her advice. And I'll be looking around. There will be opportunities."

Opportunities. That sounded to me like the old corporate line: "Mr. Who's-it has left to pursue other opportunities." Sure.

I smiled reassuringly. "Everything will work out." Yes, it was inane, but bromides paper over moments that would otherwise be too uncomfortable.

Lloyd's glance was grateful. Then he scowled.

I looked at him in surprise but his eyes, sharp now, gazed past me. I turned and glimpsed the young waiter, George, carrying a heavy silver tray covered with a damask cloth.

"I don't want to cause trouble" — Lloyd's voice was tight with anger — "but Jasmine told me something that George said to her. And if Connor hears about it . . . Lloyd shook his head. "I'd talk to Mrs. Worrell, but it's a damned awkward situation."

"Mrs. Worrell appears rather tense. Do you know what's troubling her?" This morning the manager had looked up the main steps and given Connor a look of utter loathing.

Lloyd gazed carefully about. "You never know when Mrs. Worrell's going to pop around a corner. Nice woman, but like having a death's-head at a party. Damn awkward."

Death's-head. I felt a moment's chill. When Jasmine chattered about the skeleton at the feast, I'd been amused. There was nothing amusing about Lloyd's observation.

He leaned closer to me, dropped his voice. "Of course you wouldn't know anything about it. There was a very unfortunate accident here last year. It was awful for Connor because the fellow'd been a bit too friendly. I was about ready to put him in his place, but I was glad later that I hadn't said anything. Poor devil got drunk and fell out of the tower. Or jumped. Mrs. Worrell's husband. A blowhard."

Jasmine had liked Mr. Worrell. Obviously, Lloyd had not.

Lloyd looked suddenly forlorn and uncertain. "Maybe I shouldn't have insisted we come here for the wedding. But this is where we met . . ." His voice trailed off.

I understood. Lloyd was sentimental. That didn't surprise me. Oddly, I was swept by a mixture of anger and compassion, anger at the forces combining to ruin this special journey for Lloyd and compassion for his very human hunger to love and be loved. I wanted everything to go well for him. Yes, he'd caused my daughter great un-happiness, but I was sure he'd done his best. The haunting truth is that most of us at most times do our best, no matter how short we fall.

"So the good outweighs the bad." I gave him a reassuring smile.

"I thought it did. But ever since we got here, Connor's been on edge. She wanted us to get different rooms so she wouldn't see that damn tower. They couldn't make a change because they're painting a bunch of the rooms and they don't have enough that are all together. But if Connor hears what that waiter's saying, I don't know what will happen." Lloyd rubbed the back of his neck.

"What's George saying?" I wanted to hear what Lloyd knew.

He slammed a hand against his leg. "He's been spreading all kinds of nonsense about, saying that Roddy Worrell's ghost is walking. That would upset Connor a lot." Lloyd's face flushed.

I looked at him curiously. I almost inquired why a rumor of ghostly doings would be especially distressing to Connor. I would have thought that Mrs. Worrell would be most affected. As, of course, she probably was.

"Something's got to be done." His face was grim.

"Would you like for me to speak to George?" I heard my own words with surprise. I'd intended to talk to Diana, of course. I didn't like her taking part in what appeared to be an effort to harass Connor. I'd not cared, frankly, what the young waiter did or why. But if I could help Lloyd . . .

His face lightened. "Would you do that? Listen, if —" He broke off, looked past me. "Here comes Connor." He spoke in an undertone. "Don't tell her what we've been talking about." He scrambled to his feet.

I nodded, then turned toward the walk.

Connor hurried toward us, dark head bent. She had changed sweaters. This one was a pale yellow patchwork with a sea motif, embroidered with shells and starfish. I wondered if she'd bought it at Trimingham's.

She broke into a stumbling run.

I came to my feet, realizing that something was wrong. Lloyd hurried toward her, calling out, "Connor, what's wrong? The children . . ."

I felt a quiver of fear. Those damn mopeds.

Connor never even saw me. She flung herself into Lloyd's arms. "In my room! The tower . . ." She shuddered. "It's smashed —"

Automatically, my head swung toward the hillside and the shining white tower, a dramatic beacon.

"— and there's a smell of gin. Oh, God, Lloyd, I'm frightened."

Lloyd frowned. "I don't see how it could have fallen —"

Abruptly, I understood. In my room, a miniature white porcelain tower sat in the middle of the circular table near the sliding glass door to the balcony. The legend TOWER RIDGE HOUSE was printed in dark blue Gothic script on one side. Likely, there was an identical miniature tower in every room. Connor was talking about a decorative tower, not the actual tower on the ridge.

"— unless someone bumped the table. Maybe Jasmine . . ."

Connor jerked away from him. "It wasn't an accident." Her voice was tight and strained. "It couldn't have fallen where I found it." She shuddered. "Lloyd, that last night, Roddy was angry with me." Connor reached out, clung to Lloyd, her face imploring. "He's come back. He's come back and he hates me —"

"Nonsense." Lloyd was gruff. "Just because that stupid tower got broken —"

"Gin. I smelled gin. That's what Roddy smelled like, a sea of gin." She flung away from Lloyd. "I want to go home." Her voice could scarcely be heard.

"Connor, it's all right. I'm here." His voice softened. "Honey, it's all right. You're upset over nothing. Maybe a maid knocked . . ."

I slipped away, left them there, and hurried across the grass. I looked back as I opened the door to the corridor to our quarters. They had not even noticed my departure. I walked swiftly up the hall. I always like to see for myself. I paused outside Connor's room. The door was wide open. I wasn't surprised. She'd seen the smashed tower and turned and run away.

I poked my head into the room. "Hello," I called softly.

There was no answer. I looked down the hall. I was sure that Connor and Lloyd would soon be here. I imagined that Lloyd would make every effort to reassure

Connor, but she would insist that he see the breakage.

I moved quickly. This room was much like mine, only the walls were a pale cream instead of rose, the pillowcases silk instead of cotton. I wasn't surprised that Connor traveled with her own pillowcases and likely with her own sheets. I knew if I opened the closet, her dresses would be hanging neatly. Connor had never, I was sure, lived out of a suitcase. Cosmetics in gold-accented ebony cases were neatly arranged on the dresser. Wire-rimmed glasses were lying next to a magazine. There was a faint scent of lilac, either bath powder or cologne. My nose wrinkled. And the even sweeter smell of gin.

A white wicker sofa with cheerful yellow chintz cushions sat along the wall to my right. The print containers lay in a casual tumble on the sofa. The bathroom opened to the left. Light burned there.

Lloyd and I had engaged in a fairly long conversation, which likely meant that Connor didn't see the broken tower when she first reached the room. No, she'd stepped inside the door, dropped the cardboard cylinders onto the sofa, stepped into the bathroom. No doubt she'd redone her makeup, brushed her hair, then returned to the bedroom.

I walked into the bedroom. The sliding glass door to the balcony was open. I passed the bed, stopped at the balcony. The gardens spread below. The tower loomed on the ridge to the right. Perhaps Connor had stood a moment enjoying the view. Then she'd turned . . .

I swiveled. A table and three chairs were between me and the bed. I skirted the table. Midway between the table and the bed lay a half dozen pieces of broken porcelain. I stepped close, knelt. I swiped one finger against the smooth glaze of the largest piece. My finger came away damp. I poked the rug with another finger. The rug was moist. I sniffed each finger in turn. It didn't take a bartender to identify that odor.

I pushed up from the floor and wavered on my feet, dizzy for a moment. Damn, would I ever be over the aftereffects of the pneumonia? I moved as fast as I could, if a little unsteadily, concerned my examination was taking too long. I went out to the balcony, glanced quickly about. I reached down near the metal railing and touched a sliver of porcelain. That sliver told me everything.

I left it where it lay. Perhaps Lloyd would find it. I wondered, as I hurried back across the bedroom, reached the door and poked my head into the hall, whether Lloyd would reach the same conclusion as I. The hall was empty. I plunged into the corridor and was at the door to my room when Lloyd and Connor came through the entrance. I pretended to be closing my door. I smiled. "Will I see you at tea?"

Lloyd was hearty. "We'll be down in a few minutes."

Connor, staring straight ahead, made no reply. She stopped in the hall outside her room. "I'll wait here."

I was thoughtful as I walked down the hall and out the entrance. I don't believe in poltergeists, disembodied spirits or any of the other folderol of psychic phenomena. There is always a rational explanation of any occurrence.

A reasoned appraisal of the smashed tower suggested a carefully set stage rather than a spirit's violent effort. The tower could not have broken as it did by being dropped or thrown onto the floor because that floor was carpeted. In fact, I was almost certain that someone took the tower out to the balcony and struck it hard against the railing to break it into several pieces. The pieces were then placed where they were found. As a final touch, gin was splashed generously over the broken shards.

Obviously, the intent was to disturb Connor. Why? Simply for sheer malevolence? I pushed away the memory of Diana's angry young voice. Whatever the purpose, it seemed clear that Connor was to be frightened by the prospect that the ghost of Roddy Worrell was near.

I put aside for the moment speculation as to why Connor should be afraid. Had her connection to the dead man been stronger than Lloyd believed?

Worrell died in a fall from the tower. George told Jasmine about his fall. Moreover, George had apparently told Diana about the tower and Roddy Worrell's death and the connection between Roddy and Connor. The place to start was with George. I checked my watch. Almost four. Tea was offered every afternoon at three on the patio near the pool. George was the server. I walked faster.

five

I was almost to the steps leading down to the lower terrace when I heard the rumble of mopeds. I hesitated. Yes, I wanted to help Lloyd. But first things first. I turned and hurried to the limestone wall that overlooked the drive. I was leaning over the top of the wall when the mopeds — Neal's red, Diana's green — careened around the curve, so fast my heart thudded. Children, slow down, slow down, take care.

They were laughing. The mopeds slowed. Neal looked up, saw me, waved. They parked. Diana climbed off the bike, removed her helmet and ran her fingers through her reddish-gold hair. She called up, "Are we back in time for tea?" Neal looped his helmet over the handle.

"Plenty of time." I would catch George after tea.

Neal and Diana ran lightly up the steps, Diana in the lead. "Grandma, tomorrow we have to take you to see the Spanish Rock. It's amazing. It has the date 1543 on it and they think a sailor —"

"Portuguese, not Spanish," Neal interrupted.

"— whatever," his sister said impatiently. "He was shipwrecked here and he climbed to the top of a cliff and scratched the year and his initials on this rock —"

"But now they think the letters aren't his initials after all, but an inscription meaning *Rex Portugaliae*, for the 'King of Portugal.' The date and initials are cast in bronze because they were wearing away from the rock. It's really neat," Neal exclaimed. "It's right on the edge of the cliff, seventy feet high."

"— and a cross," Diana continued, "and you have to wonder if he died here like Amelia Earhart did on that island in the Pacific —"

Neal shook his head. "Nope. I read about it. Their ship foundered on a reef but they built a new boat and made it back to Santo Domingo. Earhart and Noonan crashed on an atoll and there was nothing to build with. So they died unless they were captured by the Japanese. But that's been generally discredited." He stared out at the water, richly blue, inviting, beautiful, merciless. "Pretty awful. To crash-land and think you're going to live and find out you're on a scrap of land without any water. No water, only scraps of food in the cockpit; no way to get help, no way to build a boat."

I was proud of him, proud that he looked

beyond a glib recital of Earhart's end, sensed the pain, understood the fear. Neal's imagination would make his life harder, sometimes almost unendurable, but far, far richer.

Then he was young again. "Think I'll go put on my suit, take a swim. Coming, Dinny?"

I spoke quickly. "Stay with me, Diana. We'll go down for tea."

"See you later." Neal strode quickly away.

Diana smiled, took my arm. We walked slowly down the path. I wondered how to begin. Diana looked out toward the sea. The pleasure of the outing with her brother seeped away, leaving her face somber. Her delicate features sharpened. Her lips pressed together. She should have been lovely, with strawberry-blond curls framing finely chiseled features. But if I were in the business of giving beauty advice, I'd be succinct: Be happy.

I've spent a lifetime asking questions. All reporters know that the unexpected question can yield enormous dividends. It's not a polygraph, but definitely the next best thing. Even the slickest liar can be startled by a totally unexpected inquiry. My granddaughter was not a slick liar, but she was a very unhappy young woman.

We were at the top of the steps leading down to the lower terrace. The sounds of conversation drifted up to us. Abruptly, I demanded, "Diana, was the tower hard to break?" I watched her closely, alert for the flare of eyes, for the sudden immobility of shock, for a quick-drawn breath.

Diana stopped, puzzled. She bent toward me. "I'm sorry, Grandma. What did you say?" Her voice was polite. And untroubled.

Not even a trill of joy by a choir of angels could match the relief that flooded through me. "I said that you look as though your heart was about to break."

"Oh, Grandma." Tears welled in her eyes. "I can't stand it if Daddy marries her. She's a mess. You saw the way she acted in the bar last night, playing up to that awful man from Texas. It made me sick. And she doesn't care a bit about what matters to Daddy. He's going to leave Dallas and you know how he's always loved Dallas. And he's going to leave his law firm. And all of his friends."

I could have told her that a city, no matter how much enjoyed, and friends, no matter how treasured, are cold comfort in a double bed alone. I reached out, took her hand. "Diana, don't make your father unhappy. I know it's hard for you and Neal, but try to see this from your father's —"

She gripped my hand in her hands, held it tightly. "Grandma, she's a tramp. Listen, I've found out all about her. They've been coming here for years and she always had men clustered around her, even when Marlow and Jasmine's father was alive. Just like that Mr. Patterson. She's always stayed up late in the bar and there was always somebody drinking with her. And Mrs. Worrell's husband followed her around and he'd get drunk and sing to her. Mrs. Worrell got really upset. But last year, Dad was here and Connor went after him and that made Mr. Worrell mad. He and Connor had a big fight and the next morning they found his body at the foot of the tower."

"Is that why you engineered the picture on the point this morning?" My tone was sharp.

She dropped my hand, looked at me defiantly. "All right. It bothered her, didn't it? Why should the tower upset her unless there's something about it she doesn't want to think about? Like a man getting drunk over her and falling off and getting killed."

"You said you've found out all about her . . ."

"She's a slut." Diana was disdainful, her voice hard.

"Really. And how did you achieve this intelligence?" I gazed at her steadily.

Diana's eyes fell away. She fingered a shell button on her cardigan.

"From George? The ever-helpful young waiter?" My tone was cool.

"He knows." Diana's retort was impassioned. "He sees everything. He knows all about her."

"And apparently can't wait to broadcast it to others. Diana, look at your source. Why is George doing this?" If Diana didn't wonder, I damn sure did.

"No, no. It isn't like that. He didn't even want to tell me," she protested. "Here's what happened. I had lunch down at the pool yesterday. And he was nice —"

Read "cute." Diana is at the age when all young men are interesting.

"— and we got to talking and I asked how long he'd worked here. He's Canadian and he dropped out of college. He's been here three years but he's thinking of going back to school —"

Always a good line with a college girl.

"— and I asked if he remembered my dad being here last January. He said he'd never forget last January because that was when Mr. Worrell got drunk and fell out of the tower. And George said it was all because of

81

the American woman. Then he broke off and looked embarrassed and tried to change the subject. But I got it out of him. I told him I didn't like her at all and she was going to marry my dad and I was just sick about it."

Two sides to every story. At the least. George's revelations to Diana could be as innocent as she claimed. As for his dramatic description of a ghost to Jasmine, he might simply enjoy entertaining, and all the world loves ghostly tales. None of that, however, explained the knock on Steve Jennings's door last night. Moreover, Jennings obviously saw something near the tower that disturbed him. Or he thought he saw something. And the broken ceramic tower in Connor's room argued a degree of hostility that was disturbing. I wasn't persuaded that Roddy Worrell's purported ghost could be responsible. I believed a living hand knocked on Steve's door and broke the pottery tower in Connor's room. If the young waiter was behind either event, it needed to be discovered because the happiness of both Connor and Lloyd was at stake. As for my granddaughter . . .

"Diana." I spoke gently. "I understand your concern about your dad's marriage. But you should remember that George's description of last January is that of one person. Is it smart — or fair — to rely on a single source?"

Diana grew up in a newspaper family. She understood what I was telling her. George could be right or wrong, he could be mistaken, he could be hostile, he could be credulous.

"One source?" I let the question hang, then said quietly, "Talk to Steve Jennings."

"He's in love with her, too," Diana said bitterly. "I don't need anyone to tell me anything about her. I know what she is and she's nothing but trouble. And I'll do anything I can to get rid of her." She whirled and ran away.

I almost followed Diana, then, lips pressed together, I walked down the steps to the lower terrace. I paused in the shadow of the arbor to look over the clusters of guests on the sunny side of the swimming pool. In summer, of course, most would likely have chosen a table beneath the arbor, but the January air was cool in the shade. In fact, I doubted that tea was served around the pool during the summer months, more likely in the drawing room that overlooked the upper terrace. This January afternoon, only a half dozen tables were occupied. Voices murmured, teacups clinked. The two angular women who'd sunbathed despite the cool air were now dressed in dark sweaters and slacks and accompanied by their husbands. Two couples in their thirties, unmistakably New Yorkers, talked loudly, as New Yorkers do, about the mayor and police reform and what might happen if there was a transit strike. An austere old lady in a well-worn tweed suit listened with a slight smile as her companion, his gentle features intent, gestured enthusiastically. He was possibly in his forties. Two cheerful young women shared a magazine. One turned the page and the other giggled. They both had soft blond curls and bright blue eyes. I wondered if they were sisters. Curt Patterson held court at the table nearest the arbor, lounging back in a webbed chair. His sister looked much like him, bright red hair, lots of freckles and a confident face. Her dark-haired, burly husband munched tea sandwiches and listened, occasionally nodding as Patterson jabbed the air for emphasis. A young family occupied the farthest table. The sweet-faced mother placed tea sandwiches on the plates of her little boys, perhaps four and seven. Her husband sipped tea and spoke in a voice too low for me to hear. She replied and they chatted. The children sat so patiently and quietly, their sneakered feet dangling from the adult chairs, that I was quite sure they were not American.

I chose a table in the partial shade of the arbor, as it afforded the best view of the steps leading down from the upper terrace as well as the walk that curved past the cabana toward the garden. The tower loomed high above the garden. This morning George claimed to have seen something white near the tower, then said he was mistaken. A seagull flashed past the tower. Yes, he might have glimpsed a bird. Or, if someone was on the platform and stepping inside, there could have been a brief flash of white. Those who fancy the supernatural might believe George was psychic and that he saw Roddy Worrell though there was actually no one there. Or he might have seen nothing at all. It was the latter possibility that most intrigued me. If he invented the glimpse, he did so for a purpose and it was that purpose I wanted to divine.

George was serving the tea by himself. He came out from the pool food-service area and immediately saw me. He paused on his way to replenish the other tables. "Would you like tea, Mrs. Collins? Or would you prefer sherry?" He leaned forward, his bony face attentive. In his role as a waiter, there was nothing to distinguish him from a hundred other young men. He had the attractiveness of youth — bright eyes, smooth skin, an insouciant confidence. After all, he wouldn't have traveled so far from home unless he was eager to see new places, learn other ways. He had a nice face, wide-spaced eyes, a spatter of freckles, lips that often curved into a grin. He served with an easy banter that was friendly, yet not overly familiar.

"Tea, please." I had plenty of opportunity to observe George as I enjoyed the tea and the little sandwiches, salmon-and-cream cheese, tomatoes-and-cucumber, the flaky scones with clotted cream, and the delicate fruit pastries. He addressed every guest by name, which argued a good memory and some effort. He served our table in the evenings.

I wondered what he was like at his local pub drinking a beer with friends. I guessed boisterous, cheerful and outgoing. He was thin but athletic, with a lanky build. Diana thought he was cute.

I deliberately dawdled until everyone else had left. Dusk was falling. The lights came on around the pool. He was clearing the last table except mine. "George . . ."

He turned toward me. If he was impatient

to be done, he gave no hint of it, his gaze polite. "More tea, Mrs. Collins?"

"No, thank you. It was lovely. Actually, I'd hoped to have a visit with you. My granddaughter told me about Roddy Worrell's ghost. She said you know all about it." I looked at him earnestly. "I've always been fascinated by ghosts. Is there really a ghost in the tower?"

He picked up his tray, stepped to my table. "I know it sounds crazy." His voice held a note of embarrassment. "My grandmother always said there were ghosts. I didn't believe it until now. But a couple of nights ago I was on my way home and I heard a kind of odd sound, kind of like a rustle, and I looked up and saw this white glow near the top of the tower. I'll have to tell you" — his eyes were wide — "it got my attention." He rested his tray on the table. As he cleared the tea service, he lifted his shoulders, let them fall. "I knew it had to be Roddy. This Saturday night it will be a year ago that he died." The dishes clinked as he placed them on the tray.

"Do you really think you saw a ghost?" I didn't try to keep the disbelief from my voice.

"It's not just me." His reply was sharp. "Frederick told me this morning that he saw something last night. He said he was walking down the back steps." George nodded toward the wall that curved behind the pool. "That's where we park our mopeds, out of sight of the guests. He said it was right about midnight. He got his bike and he was just at the curve when he looked up" — George stopped, pointed up the hill at the tower — "there was a shiny glow. He said the whiteness moved around the tower like it was hunting for something. Then, all of a sudden, it was gone. Nothing. There one minute, gone the next. He said it scared the hell out of him." I heard the reflection of Frederick's fear in George's voice.

A shiny glow. Was this what Steve Jennings wouldn't describe to me?

"A shiny glow." I repeated his words. "Why do you think it has anything to do with Mr. Worrell?"

"That's where he died. He fell out of the tower a year ago." He swiped his cloth on the tabletop. "I guess Roddy's come back to haunt the place where he died."

I pushed back my chair, rose, faced him. "Interesting." My tone was no longer credulous, nor my gaze. Time was running out before the wedding on Saturday. Connor was upset, but perhaps the remaining days could be salvaged. "You've talked it up, haven't you? Told Diana and Jasmine and others —"

He watched me intently.

"— perhaps Mr. Jennings and Aaron Reed?"

We stared at each other, our faces combative.

"It's all true." He clenched his hands into fists, frowned at me. "And I'll tell you something else" — his eyes narrowed — "I've been thinking back. How could Roddy have fallen out of the tower? Even drunk, he could handle himself. And he wasn't that drunk. He was just damn mad at her. The more I've thought about that night . . ." George took a deep breath. "They say a murdered man won't rest until justice is done."

I was startled. I'd not set out to explore the death of Roddy Worrell. That event, in fact, was not of interest to me. But there was something here I had not expected. I felt a prickle of unease as I looked into his frowning face. "Are you saying someone pushed him off the tower?"

He turned to look up toward the tower. "Yeah. Roddy could handle himself. He never fell."

The words hung between us. If Worrell didn't fall, he was pushed. And if a ghost sought justice . . . I saw an ugly link between the ghost of the man who died in a fall from the tower and the broken ceramic tower in Connor's room.

"You can't prove that." I was brisk. "So what's the good of talking about Worrell? Or the tower?"

He didn't look at me. He rubbed his sunburned nose. "I've been thinking about that night . . ." He picked up the tray, stepped away into the shadow of the arbor.

I wished I could see him more clearly. I took a step nearer. "You know that Mrs. Bailey and Mr. Drake will be married Saturday afternoon."

He nodded.

"As an employee of the hotel, I'm sure you want to do everything possible to make the guests comfortable." I gazed at him sternly.

He took a step backward.

"In fact, George, you can easily be of great service to our group."

"Yes, ma'am?" His tone was cautious.

I spoke slowly with emphasis. "Do not discuss the tower or Mr. Worrell again with anyone in our party. And let's have no more talk about ghosts."

He lifted his shoulders, let them fall. "I can't help what people see." There was just a hint of insolence.

As he moved toward the service area, I knew that my stricture was too little, too late. After all, the damage had already been done. Then I had what seemed like an inspiration. After all, George worked here at the hotel. Surely he must have some idea what — and who — was behind the whiteness that came late at night to the tower.

"George." My tone was peremptory. "I want more than your silence."

Slowly, he turned, faced me. He stood in a bar of light from the pool canteen, his face respectful but his eyes defiant.

"I don't believe in ghosts." I took a step toward him. "Somehow I doubt that you do, either."

"I saw —"

"Special effects," I interrupted impatiently. "If there is an apparition late at night near the tower, someone created it and did so on purpose."

George stood very still, his eyes alert.

"I don't give a damn who's doing it." I wanted to be clear about this. "I don't care why they are doing it. But I'm willing to pay a substantial sum to make sure that Mr. Worrell's ghost doesn't stir again until after we leave the island." I watched his dark eyes, unusual eyes flecked with green and gold.

He was still for so long that I knew I'd played the right card. Money not only talks, it whistles and dances.

George gave a sudden decided nod, as if he'd made up his mind. "How much?"

I didn't hesitate. I was confident Lloyd would pay a good deal for peace and harmony. "A thousand dollars. To be paid in full upon our departure if the ghost does not walk again."

He gave a swift nod. "I'll see what I can do."

six

I luxuriated in the hotel's thick, soft terry-cloth robe as I rested on the chaise longue, sipping a cup of decaffeinated tea. I'd brewed the tea after my quick shower, quick in deference to Bermuda's paucity of water. This fall, a placard announced, rainfall was below average, so guests were asked to be sparing in the use of water. I felt tired but content. On reflection, I believed I'd solved Lloyd's problem. The more I considered my interview with George, the more confident I felt that Roddy Worrell's ghost would walk no more. George obviously wanted the thousand dollars. He would not get the money unless all was quiet around the tower. Therefore, he either knew what or who was causing the apparition, or he himself had created the ghost. I rather leaned toward the latter proposition. Although he'd made no promise, he'd said he would see what he could do. I took that as a clear indication he thought he could prevent the reappearance of the ghost.

I sipped the tea and listened through the open balcony door to the distant crash of the surf. George's willingness to cooperate was simply more proof, though I'd never needed any, that the visitation was not supernatural. I wondered idly why George (or someone) had gone to so much effort. What was the objective? I wondered if Mrs. Worrell was a demanding boss. Was the answer that simple? Was George merely a disgruntled employee?

None of it really mattered, not so long as Connor was left in peace and she and Lloyd were permitted to take their vows Saturday afternoon with smiling faces and untroubled hearts. A large order, actually. One I couldn't hope to deliver. There was too much unhappiness emanating from too many people, especially Diana and Marlow. Moreover, I doubted that Steve Jennings was overjoyed at the prospect of Connor's marriage. Would he like having Lloyd as an overseer to Connor's business interests? Diana thought that Steve was in love with Connor. And though Neal put a good face on it, he was worried for his father. Curt Patterson was one more complicating factor. I doubted the likelihood of an unblemished wedding day. But I was doing my part. At least everyone would get an unbroken sleep tonight.

The small clock on the mantel chimed the quarter hour. I finished the tea and walked to the closet. Dinner was at seven, a series of courses in the formal dining room. I'd brought a black rayon georgette dress. It was simple but elegant and the boat neck was a perfect setting for my necklace of matched pearls. I slipped on silver cross-strap slippers, I drew my hair back, fastened it with a seed-pearl ribbon. I dropped my key, a lipstick and a comb into the small black evening bag. I checked my reflection as I opened the door. I looked festive and cheerful.

The hotel had grown, a new room here, a wing there. According to the brochure in my room, it had been built in the late eighteen hundreds by the Palmer family and still belonged to the family, although the current owner, Burton Palmer, was an international banker in Singapore. The original structure provided the public rooms. The dining room stretched long and narrow, with a high tray ceiling. Coppery planks of Bermuda cedar gave the walls a rich, mellow air. The draperies, bright red and yellow peonies against a cream chintz, embraced wide, high windows. Damask cloths covered the five tables set for dinner. In high season, the dining area accommodated some twenty round tables, each capable of seating ten, as well as a number of smaller tables designed for two or four guests. Tonight the far portion of the room was unlighted, so the bare tables weren't noticeable. The chandeliers in the front area spilled golden light over the appointed tables, the crystal and china glistening in the glow.

Holly wreaths encircled the ceramic tower in the center of every table but ours. On our table, there was a different centerpiece, a slender chalcedony vase containing a single majestic stalk of bird-of-paradise, the orange sepals bright as sails at sunset. The faint strains of a Debussy waltz provided a gentle accompaniment to low-voiced conversations.

As I slipped into my seat next to Connor, I wondered who had ordered the miniature tower removed from our table. But I knew it was a topic better left unexplored during dinner. Lloyd had rather fussily arranged the seating on our first evening and, not surprisingly, we all returned to our original spots. In a circle, beginning with Lloyd and running clockwise, were Connor, myself, Steve, Marlow, Aaron, Jasmine, Neal and Diana.

George served our table deftly. The first course was a fish chowder, followed by mixed greens. There was a choice of grilled red snapper or curried lamb for the entrée. As I ate, I glanced around the table. Connor, to my right, had nothing to say, and Steve, to my left, was rather quiet, so I was free to observe my companions.

The splash of golden light from the chandelier emphasized the forlorn droop of Lloyd's face. He didn't look like a man about to go on a honeymoon. He toyed with his spoon and it made tiny little chimes against the fine crystal base of his wineglass. He ate mechanically, every so often attempting to engage Connor in conversation.

Connor's ebony hair, smooth and glistening, cupped a white, strained face. Her lipstick was startlingly red against the waxy paleness of her skin. Her shoulders hunched beneath a black silk jacket with a dramatic crimson piping, her posture at odds with the effervescence of her costume. She stared blankly at the table, making little pretense of eating.

Steve Jennings passed an occasional comment my way, but his glance always edged past, seeking Connor. I thought that Lloyd's choice of seating had been quite deliberate. Steve Jennings and Connor would have no tête-à-têtes at meals. Steve's usually genial expression was somber.

Marlow spoke too loudly. Her voice resounded in the quiet of our table, caromed across the room. ". . . don't have any patience with people who always want to be safe. You know what Katharine Hepburn said: 'If you obey all the rules you miss all the fun.' " There was an unaccustomed flush in her makeup-bare cheeks. She was her usual uncompromisingly plain self, the too-large, heavy glasses perched on her straight nose, her dark hair confined to an unadorned bun. She wore no jewelry with a purplish velvet dress that fitted her so loosely she might equally well have chosen a sweatshirt.

I wondered about Marlow. Did she eschew fashion because her mother was always exquisitely dressed? Or was Marlow simply disinterested, not rebellious? Marlow might not care about her own appearance, but she was engaged to a young man who was extraordinarily handsome, the kind of young man accustomed to dating the prettiest girl in the class. Perhaps I underestimated both Marlow and Aaron.

Aaron was ebullient tonight, laughing, throwing back that handsome head of brown curls, gently teasing Jasmine, making sure his little sister-to-be had plenty of rolls and a fresh pot of hot chocolate. I was certain Aaron always gave thought to his appearance, the dark green stripe of his tattersall shirt just the right contrast to his navy blazer. And his tie, though I was no authority, looked like an Hermès, and definitely had not been bought at a discount store.

Jasmine ate voraciously. Her response to Aaron's charm was perfunctory. She stared unwaveringly at the small table near the main door where Mrs. Worrell sat in the shadow of a fern flourishing in a bright green pot. Mrs. Worrell was in profile to us. No more than ten feet separated the tables. I wondered that the manager didn't sense the intensity of the child's gaze.

Neal poked at a curl of red pepper on the snapper, looked at it curiously, speared a mouthful and ate. He gave a little nod, tried the sautéed eggplant. This was not the usual meal for a husky teenager and I was pleased that he was open to gustatory adventures, Just for a moment, I permitted myself a grandmother's delight, the sheer wash of pleasure that wells from observing an adored grandchild: coal-black hair, light green eyes, strong-boned face; but most of all I treasured the intelligence in his gaze, the good humor in the easy set of his mouth. Neal was a nice kid. He was growing up to be a solid, dependable, honorable man. He looked up, caught my gaze, and grinned. He pointed with his fork at the eggplant. "Hey, it's good."

Diana ignored her plate. "Dad, I'm counting on your coming to Austin for my birthday." Her tone was brittle. Did she intend the demand — and clearly it was a demand — as a challenge? Her thin face was stiff, her eyes blazing.

Lloyd bent closer to Connor. He didn't respond to Diana's question. Clearly, he'd not heard her. "Connor, let's go out after dinner. There's jazz tonight at Cambridge Beaches."

Connor's voice was clipped. "I have a headache. I think I'll go to bed early."

Diana gripped her fork. But she didn't eat. She stared at her plate, the corners of her mouth turned down.

Neal picked up the wine bottle. "Here, Dinny." He filled his sister's glass. He looked politely across the table at Connor. "Connor, would you like some more wine?"

"Wine?" Connor shook her head, then touched her temple and closed her eyes.

Marlow's too-loud voice was sharp. "Jasmine, stop staring at Mrs. Worrell. It's rude to stare."

Everyone looked toward Jasmine, who ducked her head.

"Honestly," her sister continued, "you

haven't taken your eyes off her since we sat down."

"Shh," Jasmine warned. "She'll hear you. And I can look where I want to." She gave her big sister a defiant glare. "I was waiting to see if the ghost came. I'd know by the way she acted. Everybody says she knows he's walking. They say ghosts come back to where they spent a lot of time and that's where Mr. Worrell sat every evening and I remember last year he —"

"Jasmine, hush." Connor's voice was harsh. "There is no such thing as a ghost."

Jasmine's blue eyes widened. "Oh, yes, there is. Didn't you know? Mr. Worrell's come back." Her voice was excited. "They've seen him late at night near the tower. I want to stay up and —"

"Jasmine." Connor held tight to the edge of the table. Her eyes were glassy. "What are you talking about? That's impossible."

Jasmine stared at her mother, her face uneasy but stubborn. "It's true. Mr. Worrell's come back."

George replenished Marlow's water glass, moved on to Aaron.

Jasmine pointed to the waiter. "He knows all about it. Ask him. He's seen the ghost."

Connor's head jerked toward the waiter. "Come here."

George stood stiffly for a moment, then took a slow step toward Connor.

"What is this nonsense?" Connor's voice was sharp.

George glanced uneasily toward Mrs. Worrell, who was watching our table, her face intent, her eyes cold. "I don't know much about it, Mrs. Bailey." He spoke almost in a whisper, obviously fearful of being overheard by Mrs. Worrell. "There's been something seen late at night near the tower. Nobody knows what it is. A white shape. That's all I know." And he turned away, hurried toward the kitchen.

Lloyd reached out for Connor's hand, but she was pushing back her chair, coming to her feet, face blanched. "Steve." She turned toward him, a trembling hand outstretched.

Steve rose, cupped an arm around Connor's shoulders. "It's okay, Connor. I'm here. Come on, I'll take you to your room." They moved toward the door, Connor clinging to him for support.

All the men were standing now. Aaron looked uncomfortable, Neal uneasy, but it was Lloyd whose face was stricken. I looked down at my plate. I didn't want to see the pain in his eyes, the flush of humiliation, the flicker of jealousy.

Marlow said quickly, and this time I welcomed her loud, carrying voice. "Mother doesn't mind looking like a fool in front of Steve. She'll be embarrassed in the morning, Lloyd. We'll pretend none of this happened. You know, she always wants you to think she's totally cool." Marlow poked her glasses higher on her nose.

It was as graceful a face-saving gesture as any I'd ever seen. And a total surprise to me. It had been clear throughout the trip that Marlow was not enthusiastic about her mother's remarriage, yet at this moment she had gone out of her way to spare Lloyd public humiliation. It argued a kind and thoughtful nature. I looked at Diana, wondering if she understood what Marlow had done. Diana's gaze was thoughtful.

A look of relief eased the tightness in Lloyd's face. He said eagerly, "I'll bet you're right, Marlow. We won't talk about any of it again. After all, Connor's very sensitive."

Diana frowned, heaved an exasperated sigh.

Neal gave his sister a warning poke with his elbow.

Jasmine frowned. "But we have a chance to see a ghost and —"

"Shut up, Jasmine." Marlow reached over, put her finger on Jasmine's lips. "I'll get you your very own copy of *Ghostbusters* on the condition" — she drew out her words "that you do not mention Mr. Worrell again. Or his so-called ghost." Her tone was light, but there was a steely glint in her eyes.

Jasmine heaved a sigh. "Okay." Her face was glum.

George had quietly removed the dinner plates and was pushing a dessert trolley toward the table, laden with assorted French pastries, cherry and apple pie, and trifle. As the desserts were served, Lloyd said, "Okay, everybody." His tone was expansive, including them all in a team effort. "No mention of anything unpleasant to Connor. And tomorrow we'll have a great day. We're going to Spittal Pond in the morning. The afternoon's free, but I think I'll see if Connor would like to go to the Bermuda Perfumery. I'll keep her really busy." Lloyd was upbeat again.

As George poured coffee, I decided to add a little insurance. "I think this ghost business is going to be resolved."

Everyone looked at me, including George.

I gave the waiter a swift, hard glance. "I did a little investigating today. In fact, if my inquiries work out, we may discover who was behind it."

George's face was an expressionless mask.

For good measure, I added, "In any event,

I've learned enough to know it's all a prank. I don't expect the ghost will walk again. At least, not while we are in Bermuda."

Jasmine opened her mouth. Marlow shook her head and the little girl said nothing, but her eyes flashed with disdain.

Jasmine wasn't convinced. But that didn't matter. My words had not been intended for her.

I smiled as I turned the page. Jules Verne certainly knew how to tell a good story. It was fun to reread this classic entertainment, a reminder that readers once were pleased by humor and adventure sans violence. An extraterrestrial trying to understand our world by reading current fiction would very likely conclude serial killers were the norm. I put down my book and relaxed sleepily against my pillow. I suppose I'd drifted off because it took me a moment to realize someone was knocking on my door.

I pushed up from the bed and glanced toward the clock. Almost eleven. I hurried toward the door, remembering Steve Jennings's experience the night before. I looked through the peephole and felt an instant shock. I would not have been surprised, frankly, had the hallway been empty, or to have seen one of my grandchildren. But I would never have expected to see Connor Bailey. She'd changed after dinner to a silver silk blouse, red linen slacks and woven sling sandals. She pushed a pair of glasses higher on her nose, looked uneasily up and down the hall.

I opened the door. "Hello, Connor. Please come in."

"I wanted to talk to you." Her words were faintly slurred. As she brushed past me, I smelled a heady mixture of Scotch and perfume. I closed the door and followed.

Connor stood by the circular table, staring at the miniature tower. "Mine got broken." She shivered.

"Please sit down." I gestured toward a chair.

She reached out, picked up the tower, and flung it to the floor.

I was startled and my voice was sharp. "Connor —"

"See?" Her tone was triumphant. She wavered on her feet, but her gaze clung to the tower. "It didn't break. Lloyd kept saying the damn thing fell off the table. He said maybe Jasmine knocked it over. But see" — she pointed with a bright red fingernail — "I threw that one down and it didn't break."

I saw. I also saw that her hand was trembling and her eyes, magnified by thick lenses, were wide and frightened. I'd never seen her in glasses.

A woman intensely attuned to others' perceptions of her, she touched the gold wire frame. "Already took out my contacts, decided to talk to you." She blinked, stared down at the ceramic tower. She took off her glasses, rubbed her eyes.

"It's breakable." I picked up the ceramic piece, put it back on the table. "Someone broke the one in your room."

She swallowed convulsively, wrapped her arms across her front. "How?"

I wasn't at all certain she'd believe me. But she needed help and I thought I could reassure her. "Some person — some living person — carried the tower out onto your balcony and whacked it on the railing. There's a sliver of ceramic out there." I wondered if she'd challenge me. Demand to know what I was doing on her balcony. I was ready to admit to curiosity and hoped she wouldn't be angry. But she didn't say a word, she simply stared at me with those huge, frightened, myopic eyes. "I found a piece of ceramic on your balcony this afternoon. Someone's playing tricks —"

"Marlow told me what you said at dinner." She slipped the glasses on, then moved forward so eagerly that she stumbled, caught herself on the table. "What did you mean?" She wavered against the table. "I need a drink. Fix me one."

I don't usually respond to peremptory orders. But I didn't hesitate for that reason. Connor shouldn't have another drink.

She didn't wait for me to answer. She moved with great determination to the bar provided by the hotel. I never use mini-bars. I prefer tea to whiskey and it's cheaper to travel with my own candy.

Connor fumbled with the key, pulled open the door, reached without hesitation to the second shelf for a small bottle of Scotch.

I tossed some ice cubes in a glass and handed it to her.

She waved away my offer of soda, poured the whiskey, drank deeply. "You told everyone the ghost was a trick. How do you know?" She paced unsteadily back toward the table.

"I heard about the ghost, so I checked around with some of the staff." I dropped into a chair, looked up at her. "There's nothing much to it. And actually, nothing to connect the 'ghost' to Mr. Worrell." I gave her time to digest that. "Something white moves around the top of the tower . . ."

"White," she muttered. "That's what that

waiter said out on the point this morning. He said he saw something white. White." She shuddered. "Roddy always wore white — white shirt, white trousers, a white hat when he was out in the sun. She thumped onto the end of my bed, stared at me.

"That's why something white's been seen there." I was impatient. I have little tolerance for credulity. "Someone planned it that way."

She lifted a shaking hand. "What if it's Roddy? What if he's come back?"

"It isn't. He hasn't. Connor, relax. The ghost isn't coming back. Trust me." And I'd better talk to Lloyd first thing in the morning, make sure he would ante up the thousand.

Connor stared at the tower on my table. "Roddy was mad at me that night." She pulled off her glasses, rubbed her eyes. "I didn't do anything." The denial was that of a frightened child. "Roddy fell in love with me. Men do. I can't help it. R.T. understood." Her voice was soft and the words folded into each other until the syllables were hard to discern. "And now" — she swallowed and tears spilled down her cheeks — "Lloyd wants me to leave Steve out of things. He didn't want Steve to come to the wedding. I told Lloyd that I had to have him here. Why, Steve has been wonderful to me. And that nice man from Texas — Lloyd doesn't like him. I don't want to marry someone who doesn't like people."

"Oh, Lloyd likes people well enough, but he loves you, Connor, and he wants to spend time with you. Perhaps this trip isn't the time to make new friends." It was the best I could do in the Ann Landers line.

"I can't help it if men fall in love with me." Her look at me was an odd mixture of defiance and sadness. "Why can't Lloyd understand?"

I didn't have an answer for that.

She tried to stand. Some of the whiskey splashed out of the glass. Her face puckered in dismay.

I reached down, helped her rise. "It will evaporate," I said briskly.

She patted ineffectually at her blouse.

I smelled the Scotch. It reminded me of the odor of gin in her room that afternoon. "And it was real gin someone spilled on your floor today. No ghost did that." I shepherded her toward the door. "Don't worry anymore, Connor. Get a good night's sleep. Tomorrow will be fun. Remember we're going to Spittal Pond."

"Spittal Pond," she murmured as I turned the knob, stood aside for her. "Yes, Spittal

110

Pond." She walked unsteadily down the hall. I waited until her door shut behind her before I closed my own.

I walked slowly toward the phone. Should I call Lloyd? I shook my head. They were in adjoining rooms. If Connor wanted his help, she could knock on that door. I doubted that she would. She was half-drunk, scared, upset. I wondered if I should call Marlow. I decided to stay out of it. Connor was a grown woman and, when distraught, as vulnerable and lost as any child. But surely if the night went without incident, Connor would be in better shape tomorrow.

I stepped out on the balcony, grateful in the cool of the night for the heavy terry-cloth robe. The tower glimmered in the moonlight, silent as a grave, unnerving in its pale whiteness. I turned away, impatient with myself. The memory of violent death tainted the tower. Tomorrow I would climb those curving steps again, stand on the platform in bright sunshine, banish any and all ghosts.

Seven

A scream roused me. I struggled out of bed, flailing and disoriented. The ragged, tortured cry penetrated the walls, punched deep into my mind. After a frozen moment, I ran to the sliding glass door of the balcony, lifted the bar, flipped the lock, pulled the glass wide. A second scream rose to a piercing crescendo, higher, higher, then abruptly cut off.

Doors scraped open on the other balconies. Voices rose in frantic calls.

"Where is it?" Lloyd's voice was gruff, sodden with sleep. "What the hell is it?"

"Oh my God," Connor moaned. "Look, look!"

I was aware of so many fleeting images at once:

Connor clinging to Lloyd's arm on her balcony and my scarcely conscious realization that she must indeed have knocked on their connecting door.

Neal clambering over the railing of his balcony, climbing down a wrought iron pillar toward the ground.

Diana whirling toward my balcony and the obvious relief when she saw me. Dear child.

Aaron Reed shouting, "Stay where you are, Marlow," and throwing one leg over the railing of his balcony.

Marlow holding Jasmine tightly in her arms, but Jasmine struggled to see and her high voice rose, "He's there. Mr. Worrell's there!"

Steve Jennings pointing toward the tower.

But all of these images were peripheral to the luminous glow that moved as softly as a drifting cloud near the top of the tower, formless, insubstantial, frightful.

"Oh God, oh God, oh God . . ." Connor's voice wavered. She buried her face in her hands.

The silvery glow hovered near the platform, slid sideways, dipped, rose, disappeared behind the tower.

The scream sounded a third time, its intensity shocking, so loud I cupped my hands over my ears.

Neal thudded to the ground, ran toward the tower, his bare feet slapping on the cement walk. Aaron was only a few feet behind him, shouting, "I'll circle to the right, you go to the left. We'll catch them." Aaron was fastening his jeans as he ran.

Lights glowed along the garden paths, but the shadows were dark and deep away from the paths. Neal and Aaron ran toward the tower. There was no movement at all in the shadows near the base of the tower. The white radiance that had hovered near the platform was gone.

Was it gone? Or hidden behind the tower? Or was the glow now inside the tower?

I turned and hurried into my room. I always travel with a small flashlight, a precaution against a hotel fire and loss of electricity. I've been lucky enough to avoid a fire, but was grateful once to have the pocket flash in California when an earthquake downed electric lines. Tonight I snatched it up from the top of the TV, ran to the hall. I couldn't move nearly as fast as Neal and Aaron, but I was only a few minutes behind them.

As I hurried up the garden walk, Diana called out, "Grandma, wait for me."

I didn't wait but she, too, swung over the edge of the balcony, dropped to the ground and, running fast, caught up with me. When we reached the tower, the door was open. The boys' voices echoed hollowly inside.

I flashed the light and began to circle the tower.

Diana caught my arm. "What are you looking for?"

"Everything. Nothing." I didn't know. But surely somewhere there would be some trace of what had just occurred. Except, I thought coldly, the glow had moved high in the air, had never come near the ground. The excruciatingly loud scream — wasn't it almost too loud to be real? — had seemed to come from the tower, though at night it was hard to pinpoint the source of any sound. It was easy to imagine the cry was that of a man plummeting to his death, falling and knowing he was going to die, having just a few seconds left, and those seconds hideous with an agony of fear.

My light swept back and forth across the walk. A few fallen leaves, a crumpled cigarette package, a discarded cup.

Diana held tight to my arm. "Grandma," she whispered, "someone must be hurt. Do you think we should look in the garden?" She stared out into the dark grounds beyond the lighted paths.

"I don't think we'll find anyone." We had circled the tower, were once again at the entrance.

Steve Jennings stood in the doorway, peering inside. "Hello. Who's up there?"

Far above, Neal leaned over the platform railing. "It's okay. Nobody's here. Nobody's been here so far as we can tell."

I believed him, but I wanted to see for myself. "I'm going up."

"I'll go with you." Diana still held firmly to my elbow.

Jennings shrugged and moved out of the doorway. "Maybe you'd better wait a minute."

"Yes?" I frowned. Why shouldn't I go up in the tower?

Jennings rubbed his bristly jaw. "There's a light coming up from the lower terrace. I'm afraid it's Mrs. Worrell. She lives in a cottage down that way."

The light bobbed toward us.

I hesitated, then decided to wait.

The flashlight in her hand was huge, throwing our shadows thin and black against the tower. Neal and Aaron clattered down the tower stairs and spilled out beside us.

"There's nobody up there, absolutely nobody!" Neal announced. He was shirtless. Red reindeer pranced on his boxer shorts.

Aaron squinted up at the platform. "Hell of it is, nobody came away from here. Neal and I ran up on either side of the tower. I don't see how anybody could have been up there and had time to run down and get away before we came. So what the hell do you suppose that white thing was?"

Mrs. Worrell's shoes clipped against the flagstones. She stopped a few feet away. Her light, stark and harsh, flooded over our small group, all of us in various kinds of night attire.

"May I ask what is happening?" The light revealed her mercilessly, too, her hair tucked tight beneath a pink cap, her face colorless, one hand tightly clutching the lapels of her red corduroy robe.

No lawyer ever lacks for an answer. Jennings was combative. "Who the hell knows. Did you hear the screams?"

"Screams?" Mrs. Worrell forced out the word.

"Yells. Shouts. Loud enough to wake —" He broke off, cleared his throat.

"A scream. The same sound. Three times." I was sure about that. Although the first cry had awakened me and I could not re-create it exactly in my mind, the second and third were the same in tone, in duration, in scale. "The sound seemed to come from the tower. And up there" — I pointed toward the platform — "we saw some kind of white glow."

Aaron jammed a hand through his tangled curls. "Yeah, kind of white, kind of silver. Maybe two feet by five feet. Bobbing around by the platform."

"Not on the platform." Neal was precise. "Off to the side. And then, all of a sudden, nothing."

Mrs. Worrell stared up at the tower, one hand pressed against her lips. "A bird," she began.

"No way," Aaron said flatly. "Not unless it was as big as a moose."

"We all saw it." Jennings shrugged. "Not a bird, Mrs. Worrell. As for what it was, I don't think we'll ever know. Not in this lifetime. And I don't think we'll accomplish a damn thing by standing here talking about it."

Mrs. Worrell's voice was thin and tired. "I regret very much that some prankster . . ."

Neal stared up at the tower, his face creased in a frown. "You can call it whatever you want to, a joke, some crazy deal. But how? We all saw it and it wasn't even in the tower, it was out there in the air."

"We'll find out." I spoke with more confidence than I felt, but I was damned if I was going to succumb to hysteria. Even though there didn't appear to be a rational explanation, I had to believe that somehow, some way, the apparition had been rigged. "I'm going up there."

Mrs. Worrell shivered. "Mrs. Collins, perhaps it would be better if you stayed here. I'll get the keys, lock the tower. Then there can't be any more of . . ." She trailed off.

Any more of what? Mrs. Worrell didn't

know. None of us knew.

"There's nothing up there, Grandma." Neal shook his head, folded his arms across his chest.

"I know. But the exercise will do me good." I moved through the tower door.

"Mrs. Collins . . ." Mrs. Worrell's voice was sharp. I kept on going.

Diana and Neal climbed right behind me. When we stepped out on the platform, I drew in deep breaths, trembling a little from the effort. We looked over the railing at the dark masses of shrubbery far below. The lights on the paths didn't penetrate the dark grounds. Beyond the shoreline, surf foamed bright in the moonlight on the black surging water.

Neal gestured over the parapet. "That stuff was right out there. Maybe five or six feet from the platform. I don't see how anybody could have held something out there. Besides that, there wasn't time for anyone to run down the stairs and get away before Aaron and I got to the tower."

I turned away from the railing, held up my pocket flash, swept the light up and down the white limestone slabs of the tower.

Neal understood at once. He moved faster than I did. But when we'd circled, reached the spot where we started, he ran his hand over the unbroken slabs. "Nope. No ladder. Nobody went up. Nobody went down. Where does that leave us?"

"In the morning, we'll look thoroughly through the garden —"

Diana gripped my arm. "That won't do any good. There wasn't anyone in the garden. We'd have heard them running away. There wasn't anyone anywhere."

"No one," Neal said reluctantly, "alive."

"We'll look in the morning," I said firmly.

We didn't talk as we climbed down the curving steps. When we reached the garden, Mrs. Worrell was waiting, holding a padlock in her hand. The others were gone. The manager said nothing to us. She waited until we were outside the tower; then she pulled the big wooden door closed, slipped the padlock through a hasp, clicked it shut.

The snap of the lock had a permanent sound.

But as we walked back toward the hotel, Neal bent and whispered in my ear. "Locks can't stop ghosts."

I splashed water on my face, scrubbed it dry, wishing I could wash away the memory of the night. I was unhappy on several counts. I didn't like remembering the frightened sound in Diana's voice or Neal's dogged insistence that there was no one near the tower, no living person. I didn't like the fact that I'd reassured Connor, insisted the ghost was a prank. Most of all, I didn't like the fact that George had played me for a fool.

I intended to have a talk with George. As soon as possible.

I plugged in the coffeemaker. The coffee perked as I dressed, a white cotton turtleneck and navy slacks. But it wasn't until I poured the steaming dark brew into a mug, a blue mug with a white tower on one side, and moved toward the closet for my shoes that I saw the square white envelope lying on the floor where it had been slipped beneath the door.

I stared at the envelope. Obviously, it had been put beneath my door after our wing quieted down. As we came back into the hotel, Aaron was insisting that a chaise longue was a great place to sleep as he stepped into Marlow and Jasmine's room. Connor clutched Lloyd's arm and said, "We'll pack. We'll pack right now." As their door shut, Lloyd said sharply, "But we can't leave . . ."

Jennings and I had exchanged swift glances as we stood by our doors.

"That's what you saw last night." I made it a statement.

He grunted, "Yeah," stepped into his room, slammed the door.

Neal had checked my room and Diana's, making sure the balcony doors were locked, waiting to hear us snap the chains in place.

It was almost two before I'd turned out my light, lain wide-eyed and angry in my bed, rerunning the moment in my mind, the sound of the screams — why precisely the same each time? — and the luminous swath of whiteness so tantalizingly near the tower, so far from the ground, so inexplicable.

No one there.

The words had ricocheted in my mind for the remainder of the night, sometimes an angry shout, sometimes a forlorn mumble, but over and over again, an ugly counterpoint to recurring screams.

But now in the brightness of a new morning, I was not so much angry as determined. I was going to find out what had happened last night. And maybe this envelope would show me the way. I bent down, snatched up the envelope. I didn't know what was in it, but I knew that I held in my hand the beginnings of a trail, one that I could follow with sharp questions and quiet observations. By God, here was a specific discrete entity. Somebody had slipped a message beneath my door and I never doubted that it was connected directly to the apparition near the tower.

I put the mug on the table, studied the envelope, turning it over in my hands. It was hotel stationery, the Tower Ridge House address in the upper left corner, and, of course, the white tower, outlined in blue. My name was printed neatly on the outside in red ink:

MRS. COLLINS

The envelope was sealed. I loosened the flap, pulled out a folded sheet. The message was printed in bright red block letters on a sheet of hotel stationery:

$1000 — NO GHOST
$2000 — GHOST
$5000 — PARTICULARS???????

The first sum was crossed out, the second sum circled.

A simple sketch at the bottom of the page showed a headland jutting into the water, sharp rocks below the prong of land. The time — 8 A.M. — was written below.

There was no signature, of course. But George didn't need to sign this missive.

Only he and I knew that I had offered him one thousand dollars to lay the ghost to rest. Oh, well, to be precise, perhaps he and I and one other person were aware of that fact. Because someone else, obviously, had paid him two thousand to raise the ghost last night. And now, for five thousand dollars, he was willing to reveal the truth behind the screams and the luminous apparition near the tower.

I was amused in a grim way. But I intended to get the information out of George without paying a cent. And I certainly didn't need to ask Lloyd for the original one thousand. George's double-dealing scotched that debt. I was looking forward to 8 A.M. I put the sheet in the envelope and tucked it into the pocket of my slacks.

I detoured through the garden on my way to breakfast. The garden at Tower Ridge House was almost as spectacular as that at Rosedon with a profusion of poinciana, frangipani, and palmetto trees. I climbed the steps of a pink gazebo that overlooked the grounds. Diana had been right the night before. It was quite obvious in the brightness of the morning that no one could have run away from the tower without being seen. Three lighted paths led from the tower, all of them visible to those of us on the balconies. If anyone had plunged into the flower beds or tried to skirt the shrubbery in the darkness, we would have heard the thrashing, been able to follow the movement.

What about the far side of the tower? The tower sat high on a ridge and just beyond ran a limestone wall. I shaded my eyes. Not a very tall wall. Could someone have ducked away from the tower, run to the wall and climbed over without being seen from the balconies or the garden?

I climbed down the gazebo steps, followed a winding path bounded by masses of crimson blooms. There were delicate camellias, cheery daffodils, pink and white and red hibiscus. The sweet scent of frangipani mingled with the ever-present salty tang from the ocean.

Frangipani . . . I rested for a moment before climbing the far slope. In Hawaii, the tree was known as plumeria. In early days there, it was often planted around graveyards, and its delicate white, apricot, yellow or maroon blossoms were associated with death. Millions of tourists never knew this, so today the blossom is the mainstay of leis and its sweet scent automatically invokes the Islands.

The wind rustled the frangipani. I reached up, carefully pulled loose an apricot flower. I would give it to Connor, if all went well in my interview with George. Success would mean the tower could once again be enjoyed for its view, not avoided as a haven for a vengeful spirit. I wondered if Connor knew the Hawaiian custom. A single flower behind the right ear meant the wearer was available. A flower tucked behind the left ear indicated the wearer's affections were already engaged. I carried the blossom loosely in my hand, careful not to bruise it.

Once on the ridge, I looked out at the ocean first. No one could attain this clear, sweet, clean eminence and ignore the thrusting black rocks, the crashing waves with foam that sparkled like diamonds, and water so brightly blue it looked like turquoise glass. Bermuda, beautiful Bermuda. I took a final glance, then turned and walked briskly toward the tower. A lawn stretched another fifteen feet past the tower, ending at a limestone wall covered by honeysuckle. The wall curved to the farthest point of land, where a huge magnolia splayed its branches almost forty feet high.

I imagined a figure darting from the tower to the wall . . . I reached the wall, looked over, and saw a drop of more than twenty feet to a curving road. No one could escape this way without a ladder of some sort. I walked the length of the wall and, near the magnolia, looked down at the pounding surf crashing against black rocks.

As I sauntered back through the garden, I faced facts. Whatever moved briefly in the night sky near the tower, it hadn't been engineered from either the tower or the garden. A beam of light, perhaps? But once again, beamed from where?

It was irritating not to have an idea. But George knew. And George was going to tell me.

It was a few minutes past seven when I reached the dining room. Three tables were occupied, but no one from our group was there. I settled at a table for two with my back to the door. I didn't want to converse with anyone. I drank the freshly squeezed orange juice and enjoyed every bite of my bacon and eggs as I considered what I knew. I needed to be clear in my mind.

I pulled the envelope out of my pocket, opened it, studied the sheet as I ate.

I was sure the marked-out "$1000" meant that George had taken my offer to someone who topped it, paid him two thousand to be sure that the ghost appeared last night. Clearly, the appearance of the ghost — or its nonappearance — was within George's control. So he either created the phenomena himself or he knew who did.

If George did not himself arrange the ghostly doings, how could he prevent another person from doing so? Persuasion? Money? Fear of public revelation?

I finished my breakfast, sipped coffee. It was possible, I thought wryly, that George was simply a first-class opportunist and didn't have any knowledge but was willing to take advantage of my (presumed) credulity. Under that scenario, he turned the loss of my thousand into a gain by pretending someone paid him for last night's performance and, carrying it to a chutzpah high, was hitting me up for five thousand for information he didn't possess!

It was rather like an intricate chess game. His move. My move. I was sure of only one fact: George was not going to pocket five thousand dollars.

I was almost finished with my coffee when I heard footsteps behind me, swift and purposeful.

eight

Marlow Bailey came around the end of the table, gripped the top of the chair opposite me. She studied me with cool, appraising eyes. "I went to your room." There was no bun this morning. The cloud of dusky hair made her face softer, less severe, but her pale skin still lacked makeup. I imagined at home she'd come down for breakfast in an oversize T-shirt and terry-cloth scuffies. In deference to Bermuda's formality, she wore a white cotton turtleneck and black slacks. In another era, she'd have tucked flowers in her hair and favored worn blue work shirts and likely eschewed the thought of travel here. In yet an earlier era, every woman in the Tower Ridge House dining room would have been in a dress, but not even this most British outpost could turn back that clock.

She leaned against the chair as if it were a gate to vault. "I need to talk to you." Despite the softness of her Georgia accent, her voice was curt.

I didn't like her tone. "Indeed." I put down my coffee cup with a decided click.

She reached out a slender hand, the nails

short with clear polish. "Please." She took a deep breath. "I hate doing this. I hate talking about family to strangers but I've got to do something and you're the only person I can think of who might be able to help."

We gazed at each other. Taking measure? I wasn't quite certain, but the depth of worry in her eyes tempered my irritation.

I gestured toward the chair.

Marlow pulled it back, slipped into the seat, never taking her eyes off my face. She was pale and her eyes were worried, yet hopeful.

I glanced at my watch. I had twenty minutes. And I was curious. Why had this self-possessed young woman sought me out?

Brian, thirtyish, slender, self-effacing, was our waiter this morning, not George. When I'd arrived, I'd glanced around the room, wondering if George was near. But I doubted it. He must have the morning off if he'd planned our appointment for eight o'clock. As Brian poured more coffee for me and filled Marlow's cup, she waved her hand. "Fruit. And oatmeal. And orange juice, please."

But when he moved away, she was silent. She looked tired, bluish half-moons beneath her eyes, a droop to her mouth. She picked up her napkin, spread it on her lap.

Her fingers nervously worked one corner. "I went to Emory. I wanted to go to Pomona."

I didn't say anything. I must have looked blank. I felt blank.

She bit her lip. Her look was both scathing and defensive. "You're a rather formidable woman, you know. So arrogant. I wouldn't even try to talk to you, but I have to. I mean, I know you're kind of famous, but do you have to be so damn sure of yourself?" She rolled the napkin into a strip, held it like a rope. "You won't understand. You're too capable, too controlled. You've never been afraid everything would smash to pieces."

"Smash to pieces . . ." I didn't look at her. I wasn't seeing her. I was seeing my little boy and the bloody bruise on his temple where his head struck the side of the car that night so long ago. If we hadn't gone to the fiesta, if I hadn't insisted we go, the ramshackle truck would not have rammed us and Bobby wouldn't have died. "Smash to pieces . . ." And the emptiness that enveloped me, cold as a shroud, when the phone call came that my husband, Richard, was dead in a fall from a cliff and the corrosive flicker of anger at the place of his death.

We sat at the breakfast table, each of us quite alone.

Neither of us spoke while Brian served her breakfast.

As he walked away, I said in as level a voice as I could manage, "Not arrogant, Marlow. I have too much guilt ever to be arrogant. I know what happens when things smash." Yes, I knew. I knew how it felt when life was like a small boat caught in huge waves and everything on deck slips and slides. But obviously this young girl, too, knew uncertainty and fear. I asked gently, "Why didn't you go to Pomona?"

"I couldn't go away and leave Mother." There was utter weariness in her voice. She brushed back a soft pouf of black hair. She was plain, but there was a grave dignity, a kind of beauty in her strong, sad face. "You see, Daddy understood Mother. Everybody always thought she married him because he was so rich. She didn't. She married Daddy because he was strong. He understood her, how vulnerable she is, how easily frightened. And he knew she couldn't help it about men. She doesn't try to get them, but they can't stay away from her. Oh, I know, I know." Her head shake was impatient. "Sure, it takes two . . . but Mother has to have attention. That's what keeps her going, attention and admiration and love. But she doesn't mean anything by it."

I thought I understood. "But if a man means it . . ."

"Things get difficult." She spooned brown sugar over her oatmeal.

"Was it difficult with Roddy Worrell?" I wondered if Mrs. Worrell was near and what she would think about this conversation.

Marlow sighed. "None of it would have happened if Daddy had been here . . . But he wasn't here. Roddy was pressing her. He knew she was rich. He wanted to go back to America with her. He didn't understand."

No, I doubted he understood a woman who beckoned, but was always out of reach to those who followed.

"It was awful . . ." Marlow put down her spoon, her face heavy with remembered pain.

"When he fell?" I imagined the shock had been enormous.

Marlow blinked. "Oh, that. Yes, of course." She sighed. "They didn't find him until daylight. Somebody went for a walk in the garden. If Mr. Worrell cried out as he fell, no one heard him." She frowned. "That yell last night was dreadful, just the way you'd think someone might cry out if they fell and knew they were falling, but we didn't hear anything the night he died. It was the next morning — Mrs. Worrell screamed and screamed. I remember that. I was coming up the steps from the pool and so I saw her — Mrs. Worrell — she was on her knees beside him. I didn't know it was him. It looked like a bunch of clothes or a heap of trash. Nothing live. But he wasn't alive. Later they said he'd been dead for hours, that he must have fallen out of the tower not long after he left the bar. He slammed away, yelling that Mother was . . . It was hateful. And of course that's what she remembers. When we got home to Atlanta, she didn't want to come out of her room. She huddled there. She said he — Roddy — had told her she was cruel and that if anything happened to him, she would have to bear the blame in her soul forever."

"A bit extravagant, I think." My tone was dry.

Marlow looked at me eagerly. "You see that, don't you? It's the kind of thing a man says to make a woman feel bad. He doesn't mean it, not really."

Not unless he intended to commit suicide and wanted to make his lover suffer. Was that the kind of man Roddy Worrell was?

Marlow pushed her hands against her hair. "Mother was absolutely distraught.

She withdrew. I was frightened for her. It was awful."

This was what Marlow found awful, Connor's depression after Roddy Worrell's death, not the fact of his death.

"Lloyd helped." Marlow's tone was grudging. "Of course, Lloyd was part of the problem with Roddy. Lloyd went after Mother the minute he saw her. That really ticked off Roddy. But after Roddy died, Lloyd was really kind and gentle. Still, when we got home, Mother had nightmares and she holed up in her room and wouldn't talk. I could scarcely get her to eat. Then Lloyd started coming to visit and she was more and more like her old self. I encouraged him." Her tone was bitter. "God, what a fool I was."

"Why do you dislike Lloyd so much?" That dislike made all she said suspect. If she wanted her mother's happiness, why was she opposed to a man who obviously adored Connor?

"I don't dislike him." Her tone was dismissive. "But he's all wrong for Mother. He absolutely doesn't have a clue. I mean, he insisted they come here for the wedding. He kept going on and on about how romantic it was that he and Mother met here and that Aaron and I met here and it would be so much fun for all of us to come here for the wedding. All because this is where they met. He seemed to think it had some kind of cosmic significance that Aaron and I met here on spring break instead of at school. He went on and on about how he'd wanted to stay at the Southampton Princess but came here instead and met Mom, and Aaron was only here because his roommate had planned to come here on a spring-break trip but couldn't and Aaron took his place at the last minute. I mean, people have to meet somewhere! But to Lloyd, it's part of some divine plan. I mean, he is really a sentimental ass, all without having any real empathy! He didn't give a thought to how Mother might feel about coming back here. And anybody who looked back at last year should have known that it would be an awful mistake. Anybody but good old Lloyd. Doesn't he have any imagination —"

Lloyd had good qualities. He was honest, steady, and kind. But imaginative? No.

"— at all? Mother kept saying no and finally he booked everything without telling her and showed up with the tickets, looking like a lovesick calf. I honestly think she felt sorry for him. But she never should have come back here. Never, never, never. But that's not the big problem." She looked at

136

me, her eyes desperate. "Listen, you must know him really well. I mean, he was married to your daughter and he asked you to come to the wedding. He must think a lot of you."

I understood her reasoning. But she was wrong on all counts. I never lived in the same town with Emily and Lloyd and so had very little close contact with Lloyd over the years. I was his mother-in-law and therefore treated with respect and thoughtfulness. But my conversation with Lloyd on the terrace here in Bermuda might have been the most in-depth communication we'd ever had. Moreover, I was sure he'd invited me because Emily had asked him to do so and perhaps he felt, too, I'd be a buffer between him and his children.

I shook my head. "Marlow, I have scarcely ever spent a moment alone with Lloyd —"

"Oh, God." Her voice was ragged with despair. "Somebody has got to talk to him. I can't. Maybe Uncle Steve . . . But that won't work. Lloyd's jealous of him. And that scares me. And I don't think he'd pay any attention to Aaron. I thought maybe you . . ."

"Talk to Lloyd about what? Roddy Worrell?" Talk to a man I'd exchanged pleasantries with over the course of twenty-some years about the woman he was going to marry, a woman too attractive to too many men?

"Roddy. No. Not really." Marlow's eyes widened. She clapped her hands together sharply. "Or maybe that's exactly what Lloyd needs to know about. Roddy Worrell. And all the men before him." She ticked them off on her fingers: "Bob Simpson at the tennis club and Coley Howell at church and George Fisher in Daddy's office and" — she drew a deep breath — "all the others. And maybe about here and now and that jerk from Texas. Lloyd was furious when he —"

Oh, yes, the big redhead, Curt Patterson.

"— tagged along yesterday. If Lloyd will understand about him, it will be all right. Because there will always be men tagging along." She managed a smile. "So please, if you can, if you will, talk to Lloyd, try to explain that men come after Mother and it doesn't do any harm, but he can't be jealous. If he's jealous, it will ruin everything. If he's jealous" — she pushed back her chair, stood, looked down at me with grave, sad eyes — "he mustn't marry her."

I tried to walk fast, realized I simply didn't have the energy. I was late for my meeting with George. Marlow's unexpected revelations — and how much of those I could accept as truth and how much was a daughter's defense, I wasn't sure — had taken all of the allotted twenty minutes and a few more.

And I walked slowly because I was troubled. I should have told Marlow emphatically that I could not be an emissary to Lloyd. But I had not done so. That lack of refusal was tantamount to acquiescence. Was I willing to embark on a futile and potentially distressing mission simply to improve Marlow's opinion of me? I'd been shocked at her picture of me. Arrogant? No. Aloof, perhaps. Reserved, yes. Sometimes weary, tired of insincerity and triviality and unwitting cruelty. But she had seen me as a cold and dismissive woman. Why should I care what Marlow thought of me? It is not only Rhett Butler who doesn't give a damn. No one over sixty gives a damn. That is a very great freedom and one to be prized.

The sea breeze stirred the branches of a glossy-leaved magnolia. Sunlight speared between the branches, dappling the dew-laden grass. I pulled my cardigan tight. Although the early-morning air was cool, it wasn't the air that chilled me. It was almost as if I walked alongside myself, saw the dark-haired woman with a worn face and thoughtful eyes. I valued the freedom of age, but I didn't want to be hard, encased in an impervious shell. I didn't want to be arrogant.

Everything had seemed simple this morning. I'd had a clear-cut plan: Confront George, roust out the truth of Roddy Worrell's ghost, convince Connor she had nothing to fear. Marlow's request and her cold-eyed appraisal of me had re-sorted my priorities. I was afraid Lloyd would refuse to listen to me, but, damnit, I would try. As for George, now it was even more important for me to determine the truth of the visions at the tower.

I glanced again at my watch. I was more than a half hour late. I started down the steps to the lower terrace. However, George had an incentive to be patient. He was hoping to reel in a five-thousand-dollar fish. I hadn't decided how to proceed, but I had no compunction about misleading him. In my view, George wasn't due honest dealing.

I stopped a moment at the bottom of the second flight of steps. The long, inviting green tunnel to the beach was another hundred yards along. I was very late. But if George had given up on me, I'd seek him out. I didn't hurry. I had plenty to think about. I understood my options:

1. Promise George the five thousand but

on the condition that he explain the ghostly phenomena first.

2. Tell him his easy-money days were over and either he revealed what he knew about the tower or I would take the note he'd left in my room, give it to Mrs. Worrell, and inform her of my conversation with him after tea.

I inclined toward the latter. I doubted George would provide what I wanted to know without actually receiving money and, since I had no intention of paying him, I might as well see what I could learn by threat.

I wondered if it had occurred to him to wear gloves when he handled the envelope and note? After all, Mrs. Worrell would be justified in taking the note to the police on the basis that her livelihood was being endangered by the disturbances.

Actually, I felt fairly confident. George had made a mistake when he'd agreed that he could prevent the apparition at the tower. That was a clear admission of more knowledge than he would possess if he was an innocent bystander.

Last night screams tore apart the quiet, and a luminous glow hovered near the platform.

Somebody made it happen. I thought that someone was George. However, George could claim he was guilty of nothing more than trying to scam a tourist and insist he had nothing to do with the apparitions and had made the offer to me simply hoping nothing more would happen before we left Bermuda, making him the grateful recipient of an unearned thousand.

Maybe, damnit, that would turn out to be the fact and I'd be no nearer learning the truth behind the luminous glow even if I reported George to Mrs. Worrell. Still, the threat of talking to her, even if the more innocent explanation served, might be enough to scare him into cooperating. Or at least spinning another story to satisfy me. After all, his attempt to get money from a guest should be enough to get him fired. I didn't know how hard it was to get a job on Bermuda, how important a recommendation might be, how much his job mattered to him, whether a complaint could jeopardize his work permit. I might still have the upper hand.

However, I knew without doubt that George wanted money. All right, maybe I should talk to Lloyd, see how much he would be willing to pay to expose the nonsense about the tower as trickery. Maybe bargaining was still the best route. I would decide how to deal with George when we talked.

I reached the end of the tunnel of greenery. I stopped at the ridged concrete walkway that shelved down to the rocky, seaweed-strewn beach. Surf as white as Chantilly lace foamed against the rocks, rippled over the pale pink sand. The sky gleamed bright blue, shiny as enamel. If I were a painter, I'd take that sky and splash it by the handfuls on a stark-white canvas and add dollops of the lighter, richer turquoise of the water, but no art could ever match the grandeur of color in Bermudian sky and sea.

I edged down the ridged slab and crossed the damp sand to the base of the headland. I found the faint trail, followed it. When I reached the top, I could see all the way to the point and far, far out to sea, the glorious, compellingly blue sea.

"Damn." No one waited.

Was George a no-show? Had he given up on me because I was late? But if that was the case, we should have met in the green tunnel. I walked slowly toward the point, feeling the strength of the breeze, welcoming the salty scent of the water. I passed the moongate and stopped at the edge of the cliff.

The breeze was cool and fresh. I wanted to stand there and draw the freshness inside, feel young again, buoyed by beauty which feeds hope. I clung to the moment, knowing I must turn away. I needed to find George. And I must approach Lloyd. Would he listen? I believed that Lloyd loved Connor, but could he provide the accepting love Marlow thought Connor needed? And yet I lingered, still as a lizard, basking in the sun. Finally, with a sigh, I turned to go and my gaze swept out to the reef and the bubbly line of surf, then closer to shore and the sharp rocks below . . .

I froze, shocked into immobility, staring down at the crumpled body wedged facedown between black pinnacles. Foamy surf submerged the body as each wave broke and for that instant I lost sight of the lolling head.

Dead. George was dead. I didn't need to see his face to recognize him. The body was that of a young man in a white shirt and khaki trousers. I stood for another moment, listening to the crash of the surf. There was no way to climb down the cliff face without ropes and pitons. The only access to the rugged rocks would be from the beach over wet boulders and that would be a struggle. But there was no hurry. The water sloshing over the body, pummeling the inert form, had long since extinguished any spark of life that might have survived the brutal plummet onto the rocks.

nine

I paced up and down at the top of the hotel steps. I'd grabbed up the phone at the front desk to make the 911 call, ignoring the shocked questions from Rosalind, the young woman at the desk, saying only that I was going outside to await the arrival of the police. It wasn't my job to announce the discovery of George's body to the staff. But I'd known as I hung up the phone and moved toward the front door that word would spread faster than the click of castanets. I wasn't surprised a few minutes later when Mrs. Worrell burst through the main door. Lloyd was right behind her.

Mrs. Worrell's angular face was taut with irritation. "Mrs. Collins, please explain this call you've placed." Her hands curled into bony fists.

Lloyd's voice was shocked. "Henrie O, what the hell's going on? Did you really find a body? Where? What happened?" He paced back and forth beside me, peering down at the drive. "Have you actually called the police?"

I held up my hands. I spoke to the manager. "There's a body at the foot of the point, caught in the rocks." I hesitated, then, watching her carefully, I said, "I think it may be George."

Her head shake was decisive. "I just saw George a little while ago, Mrs. Collins. And certainly he wouldn't fall on the rocks. That's absurd. Besides, he'd have no reason to be out on the point. You may have seen a log —"

"In a white shirt and khaki slacks?" My tone was sharp.

Her pale blue eyes bulged.

Lloyd jolted to a stop, stared at me. "God, that's too bad." He ran a hand through his reddish-gold hair. "Oh, hell, this is going to upset Connor." He glanced down at his watch. "We're supposed to take off in the van in about twenty minutes. Maybe I can round everyone up and we'll leave a little earlier, miss all the . . ." His voice trailed off. He didn't meet my eyes.

I stared at him. "What a shame if you are inconvenienced."

"Oh, hell." He chewed on his lower lip.

I didn't say a word.

Lloyd finally met my stony gaze. "I'm sorry, Henrie O. God knows it's a shame but we can't help anything by hanging around here, and Connor . . . She's not up to any more stress. Look, it has nothing to do with us —"

The manager nodded emphatically. "That's a very good plan. The fewer people in the hotel this morning, the better it will be. Please gather up your group, Mr. Drake." Mrs. Worrell glanced down the steps. "I must stay and speak with the police, but I'll arrange for another driver."

Lloyd gave me a shamefaced look, ducked his head and hurried up the steps.

A white station wagon rolled to a stop by the front steps of the hotel. I walked down to meet the uniformed officers, two of them, a slender black woman in her forties and a young man who reminded me sharply of George, tall, gangly, smooth young skin and a sunburned nose. Mrs. Worrell was right on my heels.

The woman officer was in the lead. "Mrs. Collins?"

I'd made the call, so they had my name.

The officer observed me politely but with care, noting, I was sure, that my clothing showed no signs of disarray, that I was dry, sober, and apparently compos mentis.

"Yes, officer. The body is on the rocks below the headland. A man."

"Thank you, Mrs. Collins. I am Police Constable Howard." She nodded toward the young man. "Police Constable Dugan. We will accompany you to the beach." It was a simple statement, but it reminded me that for the time being I had no freedom of movement.

Mrs. Worrell clasped her hands tightly together. "If you could direct the ambulance to use the lower road . . . I don't want to disturb the guests. It has nothing to do with the hotel."

P.C. Howard was polite but firm. "There will be a number of cars, ma'am. In the event of an unexplained death, it is necessary for a forensics team to assemble." She unloosed a cell phone from her belt. "I will ask that the vehicles be deployed to the lower road."

Mrs. Worrell took a step or two with us.

"I suggest you remain here, ma'am." P.C. Howard was pleasant but insistent. "Access to the beach will be closed until the field search is complete."

As we moved away, I glanced back at Mrs. Worrell. She looked shaken. And frightened. I carried that picture of her with me as we walked down to the beach. My mind was jumbled with thoughts, but I was puzzled by the sense of fear emanating from the hotel manager. Certainly she should know what happened when a body was found. She'd had that experience last year with her husband's death. Why, then, did she appear to be frightened? I pushed the thought aside. I had plenty of other concerns, including what I should tell the police. The officers waited patiently as I paused twice during the descent. I began to explain, "I was walking out on the headland —"

P.C. Howard interrupted. "The chief inspector will interview you, Mrs. Collins."

And that was that. I led the rest of the way in silence, through the long cool tunnel to the outcropping of black rock above the sand, down the cement grid and the slow climb up the faint trail to the top of the narrow headland. When we stood on the point and looked down, the tide was coming in. Most of the body was hidden beneath the swirling water. As the waves broke, a floating hand could be glimpsed for an instant.

The young officer spoke for the first time. "May go out with the tide."

P.C. Howard lifted her cell phone, then looked at me. She nodded toward a rustic wooden bench some twenty feet from the point. "If you will be kind enough to wait there, Mrs. Collins."

I spent almost two hours on the bench. Occasionally, I rose and paced a few feet, careful to stay out of the way of the field search team. In the water, marine experts were at work. The forensics team included a slim young woman who turned out to be the pathologist there to view the body in situ.

I briefly met Chief Inspector Gerald Foster, who had a shock of iron-gray hair, the chiseled good looks of Harry Belafonte, and a probing gaze. His gray suit had a fine blue pinstripe and it fitted him perfectly. He spoke with the beautiful, clear diction of an educated Bermudian, his voice pleasant but nonetheless commanding.

"Mrs. Collins?" He didn't refer to notes to call up my name. "You found the body?"

"Yes." Would he ask what brought me to the end of the point?

"At what time?" He glanced at his watch.

"Approximately eight thirty-five." If I'd been on time for my appointment, would George be alive?

"There was no sign of life?"

"None." Sodden clothes and a lolling head.

"Do you know the deceased?"

I hesitated. That was a mistake. Chief Inspector Foster's gaze sharpened. He looked at me with alert interest.

I spoke too quickly. "I can't be certain. I thought it might be George, a young waiter from the hotel."

Foster studied me, then swung around and walked to the end of the point and stared down at the quiet activity on the rocks below him. He stood in a relaxed way, head cocked, hands loose at his side.

I dropped onto the bench, wishing I could hurry back to the hotel, although I wasn't sure what I would do when I got there. Because, of course, everything depended upon what had happened to George. Was his death murder, accident, or suicide? I had a cold feeling that there might not be a definitive answer and an even colder feeling that George's death might have resulted directly from my dealings with him. I'd offered George money to close down the ghost of Roddy Worrell. Had I set in motion, inexorable as an avalanche, a series of events resulting in George's murder?

I looked at it clearly. I offered George money to stop the ghost. The ghost hovered near the tower last night. This morning I found the note which, in effect, informed me my thousand dollars had been trumped but I could have the truth about the ghost for five thousand.

Had George pushed his luck? If I accepted the implications of the note, someone upped my offer to two thousand

and the ghost walked — or floated — last night. Then George asked me for five thousand. What if he'd asked someone else for six thousand — or more — in exchange for silence?

What if that person decided to kill George instead?

I rubbed my temple. Was keeping the secret of Roddy Worrell's ghost worth murder? Why?

Perhaps George fell. Perhaps he walked to the end of the point and lost his balance. I shook my head. George had been young, strong, agile. It didn't make sense. But accidents happen. Suicide? No. A depressed person contemplating suicide would not have written the note asking for money.

It came down to murder or accident. Accident or murder.

Firm footsteps sounded. I looked up. Chief Inspector Foster walked toward me.

Chief Inspector Foster sat opposite me, the width of a card table between us, in a small room along the short corridor that branched from the main lobby. To one side, a uniformed officer, a young man in his twenties, held a notebook and pen. The chief inspector rested his elbows on the table, looked at me intently. "The body was facedown in the water. It could not be identified from the headland. You thought it might be a waiter here at the hotel. The body has now been identified as that of George Edward Smith, an employee of Tower Ridge House." He cocked his head, like an old, thoughtful parrot. "I'm a little curious, Mrs. Collins, how did you know the dead man was this young man whom you called George?"

I'd known this moment would be coming, though I'd not expected his first question to place me squarely on the spot. I slipped my hand into my pocket, felt the envelope I'd tucked there. If I gave the envelope and note to him, I would have to explain the significance of those sums — the crossed-out 1000, the 2000, and the 5000. At this point, I was reluctant to tell the police of my attempts to persuade George to corral the ghost. Moreover, I didn't want to expose Connor to the rigors of questioning in a police investigation. Admittedly, Connor was upset about the ghost's appearance, but surely, whatever the truth behind the ghost, it couldn't have anything to do with the Drake-Bailey wedding party. I didn't know the whys and wherefores of the apparition, but I knew that George Smith didn't believe Roddy Worrell fell from the tower. That was the important point. I pulled my hand out of my pocket, folded my hands loosely together.

"I wasn't certain that the dead man was George, Chief Inspector. But there was something about the shape of the body," I said vaguely. "And he'd been out on the point with our group the morning before, taking a photograph for us. I suppose that came to my mind."

Foster continued to look at me.

Before the silence could grow oppressive, I said briskly, "And I had such a long chat with George yesterday afternoon. About the ghost. And about Mr. Worrell's murder."

Foster's smooth dark face remained expressionless. "Mr. Worrell's murder?"

I hitched my chair closer to the table, met his gaze eagerly. "It's an extraordinary story. Last year, as you may know —"

Of course Foster knew, but he made no response.

"— the hotel manager's husband, Roddy Worrell, died in a fall from the tower. The first anniversary of his death is apparently coming up and this week there have been several sightings of some kind of luminous cloud near the top of the tower. George told the little girl in our party — Jasmine — all about it. I was quite curious, so I spoke to

George after tea yesterday afternoon. He confirmed the sightings, but perhaps even more important" — I spoke with great clarity — "George insisted Mr. Worrell could handle himself even if he was drunk. George didn't believe he fell."

Foster leaned back in his chair, folded his arms. "What basis did Smith give for that statement?" His voice was crisp.

The young policeman wrote swiftly.

"He said . . ." I paused to try and remember George's words: " 'Roddy Worrell never fell out of that tower. Even drunk, he could handle himself. And he wasn't that drunk.' " I looked expectantly at the chief inspector.

"Worrell's blood alcohol level was point zero nine." Foster left it at that. "Did Smith accuse anyone?"

"No. He simply said Worrell didn't fall." I didn't have to point out that a killer who pushed once would be quick to push again if danger threatened. "George made the point that Worrell could handle himself. Yet he ends up dead at the base of the tower. Now George is dead, yet he appeared very athletic. Why would he fall off a cliff?"

"We don't know what happened, Mrs. Collins. Accidents occur. The young and quick are often careless. I won't have the official report from the pathologist for several days. Her preliminary judgment is that death was due to drowning, that he likely was rendered unconscious by the fall. There are no suspicious circumstances" — now his eyes raked my face — "except for your statement."

"Grandma, are you sure you don't want to come?" Diana touched my arm. Her reddish-gold hair was drawn back in a ponytail, perhaps too severe a style for her fine features. But I knew her bleak expression reflected shock at George's death.

I welcomed the soft pressure of her fingers. Yes, I wanted to climb on the pillion of Neal's scooter and ride to Harrington Sound with my grandchildren as if this were a normal vacation day and a young man's body had not been slipped into a rubberized bag for its journey to the cold air and harsh glare of the morgue.

"I'm a little tired. I believe I'll stay here and rest." I was tired, but I had no intention of resting. It wasn't fatigue that weighted me. It was the nagging worry that my less than frank interview with the chief inspector might hamper his investigation. So I was determined to nose around until I could give Chief Inspector Foster the name of the unknown figure who'd trumped my thousand-dollar offer to George.

Was I looking for a ghost-raiser? Or a murderer?

Diana shivered. "It seems all wrong to go and play — just as if nothing had happened." She looked over her shoulder at the steps leading down to the lower terrace. The paramedics had carried the body bag up those steps.

"Nothing we do will change the fact of George's death, Diana. You and Neal go now. Look for beauty." It was another way of saying a prayer.

"Are you sure you're okay, Grandma?" Neal was astride the moped, his blunt face creased with concern.

I managed a smile. "I'm fine." I waved my hand at them. "Scoot."

I stayed on the drive until I no longer heard the putt-putt of the mopeds. They were going to Devil's Hole, a clear natural pool famous for its sharks and moray eels and brilliantly hued fighting fish. For a fee, a visitor could fish with baited but hookless lines.

I was going fishing, too. I wasn't sure about my bait — a hint of dangerous knowledge? — but I hoped my line had a sharp hook.

Tower Ridge House drowsed in the afternoon sun. The presence of the police was unobtrusive. The door to the manager's office was closed. So far as I knew, no one in our party was in the hotel. Lloyd and Connor and Steve, along with Marlow and Jasmine and Aaron, were gone when I climbed up the slope from the beach, and I assumed they'd departed on their excursion to Spittal Pond and on to Hamilton for a late lunch at the Hog Penny on Burnaby Hill. The restaurant, decorated like an old English pub with dark-paneled walls, was well known for its fish and chips and steak-and-kidney pie. My last visit there was on a long-ago July day with Richard. I'd chosen a curried dish. Beneath the inconsequential thought of food, I tried to decide what I should do. I hesitated in the center of the hallway between the lounge and the bar.

Huge poinsettias in cobalt-blue pots sat on either side of the folded-back doors to the bar where wall sconces burned dimly against the coppery planks of cedar. Behind the bar, the bartender, round-faced with thinning blond hair, polished glasses. Not surprisingly on a sunny afternoon, he had no customers.

I walked in with a smile, slid atop a red leatherette seat. "I'll have a glass of sherry, please."

"Sweet or dry, ma'am?" His voice was young. He was balding but probably not even thirty yet. Long bristly sideburns framed plump cheeks.

"Bristol Cream, if you have it." I like sherry for the same reason I enjoy chocolate truffles.

"Yes, ma'am." He swung about, reached for a dark green bottle.

When he brought the glass, I took a sip. "That's very good."

"It's Harvey's, Mrs. Collins." He picked up a glass, wiped it carefully.

"Oh, yes. Thank you, James." I recognized him as one of the other waiters at lunch. "It is James, isn't it?" I held him with my gaze.

He remained opposite me. Most bartenders quickly pick up on a customer's need to talk. "Yes, ma'am."

I sighed. "I'm sorry about George."

The professional veneer almost held, but not quite. His blue eyes looked shocked. He crumpled the dish towel in pudgy hands. "I saw him this morning. Just about eight, it was." His voice held disbelief. "He was heading down to the lower terrace and I wondered about that. He should have been in the dining room, getting everything ready for breakfast. But I talked to Brian a little while ago and he told me he took over for

159

George this morning. That George had something to do."

That placed the time of George's death between eight and eight forty-five.

"Do you suppose George was going down to the beach when you saw him?" I kept my tone casual.

James swept his cloth in little circles on the mahogany of the bar. "I guess so. But what he said didn't make any sense."

"Really." The sherry was as sweet and rich as dollops of cream.

James looked at me, his round face earnest. "I keep trying to get it straight in my mind. The policeman's asking everybody when they last saw George, what he said. But see, he told Brian he had someplace to go and when I saw George, he grinned at me and gave me a thumbs-up and said he was going to get his ticket home. He was walking cocky like he'd won the lottery."

"Ticket home?" Yes, I'd known that George wanted money.

"He was saving money to go home. Toronto. I know he was a long way from having enough." He shook his head. "But that's what he said."

A thumbs-up and a cocky walk. On his way to die.

"It doesn't make any sense." James's tone

was querulous. "Who'd have money down at the beach?"

I felt empty. If George hadn't hoped I would bring a promise of five thousand, he wouldn't have been standing on the point, above the deadly rocks. "No, I wouldn't think there would be money down at the beach."

James made a sour face. "Well, I can tell you it didn't have anything to do with drugs. Not at this hotel. And not on our beach. Sure, there are drugs on the island. But George wasn't into drugs. He didn't even drink. He was a scuba diver and a Rugby player. He told me he'd quit his job before he'd work in here." James waved his hand. "The bar is the only place anybody can smoke in the hotel except in their own rooms. I told the police George didn't have any use for drugs. He didn't go down there for a drug deal."

"I'm sure he didn't," I agreed.

James's combative look eased.

"I suppose George got too near the edge of the point and slipped." I shook my head. "And I'd had the most interesting visit with George yesterday afternoon. He told me all about the ghost at the tower." I simulated a shiver. "I suppose you've heard about last night?"

"Yes, ma'am." His eyes slid past me, stared through the doorway into the hall.

"Have you ever seen the ghost, James?"

His reaction surprised me. He didn't look uneasy, as if afraid of otherworldly apparitions. Instead, he darted another cautious look at the doorway and bent toward me. I heard his quick whisper, "Look in the Sports cupboard down by the pool. Don't say I told you." The clatter of heels on the wooden floor almost drowned out the final words.

"Mrs. Collins." The voice was shaken, breathless.

I turned to face Mrs. Worrell. Behind me, James set a glass down sharply on the bar.

The transformation in the manager was shocking. The genteel, reserved innkeeper with gingery hair, faded blue eyes and worn, shapeless clothing stared at me, her eyes dazed, her face drained of color. She clung to the doorframe for support.

"Please." The words were so faint they could scarcely be heard. "I must speak with you."

162

ten

The sleek black cat on the purple silk cushion lifted his head, stared at me with unblinking yellow eyes and aloof disdain. I've always suspected that cats see beyond our pretenses and affectations, cataloging human behavior with humorless precision, unswayed in their final estimate by charm, affection, or choice cuts of meat.

Mrs. Worrell closed her office door behind us, leaned against it as if she had lost strength. Although she was a big-boned woman, she seemed small, propped against the wooden panels like a discarded rag doll. "I'm sorry," she began, "I've no right to trouble you, but I must know. I simply must." She pushed away from the door, reached out a hand toward me, though the trembling fingers didn't touch me. "I have to find out, and you must be the one . . ." She stopped, shook her head. "Please, did you tell the police officer that George said Roddy" — she drew in short, quick drafts of air as if her lungs were strained to the bursting — "was murdered?" The last word could scarcely be heard, a faint whisper.

I'd not thought what effect my statement to Chief Inspector Foster might have on others. My intent was to raise a doubt in Foster's mind that George Smith's fall from the point was an accident, to link George's death to Roddy Worrell's death, a link that seemed quite likely to me. Moreover, my statement to Foster was accurate. It was not I who questioned Roddy Worrell's death. It was George who had called Roddy's death murder.

Mrs. Worrell mistook my silence. "Oh, I thought it must have been you who told the inspector. You're the only person he's talked to. You and he were in the cardroom, and I assumed . . . but you must forgive me. He said he'd been informed that George insisted Roddy was pushed from the tower. But the inspector wouldn't tell me who told him. I have to know. I have to know what George said."

A grandfather clock in one corner ticked, the sound slow and somber in the heavy quiet, a sonorous counterpoint to the manager's shallow breaths. The wedge-shaped office was lit by a small pottery lamp on the corner of the pine desk. The single window of blue and white art glass, a wave endlessly breaking, afforded no natural light. The office ceiling sloped, giving the room a tucked-away, secretive air, as if the worn desk had been discarded there by accident. The ubiquitous computer on a metal stand looked like an afterthought, its coil of gray wires dangling to the floor like a tangle of dead snakes. A faint smell of potpourri mingled with the dry must of old books.

For a moment, I felt captured with the stricken woman in a dim circle of pain because I understood her distress. Oh, how well I understood. I would never forget the searing instant when I looked down at an anonymous letter informing me that my husband, Richard, had not died in an accident, as I had believed. That letter took me on a determined journey thousands of miles from my home, where I used guile and cold determination to gain access to a remote mountaintop mansion stalked by death.

My well-intentioned report to the chief inspector was bringing the same kind of torment to Mrs. Worrell, the swift uprush of anger that life had been deliberately wrested away, the anguish in knowing that days and hours and minutes that belonged to her and her husband had been stolen and, no matter what happened, even if the murderer was found, that the time which should have been theirs was gone forever.

"Mrs. Worrell, I'm sorry." Some of my

own anguish must have been clear on my face. "Of course I will tell you what George said. You have every right to know."

Her sandy eyelashes fluttered. She lifted a hand to her throat as if to still the pulse that throbbed there. "So it was you." She moved unsteadily, pulled two shabby green wooden chairs close together, sank into the far one. She waited, her hands twining together in unceasing movement, her unwavering gaze almost a physical pressure against my face. She didn't speak, but her eyes begged.

I sat on the second chair, so near I felt her tension as clearly as summer lightning crackling in the sky, and recounted what George had said about Roddy's death. I did not, of course, mention Connor or the broken miniature tower in her room or George's suggestion that Roddy's ghost was seeking revenge. Yes, I was still trying to protect Connor. I had not forgotten Mrs. Worrell's icy glare yesterday morning when Connor and Lloyd stepped out of the main door.

When I finished, she gave a tiny moan. "Oh my God. I should have known. I should have known." She rocked in the chair, her hands now clasped so tightly the fingers blanched. "That night" — her tone was feverish — "when Roddy slammed out of the bar, I didn't go after him." Her head jerked up. The eyes that stared at me were terrible with accusation. "Because she did. She went after him. She couldn't bear it that he was angry with her. And it wasn't as if he didn't have a right! She'd flounced around him, teased him, led him on. That's what she did. Another woman's husband, but she couldn't stay away from him. When he came after her because he was a man and he thought she wanted him, she ran to Mr. Jennings, complained as if it were all Roddy's fault. Roddy had put up with enough. He told me how she'd treated him, that she was no better than a slut." She pulled one hand free, brushed back her gingery hair. "He told me he was sorry. But that night she smiled at him, asked him to dance, one of those slow dances. And then Mr. Drake came in the bar and she went after him."

Mrs. Worrell was talking about Connor, of course. I'd not mentioned Connor's name, but I'd obviously not needed to do so. Mrs. Worrell's memories of her husband's last night of life were corroded by her unremitting anger against Connor.

Mrs. Worrell pushed up from her chair. She wavered on her feet.

I rose, too, reached out to catch her arm. I

was startled at the thinness of her forearm and the rigidity of her muscles.

She seemed unaware of my grip. "Now I know what George meant. I didn't understand until now. George knew she killed him, he knew it and tried to tell me. The day after Roddy fell" — she shuddered — "was pushed, George came in here." She pulled her arm free, pointed at her desk. "He stood right there and said that he'd seen Roddy at the tower and that the American woman was with him. I shushed George. I told him I didn't want to hear about it, that he was not to talk about it to anyone. I told him to get out. He hesitated and"— she gave a little moan — "I screamed at him to leave. When the door shut, I threw myself into my chair and I grabbed up Roddy's picture and I cried."

I looked at the desk. There were a half dozen photos in frames, mostly family shots of Mrs. Worrell with a little boy, then a slender teenager and later young man. Her son? A nephew? I didn't see any pictures of a man. Jasmine had described Roddy Worrell as smiling and with a big laugh.

"But now" — and she wasn't speaking to me, she was throwing out words as if they were knives flung toward a target — "I understand. George saw something that night.

168

He knew what happened to Roddy. He tried to tell me but I wouldn't listen. Oh, I always knew Roddy died because of her. But I never suspected her of killing him. Now I know. I must tell the police. They'll arrest her. That's what they'll do." She whirled away from me, flung open the door.

I didn't try to follow. There was no way to deflect her. She was sure of her facts, certain she now knew the truth about her husband's death. Connor Bailey's troubles were just starting.

I closed the office door behind me, walked down the short hall to an exit to the upper terrace. I was tired, so tired. I felt as if I'd fought my way through turbulent water, pummeled by currents. I realized that I'd had no lunch. But I had one more task to accomplish.

I paused at the top of the rock stairs, then took a deep breath and trudged down the steps. It seemed a long time since my early breakfast with Marlow and her request that I talk with Lloyd about Connor's penchant for attracting men and the problems that could ensue. But everything was changed now. What was I going to do about Mrs. Worrell and her accusations to the police? Certainly Connor needed to know.

What would happen if I told Connor? Was

she capable of handling this information? Damnit, she was a grown woman. Certainly I should tell her. Yet, I felt unsure. I needed to think it through. Perhaps I should talk to either Lloyd or Marlow first. My instinct rebelled. The thought of treating Connor as a helpless woman who had to be protected by her menfolk or her daughter was repellent. But was that judgment true, no matter how condescending it might be?

That was the decision I had to make and make soon. Although Chief Inspector Foster might not be in any hurry to reclassify Roddy Worrell's death as murder, he would not ignore Mrs. Worrell's accusations, especially not since my report of George's statements lent a frightening credence to her claims.

No one can be accused of murder on hearsay evidence, but Foster might reopen the investigation into Roddy Worrell's death, especially if the autopsy on George suggested any possibility of murder. Connor had to be told that this might happen because, if the investigation into Worrell's death began again, Connor would be high on the chief inspector's list of persons to interview.

As I passed the pool, I nodded a pleasant good afternoon to the two Canadian ladies, determinedly sunbathing despite a brisk wind and a temperature in the mid-sixties. The clear blue water rippled in the wind and the umbrellas over the tables were closed. No one was on duty behind the snack bar. It wasn't yet time for tea.

I passed the snack counter. Dressing rooms for men and women were next. The final door, painted a bright orange bore the legend SPORTS in capital letters. I assumed this was what James had meant when he responded to my question about the ghost: *"Look in the Sports cupboard . . . Don't say I told you."*

I'd visited this storeroom several times, ducking inside to pick up a light aluminum folding chair to carry down to the beach. There were folded beach umbrellas, a stack of foam surfboards, a folded volleyball net, a bin filled with soccer balls, plastic life rings for the pool, a croquet set. Obviously, James believed there was something here that would tell me more about the ghost. I was quite certain he would deny ever having said so.

I flicked on the light, a single low-watt bulb that hung from the ceiling and only faintly illuminated the narrow closet. The brightly striped umbrellas were bunched in the near corner. Sand gritted underfoot on the gray cement floor. I took my time, looking behind the umbrellas, peering around the bin of soccer balls, opening several wicker picnic hampers to find them all clean and empty, tugging the stack of surfboards to one side. Finally I stood at the far end of the closet and gingerly poked a mound of discards: some old croquet mallets, a hand air pump with a broken handle, a folded-up tarp, a deflated air mattress, a coil of hawser-thick rope.

I leaned against the rough stone wall and felt a wave of irritation mixed with disappointment. I'd not realized how much I'd counted on finding a link here to the tower ghost. But if there was anything secreted among the beach and water paraphernalia, I was not clever enough to find it.

I sighed and turned to retrace my steps. My head ached and my bones felt like water. Perhaps I'd better retire to my room, order a late lunch. If I was lucky, I'd get both sustenance and information. I flicked off the light. As I turned to step out of the closet, my gaze swept the darkened cupboard. For an instant, I froze into stillness. There was a faint glow at the very end of the closet, floating like a cloud of silver in the darkness.

I turned on the light, blinked. The glow was gone. A high shelf ran the length of the storage area and it was at about that level where I'd seen that silvery splotch. I walked to the end of the closet, looked up on the shelf. A ball of cord, dark paper stretched over plywood strips . . .

It took me a moment, then I understood. Oh, yes, of course. Clever. Damn clever. I reached up, then yanked back my hand. I should not touch the box kite. I didn't need to pull it down. I understood now how a luminous cloud floated near the tower. Not magic, not otherworldly, not a spirit, simply a kite liberally coated with phosphorescent paint. Clever and cruel, a child's toy used to trick and terrify.

I suppose I should have tried to find Chief Inspector Foster first, but fatigue weighted me down like seaweed dragging at a wave-tossed swimmer. Instead, I walked slowly back to my room, called room service and ordered lunch, a grilled chicken sandwich with chutney, chips, and coffee. Especially coffee. Then I dialed the desk.

A cheerful voice answered immediately. "How may I help you, Mrs. Collins?"

There are few secrets that can be kept in today's computerized world, and certainly there is no anonymity in a hotel. "Rosalind?" I thought I recognized the voice of the buxom blonde who was on duty during the daytime.

"Yes, Mrs. Collins?"

"Do you know where the police inspector is?" I was stretched out on the chaise longue, a notepad balanced on my knee. I drew a box kite. A gloved hand held the line. I blinked at my drawing. I hoped fervently that George — I was almost sure the kite expert was George — had not worn gloves. I wanted to establish the identity of the creator of Roddy Worrell's ghost. That would be the first step in discovering why Roddy Worrell's ghost had appeared.

The pause on the other end of the line lengthened.

"Rosalind?" I tapped on my pad.

Her voice dropped. "We're not supposed to talk about the police. The" — a brief pause — "accident on the beach is most unfortunate, but it has no connection to the hotel."

Interesting, Mrs. Worrell had wasted no time setting out in search of Chief Inspector Foster with her accusation against Connor Bailey, but she apparently saw no connection between George's death and her husband's. Or was she simply trying to maintain a semblance of life as usual within the hotel? Whichever, I wasn't going to be put off. "I need to speak with the chief inspector. Do you know where he is?"

"He is not presently in the hotel. But," she whispered, "he left a phone number."

I wrote down the number. My call was answered on the second ring.

"Chief Inspector Foster's office." The woman's voice was brisk and pleasant.

"May I speak with the chief inspector, please."

"I'm sorry. He is not in his office. May I take a message?" I didn't think a message about a box kite and phosphorescent paint would be intelligible. "Yes. Please tell him Mrs. Collins called from Tower Ridge House and I have some information for him in the death he is investigating here."

When I hung up, I leaned back against the chair, but I couldn't relax. Trouble was coming. Once, long ago, I watched spiked mines bob in ocean swells, coming ever nearer the ship on which I sailed. I had held tight to the railing on that calm, moonlit night and stared down, my mind and heart frozen, knowing an explosion was inevitable. The explosion came, but it was another ship that lurched, blew apart, sank in flames. I'd felt helpless then. And now —

A brisk knock on the door.

The stocky young waiter placed the tray

on the table, moving the ceramic tower to one edge.

I signed the ticket, then looked at him inquiringly, "Frederick?"

"Yes, Mrs. Collins. Is there anything else you need?" Frederick's plump black face was usually creased in a smile, but not today. His somber expression made him look older.

I was hungry and aching with fatigue, but I could handle that. What bothered me more was the uneasiness that plucked at my mind, the sense of impending doom. I wasn't going to stand there like a deer frozen in onrushing headlights. I was damn well going to do something, to claw and scratch for facts, to arrange what I had discovered in some semblance of order. "Yes, indeed, Frederick, you can certainly be of help to me."

"Yes, ma'am." A spark of interest flickered in his dark eyes.

I shut the door, smiled at him. "I've just been visiting with Mrs. Worrell and learning a great deal about Tower Ridge House and the people who make it such a special small hotel. I'm a writer and I sometimes do travel articles. Mrs. Worrell understood immediately when I explained that I like to have the viewpoints of both management and staff and I have just a few questions for you."

Frederick tucked the tray under his arm and rested the weight on his hip. He looked interested. "I'll be glad to help if I can."

"Now you've worked here . . ."

"Four years, Mrs. Collins. I started as a busboy when I finished school."

"How would you describe working here?"

He rubbed his nose. "A good place. Mrs. Worrell runs a tight ship. She oversees how things are done and she keeps a close eye on everything from the towels at the pool to the flower buds that go on the room service trays. Quiet and perfect, that's how she wants everything done. She's nice about it, but she won't tell you twice." He was respectful, not resentful. "She's been manager here for years and years."

I didn't doubt that she was a martinet. "Has anything changed since Mr. Worrell's death?"

Frederick's reply was immediate, definite. "No, ma'am. But Mrs. Worrell was always in charge." He grinned. "Oh, sure, it's changed some. It's been a lot quieter at night. Mr. Worrell liked to visit with the guests. Sometimes he played the piano in the bar, even sang a little. Nightclub songs. Yes, it's been quieter."

"Such a sad thing. To fall to his death." I

sighed. "Were you working at the hotel that night?"

"In the kitchen." He was suddenly tight with his words.

"Oh, I know all about that night." I spoke in a confidential tone. "I certainly won't put anything about the accident in my article. I know how upsetting it was for Mrs. Worrell. Of course, I understand Mr. Worrell often had a bit too much to drink. And I know Mrs. Bailey must have been sorry about everything, since she followed him out of the bar."

He relaxed. "I was carrying out some trash and I saw them walk toward the stairs down to the lower terrace. Mrs. Bailey was running after Mr. Worrell." His brows drew together. "She was calling his name."

The lower terrace? I managed not to look surprised. "What time was that?"

"Just past midnight."

"Did you see him again? Or Mrs. Bailey?"

"No, ma'am, I was busy in the kitchen. It was almost two when I left. But I took the main steps down to the lower level. I didn't pass the tower."

"So you didn't see him again." Or pass by his body. My tone was vague; my thoughts were not. Where were Roddy and Connor going? Was he drunk? What time did he —

or they — return to the upper terrace? Did Connor go to the tower with him? Was he alone? Or did someone else walk with Roddy Worrell that night? Mrs. Worrell claimed that George told her he'd seen Roddy with Connor at the tower. "To fall all that way . . ." I shuddered. "And now there's been another fatal accident here. I'm so sorry about George. He seemed like a nice young man. Was he a friend of yours?"

"Oh, sure." There was no particular warmth or regret in Frederick's voice. "He was a nice guy. He liked sports."

"Were he and Mr. Worrell on good terms?"

Frederick looked puzzled. "Mr. Worrell was nice to everybody. He never got on us about anything. He left that to Mrs. Worrell."

Frederick didn't say more, but the implication was clear that Mrs. Worrell had no difficulty keeping employees in line.

"Was George particularly grieved about Mr. Worrell's death?"

"George?" Again that tone of surprise. "He never said much about it."

So George had not created the ghost in an indirect effort to avenge Roddy Worrell's death.

"It seems odd that George would die in a

fall, too." I watched him carefully.

Frederick frowned. "Yeah. Weird. George asked me to handle breakfast. I got the idea he was going to do something for one of the guests. But I don't know why he would have been out on the end of the point. Maybe somebody left a book there and he went to get it. I guess he got too close to the edge. It's kind of crumbly."

"George told me you saw the ghost at the tower the other night. What do you think about that?"

"Really weird. George thought —" He broke off, backed toward the door. "I better get back. I've got some other trays to deliver."

It was an off time. I didn't believe him. But he abruptly didn't want to talk. "Wait, Frederick. What did George think?"

He rubbed his cheek, frowned. "Listen, I don't want to get mixed up in anything. George kept saying that the ghost had to be Roddy come back. I told him he'd better shut up that kind of talk or Mrs. Worrell would fire him in a minute. And he just laughed."

As the door closed behind him, I wondered at George's laughter. Why wasn't George worried about losing his job? Did he not care about the job any longer? Or was he sure that Mrs. Worrell wouldn't dare fire him? George told me he'd been thinking about the night Roddy died. What did George know or remember? And where was Mrs. Worrell when her husband climbed the steps of the tower?

eleven

I welcomed the tang of the chutney on the sandwich and the jolt of the caffeine in the coffee. This was the first quiet moment I'd had since I looked down onto the rocks at George's body, and I had a lot of decisions to make.

Was George's death an accident?

No. It was simply too fortuitous when I had an appointment with him to discover the truth behind the ghostly doings at the tower. Of course, there was another possible reason for him to die. George had insisted that Roddy Worrell was pushed to his death. Was that true and, if so, did George know who killed Roddy?

Knowing the identity of a murderer should surely be a good deal more dangerous than knowing the identity of the person who arranged for the ghost to appear. Obviously, they could not be the same person. The murderer of Roddy Worrell would not want attention brought to the death, nor any discussion of a ghost apparently seeking vengeance.

I finished one cup of coffee, poured another, carried it to the balcony. The balcony faced south, overlooking the gardens and the coast and the dazzling turquoise water, but my gaze slipped over the masses of poinsettias to fasten on the tower.

If I was right, the box kite tucked back on the far reaches of the shelf in the Sports closet explained the luminous apparition that we'd seen. The anguished shout last night could be explained, too. Perhaps a matchbox-sized recorder, activated by a timer, was attached to the kite. But understanding the mechanics was much less important than discerning the reason for the hoax.

I sipped the coffee and studied the tower. From what I had seen and what George had said, I was certain that the intention was to create a belief that the ghost of Roddy Worrell was appearing at the site of his death.

What would that accomplish?

It would be disagreeable to guests of the hotel. Very few persons enjoy having their sleep interrupted by screams and apparitions. Any activity which disturbed guests would surely distress Mrs. Worrell. Moreover, if the apparition was that of her late husband, her distress would be even greater, moving from a business problem to a personal problem. So, was the ghost created to cause trouble for the hotel or, more particularly, to upset Mrs. Worrell? On a more devious level, the hoax might have been planned to suggest Roddy Worrell was murdered. That was, in fact, exactly what George Smith had claimed. If George — or someone — had created the ghost as a dramatic way of demanding money for silence about Worrell's death, this might have moved a murderer to strike again.

Or was it possible that George Smith was behind the creation of the ghost and that his goal was simply malicious mischief? There was also the strong possibility that although George might have flown the box kite, the hoax was serving the ends of another person. How else to explain George's note with the crossed-out thousand dollars replaced by two thousand and the suggestion that I could learn all about the ghost for five thousand? Of course, George might have realized that the effect of the ghost on Connor Bailey was such that a good sum of money could be had by pretending to reveal the truth about the ghost.

I stared glumly at the tower. There were too many possibilities. I needed to go at it another way. I knew these facts:

Roddy Worrell was dead. From a fall.

George Smith was dead. From a fall.

George died after he claimed Roddy was murdered.

It was time to explore the death of Roddy Worrell. But first I must go down to the pool. I had an unfinished task there. I'd not yet told Chief Inspector Foster about the box kite in the Sports closet. I believed the kite to be important evidence, so it was up to me to protect it.

Frederick was serving tea when I reached the lower terrace. The westerly sun spilled gold across the pool at the tables, but the breeze was cool. The Canadian women were in shirt sleeves and shorts, the other guests in sweaters and slacks.

Neal bounded up from the farthest table. "Grandma, over here." His face was pink from the sun. "Dinny'll be here in a minute."

I smiled. Neal looked so normal and everyday, immediately identifiable as an American teenager. It wasn't simply the Tommy Hilfiger striped polo and the crisp pleated khaki trousers and the well-worn running shoes. Those clothes are everywhere around the world. It was his expression: frank, open, a little brash; his posture: not quite a slouch but close; his unmistakable accent, the flat Texas drawl.

I walked toward him. Curt Patterson sat alone at the next table. He lifted a hand in greeting and his loud tone was also unmistakably from Texas, "Good to see you, ma'am." He, too, had been in the sun today and his freckled face was almost a match for his red hair. He held a whiskey tumbler. Suddenly his sunburned face creased in a wide grin. He pushed back his chair.

I was startled for an instant, but Patterson was not looking at me. He brushed past me, booming, "There weren't any lovely ladies on the golf course today, but seeing you puts everything right."

I glanced back.

The deep warm voice was almost a caricature of a smooth-talking Lothario. I wanted to say, *Oh, come off it, fella,* but Patterson, eyes gleaming, holding out his big hands, wasn't kidding. So what else is new since the handsome rake became the staple of eighteenth-century fiction? Probably Lothario's counterpart would be found back in the dim reaches of cave dwellers — the guy with the hairiest chest and the deepest voice, swaggering in and dropping his club by the fire of the most curvaceous female. In any event, as in ages immemorial, Patterson headed straight for Connor.

It was an interesting tableau, though it lasted only a moment. Connor's eyes widened. Her pale features softened. Her lips curved in a half-sweet, half-seductive smile. His square face rigid, Lloyd poked his head forward like a bull when the pasture gate opens. Marlow's brows drew into a tight straight line. She glanced uneasily toward Lloyd. Steve Jennings gazed at Connor, and his face held a mixture of pity and dismay. Aaron jammed his hands in the pockets of his jeans and hunched his shoulders as if removing himself from the group.

Patterson wasn't fazed or dismayed. He obviously cared only about Connor's response. I suspected he'd spent his life doing what he pleased, when he pleased. Was he aware of the havoc he created in the lives of those around him? If so, I doubted that he cared.

Patterson stopped in front of Connor, looked down, his bold eyes admiring her, his burnished features glowing with sun and sheer animal vigor. He was tall enough, well-built enough that Lloyd was diminished in comparison, his office paleness accentuated, his middle-aged portliness emphasized.

Lloyd knew it, of course. His lips folded into a tight line.

Patterson stood just a little too close to Connor, but he didn't step back. "I didn't think I'd ever see anything prettier than this island, but you've proved me wrong. You're prettier than any ocean or beach. It's a pure treat to see you, and now only one thing more can be even better. I hope you folks will make this lonely Texan's day and join me for tea." It was as if he were the host and they his guests.

Connor's eyes sparkled. "Why, we'd love —"

Lloyd snapped, "Thanks, no. We're —"

Connor slipped her arm through Lloyd's, looked up at him eagerly. "Why, Lloyd, of course we can join Curt. Don't you see, he's all by himself."

Patterson took her other arm. "You're as kind as you are lovely, dear lady. My sis and her husband won't be back until late tonight and . . ."

I slipped into the chair next to Neal.

My grandson opened his mouth, pointed down his throat.

"Neal." But I agreed. And I concluded Curt Patterson had awaited Connor's arrival with every intention of attaching himself to the Drake-Bailey party.

The little group sorted and shifted near Patterson's table, Aaron muttering, "Think

188

I'll take a jog. Gonna go change," and Jennings brushing away Connor's entreaties to stay. "Still full from lunch, my dear. Believe I'll get some exercise, too. A brisk walk on the beach is just the tonic." As he moved toward the stairs, Jennings's face looked weary. That left an ebullient Patterson, focusing every ounce of his masculine charm on Connor, a coquettish Connor, a grim-faced Lloyd, and a resigned Marlow.

Neal steadily devoured the delicate tea sandwiches and watched the next table, his face a study in gluttony and disdain.

Connor was animated, her pale cheeks flushed with pleasure. "It's too bad you weren't with us today, Curt. We went up to the cliff above Spanish Rock, oh, it's so high. I didn't get close to the edge. It was scary . . ."

I wanted to march across the terrace and shake Lloyd by his shoulders. After all, Connor was going to marry him, not the loudmouth from Texas. *Smile at her,* I wanted to say, because Connor was giving Lloyd occasional puzzled, petulant glances, until she squared her shoulders and bent a dazzling smile on Patterson. But maybe this was a primer for Lloyd. Maybe, if I ever had the chance to speak with him, I could urge him to relax, let Connor soak up the attention she craved, the admiration she hungered for. Marlow darted worried looks between her mother and Lloyd. And I wished, knowing that Mrs. Worrell had undoubtedly talked to the police, that all Lloyd was going to have to worry about was competition from the brash Texan. Would the chief inspector take Mrs. Worrell's accusations seriously? If he did . . .

Diana, lovely in a swirling multicolored floral dress and butter-colored sandals, crossed the terrace with the grace of a gazelle. She scarcely glanced at the next table. She stopped by my chair and her hand touched my shoulder. "Grandma, are you okay?"

It was a reminder of the somber scene the children had left behind that morning. "Fine. The police were very nice."

Neal frowned. "Have you been here all day?"

Diana slipped into a webbed chair. She reached for the teapot.

I didn't want to talk about my day. "It's been very quiet. A bit too quiet, really. I believe I'll take a walk on the beach before it gets dark. I had a late lunch, so I don't need any tea." As I stood, I glanced across the pool area. Mrs. Worrell came quietly down the stone steps from the upper terrace. She paused midway, her glance sweeping across the tables. Her face was quite still and satisfied as she stared at Patterson's table. Patterson gave a sudden bark of laughter. Connor clapped her hands together in appreciation. Lloyd made no response at all, his face a dark glower. Abruptly, Mrs. Worrell turned and hurried back the way she'd come.

Frederick was moving from table to table, offering more sandwiches and scones and tarts. Voices rose and fell softly, except, of course, for the unmistakable boom of Curt Patterson. The sun was quite low in the sky now. It would be dark in less than half an hour. Already the portion of the pool area near the snack bar was in shadow. The doors to the locker rooms and the Sports closet were on the far side of the snack bar, as was another stone stairway rising to the upper terrace.

I smiled at the children. "Eat some whipped cream for me. I'm going to get a jacket, since it's cooling off. I'll see you at dinner." A jacket would be welcome but my main objective was to pass the Sports closet.

I moved quickly past the snack bar into the shadows. I paused by the door to the women's locker room. No one was looking toward me, including Frederick as he cleared the remnants of tea at a table. I took half a dozen steps, reached the Sports closet, opened the door. I didn't turn on the light. I saw what I wanted to see, the faint luminous glow at the far end. I reached around, checked the door and smiled. I punched the lock button, closed the door. I turned the knob. The door was locked. The hotel staff would have a key, but it was unlikely anyone would seek to open the door this late in the day. It was time to return chairs or floats, not take them out. If any were returned later, they could be propped by the door. And certainly before tomorrow, I would speak with the chief inspector.

By the time I reached my room and shrugged into my jacket, it was definitely twilight. I found my little pocket flash and headed down toward the beach. The light was useful in the tunnel beneath the greenery. My hope was to reach the beach and find either Aaron or Steve. Both of them had been here last year. I assumed Aaron had been a guest of Marlow's family. This was not a resort for a graduate student on a budget. Both Aaron and Steve could tell me more about Roddy Worrell. I had a nervous sense that I needed to gather up bits and pieces of information so that I could help Lloyd protect Connor if the need arose.

The wind surprised me when I reached the concrete grid leading down to the beach, ruffling my hair, pulling at my sweater and slacks. I stared out at the magnificent darkening reach of water, mysterious and somber as the color deepened to purple and the final pink and gold tendrils wavered on the horizon. As I looked up, I saw the moongate and beyond it a figure outlined on top of the headland, a man staring out at the sea, a tall, lanky, commanding figure. I started carefully up the narrow trail.

The wind seemed stronger on the ridge. I was a few feet behind Steve Jennings when I called out. "Steve. Mr. Jennings?" I knew he hadn't heard me approach, and I didn't want to startle him.

He swung around. It was hard to tell in the fading light, but I thought his gaze was probing. When I stopped beside him, he pointed down at the spume-slick rocks. "Is that where he was?"

No doubt everyone in the hotel had heard about George's death and the arrival of the police. "Yes."

Steve folded his arms across his chest. "You'd have to be stupid to fall from here. A clear morning. Moderate winds. Sober. Presumably."

"George was sober." According to the

young bartender, George didn't drink alcohol. Besides, the note he left me was not the work of a drunk. I kept my tone neutral. "He may have been careless."

Steve continued to stare down at the rocks. He didn't respond to my comment. Instead, abruptly he demanded, "Did George tell you that Roddy Worrell was murdered?"

I was a little surprised at the anger in Steve's voice. "Yes. He told me."

Steve's voice was hard. "I cornered him last night, asked him what the hell he thought he was doing. He acted surprised, said he was just saying what everybody thought. I asked him for chapter and verse. Of course, he couldn't come up with anybody else who was claiming Roddy was murdered. I told him he damn sure better be careful what he said or he might be in big trouble." The lawyer's face jutted forward. "The little punk laughed at me. Well, he's damn sure not laughing now."

I made no answer.

"But," and his tone was uneasy, no longer combative, "I don't see how the hell George could fall from here. I don't like it."

"There was no suggestion last year that Roddy Worrell's death was anything other than an accident?"

Steve didn't answer for a long moment.

I looked at him sharply.

He massaged the side of his face. "I thought maybe he jumped. But now . . ." He jerked his head toward the shore. "We'd better head back before it's completely dark."

I went first, using my small travel flashlight. The thin beam was some help, but we didn't speak again until we reached the hard-packed trail that led up to the hotel. I faced him. Suicide? "Tell me about Roddy Worrell." His wife remembered him as a justifiably angry man. George Smith had said he wasn't really very drunk. Frederick described a showman of sorts and recalled a burst of laughter. But I wanted to know more. "Did you like him?" And how, I wondered, did Steve feel about a married man pursuing Connor?

"Roddy." Steve's tone was dry but with a tinge of warmth. "Cocky little guy. He could be a hell of a lot of fun."

I was surprised. I'd envisioned an imposing man, someone like Curt Patterson or Steve Jennings. "Little?" Of course Steve Jennings was a big man indeed. Though lanky, he stood at six feet two, perhaps three.

He studied me. "A little taller than you.

Skinny. Think Frank Sinatra."

I smiled and understood immediately. Steve and I dealt in the same cultural currency.

"You know what I mean. A bony face," he explained, "a scrawny guy, but he had some kind of appeal for women." He sounded puzzled.

I wasn't. Sex appeal isn't limited to linebackers. I was getting a better idea of Roddy Worrell, a man who attracted women, a man with a taste for women, a man who liked to have fun.

"What kind of marriage did he have?" In a domestic crime, the spouse is always the first suspect. It's amazing how often the old dictum proves true.

"She was married to him when he died." He shrugged. "Who ever knows about someone else's marriage? A lot of women wouldn't have given him such a long lead. But maybe she didn't give a damn. Maybe she gave a big damn, but she liked being married. Maybe . . . Who the hell knows? Do I think she pushed him off the tower? She could have." I almost didn't hear his next words, he spoke so softly. "So could a lot of other people."

"People staying at the hotel." I didn't make it a question. That number, as he and

196

I well knew, included Connor, Marlow, Jasmine, Aaron, Lloyd, and, of course, Steve himself.

"There were other people here that night. And we don't know who might have had it in for Roddy." Steve took my elbow and we started up the path. "Maybe he owed his bookmaker. Maybe he'd made a pass at the gardener. Maybe he knew more than he should have about somebody."

The last might have been true for George Smith. I didn't think it applied to Roddy Worrell. I trained the little flashlight on the path, watched my step. "Was his bookmaker sighted in the garden that night? Or the gardener? Or any desperate phantom seeking his silence? And were any of them here this morning?"

Steve didn't answer.

I slowed my pace. "What time did the party in the bar break up?"

"Just after twelve."

"What broke it up?" I hoped he would be honest.

"A pretty ugly scene." The words were strong, but his tone was remote. "Connor was dancing with Lloyd. Anybody with eyes could see that he was infatuated with Connor. She loved it, of course. But I thought it would just be one of her usual —"

He broke off. "Anyway, they were dancing and Roddy was playing the piano and singing. He tried to sound like Mel Tormé. I think he was singing 'You Belong to Me.' All of a sudden, he slammed his hands down on the keys, stood up. He knocked over the piano bench."

"Were there many people there?" We were at the top of the slope and I welcomed the bright circles of light from the hotel lamp-posts.

"No. It was a quiet night. Just Connor and Lloyd and my wife and me. And Mrs. Worrell. She was sitting at one of the small tables. That was a little unusual. She didn't usually come into the bar that late. And the bartender. I don't remember who it was."

"Marlow and Aaron?" Jasmine, of course, would not have been in the bar.

"No. They turned in around ten. Thank God it was just us."

I was seeing the bar, dim for evening, the wall sconces glowing against the paneled walls, perhaps a light over the piano. And the cocky little man who looked like Frank Sinatra and the ever-seductive Connor and lovesick Lloyd, and Steve watching from a table, likely drinking a Dark 'n Stormy, and the throaty whisper of a song.

"It all happened pretty fast. Roddy

lurched across the dance floor —"

The small oblong of shiny wood floor near the piano scarcely qualified as a dance floor, but I understood what Steve meant.

"— and I got up. I thought Roddy was going to grab Connor. He had his hand out, but when he got up to Connor and Lloyd, he stopped and rocked back on his heels and pointed at Connor." He frowned. "He was pretty drunk and I couldn't hear all of it, but he kept saying he loved her and he thought she loved him and if his life went to hell it was all her fault, and then he swung around and headed toward the door. Connor was upset. She ran after Roddy." Steve gave a little shrug. "That didn't mean a thing. You have to understand that Connor can't bear it if anyone's angry with her. Lloyd started to go after the two of them and I reached out and grabbed his arm. I told him to let it go, that Connor would soothe Roddy down, that he was given to dramatics and it would blow over better if Lloyd stayed out of it. I told him to stay cool like Mrs. Worrell. She was sitting at her table, a half-smile on her face, like the music had never stopped. Lloyd was still an outsider. Connor was with me and my wife, so Lloyd dropped it."

"Did you see Connor later?"

It took him a moment to answer. He came

back from a far distance. "Ellen wasn't feeling well. We turned in."

"You didn't check on Connor?" I didn't quite keep the surprise from my voice. Connor had hurried out into the night after a man who'd drunk too much, a man in a highly emotional state.

We reached the base of the steps to the lower terrace. In the lamplight, his face was sardonic. "Mrs. Collins, if I chased after Connor every time some man went nuts for her —"

Footsteps pounded across the terrace above us.

We looked up.

Marlow Bailey flung herself down the steep stone stairs. "Steve," she shouted, "Steve, come quick."

twelve

We met Marlow halfway up the steps. She grabbed Steve's arm. "You've got to come. The police are here and they want to talk to Mother about Roddy."

I scarcely heard the rest of Marlow's frightened plea. Steve hurried up the stairs after her, moving fast but trying to calm her down at the same time. "Don't worry, Marlow, I'll take care of it." He spoke in his confident lawyer's voice, but I wondered how he felt in his heart.

I didn't try to keep up, though I followed as fast as I could. I should have warned Connor and Lloyd at teatime so that they would have been prepared. It was inevitable that the inspector would pursue Mrs. Worrell's claims. I had known what was sure to come and I had waited too passively for the right moment to speak with Connor. Part of it, of course, was my indecision about whom I should warn — Connor or Lloyd or Marlow.

I stopped for a moment's rest when I reached the stairs to the upper terrace. Mrs. Worrell must have contacted the inspector the minute Connor and Lloyd reached the hotel late this afternoon. Quite likely, Foster had asked her to telephone when Connor returned.

I found Lloyd pacing in the lobby area between the front desk and the drawing room. Marlow hunched on a narrow settee, her face bleak.

"Damn officious, if you ask me." Lloyd's face was red, his tone aggrieved. But beneath the bluster there was a thin sound of fear. He strode toward me. "You talked to that policeman this morning. What's going on? He came down to the terrace and asked Connor to come up here to help him in his inquiries." Lloyd clawed at his thinning hair. "I told him she didn't know that fellow who landed on the rocks. He had nothing to do with us and that inspector — what's his name, Frost?"

"Foster." Marlow pressed her hands tightly together.

"He said he just wanted to have a few words with Mrs. Bailey about her activities a year ago when Mr. Worrell died. I said that was nonsense, but he insisted and we came up here —"

"I ran to get Steve." Marlow's face was pale. "He's with Mother." She pointed across the lobby at a short hallway that angled away from the front desk. A door opened just past the front desk and Mrs. Worrell came out.

Lloyd nodded his approval at Marlow. "That was using your head. They wouldn't let me come in with Connor —"

Lloyd's back was to Mrs. Worrell. She hesitated, then turned away, moving up the short hall. She was quickly out of sight. Of course, she could simply have been on her way to the exit at the end of the hall. I didn't think so. She had moved so cautiously, her final glance surreptitious and stealthy. The cardroom where I'd spoken to the police that morning was one of a series of rooms that opened onto the short hallway.

"— but when Steve said he was Connor's attorney, Foster let him accompany her. I should have told him I was her counsel. Hell, why not? I'm a lawyer. I can represent her, too." He swung around, headed for the hallway.

"Wait, Lloyd!" Marlow came to her feet.

He hesitated, stopped, his face petulant.

"I know Mother would rather have you with her." Marlow ran up to him. "But don't make too big a deal of it. After all, Steve was here last year. The police talked to him at the time. Let's not blow it all out of proportion."

"Yeah. Maybe you're right." The prospect of action had given him energy. Now his shoulders slumped and he resumed his edgy pacing.

I wondered at Marlow's motives. Perhaps she didn't want Lloyd to hear what her mother might say about her actions on the night Roddy Worrell died. But I very much wanted to hear. And there might be a way.

"I wouldn't worry, Lloyd." I spoke in a soothing tone. Now was not the time to tell him of Mrs. Worrell's accusations against Connor. "It won't amount to anything and surely it won't take long." I smiled reassuringly. "I'll see you at dinner and hear all about it."

I moved toward the drawing room. I heard his nervous steps behind me. I crossed the drawing room, but instead of taking the exit that led to our rooms, I darted out through the open French doors to the upper terrace. It took only a moment to cross the smooth lawn and to reach the end of the building and the entrance to the short hall. I slipped through the door. The area where Marlow sat and Lloyd paced wasn't visible from the hallway. I walked fast to the door next to the room where I'd spoken to Foster that morning. The door was closed.

I turned the knob, stepped inside a dark room. The light from the hall flared through the shadows, illuminating the tall woman hunched near a connecting door. The merest sliver of light between the door and the jamb indicated the connecting door was ajar, that and the deep, precise voice so easily heard.

Mrs. Worrell whirled around, her features ridged with fury and fear, staring eyes, twisted lips, splotched skin.

I pointed at the sliver of light from the connecting door, touched my finger against my lips, eased the hall door shut and tiptoed across the room.

I stood so near I heard the soft rush of her breath, but, more important, I heard the voices in the next room:

". . . simply asking Mrs. Bailey to describe her actions on the night Mr. Worrell died."

"I see no purpose to that." Steve Jennings's tone was crisp. "You have Mrs. Bailey's statement from that evening. I refer you to that statement. It is complete and accurate and quite likely much more detailed than Mrs. Bailey could be at this point. After all, an entire year has passed. She would very likely not be able to remember the activities of the evening precisely."

"I will be glad to refer to the statement if

Mrs. Bailey has any difficulty —"

"I don't want to remember." Connor's voice rose. "It's horrible to have to talk about it again. That's all over and done with. I can't help what happened to Roddy. I'm here to get married and I want to be left alone."

Mrs. Worrell shifted her feet, the scrape of her shoes loud.

"Mrs. Bailey" — the inspector's voice was smooth, pleasant, relentless — "what was your relationship to Mr. Worrell —"

"Relationship! Why, he —"

"My client" — Steve's voice overrode Connor's — "declines to answer any questions concerning Mr. Worrell. She has already answered those questions. She responded to the inquiry at the time, and unless you have some reason to reopen that investigation, we shall excuse ourselves."

Papers rustled. "Mrs. Bailey, information has been received that you were seen that night at the tower in the company of Mr. Worrell —"

Mrs. Worrell leaned her forehead against the wall as near the tiny opening as possible. The sliver of light ran a silver bar across her faded red hair, glistened on a golden hoop earring.

"— yet in your statement last year you

claimed that you left Mr. Worrell on the upper terrace, returned to the hotel and never saw him again." A sheet of paper crackled. "I will read your statement of last year:

"I don't see how I can help you. Poor Roddy. I still can't believe it. He was so alive, so much fun . . . when he was himself. Sometimes he drank too much and he had a way of making everything big and dramatic. And last night . . . oh, I don't know how to tell you. It was just one of those things. He cared for me, you see, but I'd never done a thing to encourage him. That happens to me. Men, you know, and I always try to be kind. I felt sorry for him, of course. Poor boy, he was so unhappy. That wife of his —"

Mrs. Worrell might have been carved from stone, she stood so still.

"— so cold and unpleasant. You wonder why he ever married her. Not a pretty woman at all. And he rather made a scene in the bar. I suppose you've heard about that. Roddy said he loved me and he thought I loved him, and he said I was cold and cruel and that simply isn't true and then he threw himself out of the room. I went after him, of course. How could I not? Why, I had to tell him not to be silly. I couldn't bear for him to think me cruel —"

Despite the almost toneless recitation in the inspector's precise British speech, there was an echo of a woman's overweening hunger to be loved.

"— and I caught up with him on the terrace. But he wasn't like his usual self. He was gruff and angry. I talked and talked. I told him he was quite wonderful, that of course I really cared for him. And I did, you know, as a friend. That was always how I felt, that he and I were such good friends. He calmed down and we walked about the terrace. I felt that everything was all right. He asked me to walk in the gardens but I told him I was rather tired and I thought I'd go in and we said good night. I went back to the hotel and I never saw poor Roddy again."

I'd accepted Connor's version, most of it, until the concluding sentences. I didn't believe for a minute in that chaste good night at the entrance to the gardens. A truculent drunk would not metamorphose into a genial companion suggesting a stroll in the moonlight among the bougainvillea.

Chief Inspector Foster cleared his throat. "Mrs. Bailey, you were seen at the tower with Mr. Worrell. I am giving you an opportunity to correct your statement of —"

A chair scraped. "Upon advice of counsel,

Mrs. Bailey will make no further statement. Come on, Connor."

"Steve," her voice was high and frightened, "what if someone saw—" She broke off abruptly.

I almost edged the door wider. Had Steve grabbed her arm? Frowned? Whatever, Connor said no more.

There was a flurry of movement as Connor and Steve hurried out of the cardroom. Papers crackled, a briefcase clicked shut, a man's firm tread sounded. The door to the hallway opened, closed.

Mrs. Worrell pushed the connecting door shut, pushed it hard, with a violence that was the more frightening because it was directed against the inanimate door. She turned, bumped against me, the sharp bone of her elbow painful against my arm. "You . . ."

I moved, too, but she reached the hall door first, flung it open. She glared at me, her gaze venomous. "Bitch." Her footsteps clicked on the floor as she hurried away.

I looked after her and wondered. Did she mean Connor? Or me?

By the time I reached the desk in the main lobby, Mrs. Worrell was out of sight. Rosalind was still on duty.

"Mrs. Collins. What may I do for you?" She might be getting toward the end of her shift, but her voice still had an eager lilt.

Give me energy. Give me answers. Give me peace. How shocked she would have been had I answered honestly. Instead, I said briskly, "I'm looking for Chief Inspector Foster and I thought he came this way."

"I believe he and his assistant have left. You can check with Robert down in the drive. He's parking cars this evening." The hotel provided valet parking for dinner guests. The brochure proudly proclaimed the dining room a favorite of Bermuda families, and this evening that certainly appeared to be true.

I found Robert at the foot of the main stairs. "Have the police left, Robert?"

Robert had steady gray eyes, a freckled face, and, usually, a ready laugh. Tonight he looked pale and serious. "Yes, Mrs. Collins. Just now."

If I hadn't eavesdropped alongside Mrs. Worrell, I could have been in the main hallway and caught the inspector before he left. But the door to the Sports closet was locked. Tomorrow would do. I felt certain the chief inspector would be here bright and early.

Robert echoed my thought. "The chief inspector said he'd be back tomorrow. He asked for you, but there was no answer in your room. Will tomorrow be soon enough?"

"Yes. Thank you, Robert." I was turning away when I paused. "Robert, have you seen Mr. Worrell's ghost?"

"Ghost?" Robert's voice was thin. His eyes blinked rapidly. "Oh, no, not me. I don't know anything about it." He looked past me. "Excuse me, Mrs. Collins, here comes a car."

He stepped past me.

I climbed the steps, looked down to watch as Robert eased his long body into the tight seat of a VW. He carefully didn't look my way.

The hotel was falling into its evening rhythm as I walked slowly back to my room. There was no hint that a life had been lost only a hundred or so yards down the hillside, nothing to remind guests that the beach had been the scene of an intensive search, that the medics had struggled up the sloping path with a body bag. Through the open French windows, the sweet, balmy night air drifted inside with the murmurs of the birds as they settled into the soft darkness of night in the garden. The local diners appeared relaxed and cheerful, their chatter bright and animated as they walked toward the dining room or the bar.

The very ordinariness made me angry. Damnit, George was dead! But what could I do about it? Perhaps tomorrow, when I talked to the chief inspector, I would persuade him that the purported ghost of Roddy Worrell mattered. In any event, surely he would agree to test the box kite for George's fingerprints, perhaps even test the kite tomorrow night, see if he could re-create the luminous glow that had hovered by the tower.

What would that prove?

At the very least, it would prove that there was no ghost. It would prove that someone had spent considerable time and effort and ingenuity to create the semblance of a ghost. It would surely encourage the chief inspector to wonder why this effort had been made. I certainly wondered why. I was too tired now to make sense of any of it, but I was sure that the luminous apparition seen above the tower was connected to George's death.

I glanced toward the tower, a dark shape in the moonlight, and hurried into the building with our rooms. I was a little surprised to find our hall empty. I'd rather expected to catch Steve or Connor or Lloyd or Marlow in the hallway. I looked at the line of closed doors. Dinner was served at seven. It was a quarter to seven and I needed to change. My lips suddenly twisted in an ironic smile. Which was more important: to dress for dinner or to seek the truth about murder?

I took a few swift steps, knocked on Connor's door. I suppose I was impatient. I was knocking again, a demanding rat-a-tat when the door opened a scant three inches, framing a vertical stripe of Lloyd's face.

"Not now, Henrie O." His voice was hushed. "Thanks, but Connor's frazzled. Such stupid stuff, raking up an accident from a year ago. She and I are going out to dinner by ourselves. I managed to get some tickets to the ballet, part of the Bermuda Festival. After all, we're here to have fun. We'll see you in the morning."

"Lloyd . . ." But the door closed. I lifted my hand again, slowly let it fall. I wanted to talk to Connor. I'd get the truth out of her about that night. Abruptly, I swung away from the door, disliking myself for that swift, somewhat cruel thought. Yes, Connor with her insecurities and fears would be no match for me. I'd asked too many hard questions for too many years. I reached my door, opened it, stepped inside.

Did I have any right to ask hard questions

of Connor? I stood irresolute in the center of my room, swept suddenly by the fatigue I'd refused to recognize throughout the day, confused by my uncertainty about how to proceed — or whether to proceed.

I turned to the closet, selected a long-sleeved white silk blouse and a velvet skirt. I dressed quickly. In only a moment, I looked in the mirror, brushed back my hair, tying it with a dark ribbon that matched my skirt. I studied my face critically: deep-set dark eyes, the fine web of lines across my cheeks, the firm mouth, stubborn chin. I smoothed on a bit of powder, added a bright lipstick. I looked like what I was, an unsmiling, worried, rather weary elderly woman.

Connor Bailey didn't want my help. Nor did Lloyd Drake.

Why not leave it at that?

I had a sudden swift memory of the sodden lump of lifelessness on the sharp rocks beneath the headland. Yes, I'd rather thought George Smith was a brigand, ready to hold me up for whatever he could manage. Even though that might be true, he had been young and alive, perhaps heedless, but I didn't think cruel. And now he was dead, either because I'd enticed him into a game of wits with a much more dangerous player or because he knew who killed Roddy Worrell.

Was I trying to prove that Roddy was murdered to avoid any responsibility for George's death? Was this what propelled me, weary to the bone, to probe and prod and eavesdrop and conjecture?

I picked up my little black mesh evening bag and started for the door. All right. To be honest, I didn't want to be responsible for George's death. I might in the end discover that it was I who set in motion a deadly chain of events, culminating in his murder. If so, I would face the truth. But, whatever was to happen, I wouldn't stop until I knew the truth.

A swift knock sounded. When I opened the door, Marlow Bailey looked at me uncertainly. She poked her horn-rims higher on her nose. "Mrs. Collins . . ." She stopped.

"Yes, Marlow?" If she wanted a report on my promised talk with Lloyd, I would have to confess failure.

"I wondered if perhaps . . ." Her fingers plucked at the top button of her blouse. I noticed the silver sheen of the blouse and the boxy fit of her blue velvet trousers and the sleek black pumps. Even in dressy clothes, Marlow didn't look stylish. Was it her manner or the lack of makeup? The dash of pale pink lipstick only made her look paler. "Mother and Lloyd have tickets for the ballet. Aaron and I thought we'd go into Hamilton to the Coconut Rock. Neal and Diana are coming with us. We didn't want to be here for dinner. George . . ."

I understood. No matter who waited our table this evening, we could not help but think of George.

"I hope you don't think that's awful." Her tone was anxious.

"Of course not. It's a very good idea." I wished I'd thought of it, though I was much too weary to plan an outing myself.

"Then would you mind very much keeping an eye out for Jasmine? I don't want to go off and leave her all alone without someone to be with her at dinner."

I wasn't surprised that it was Marlow who was concerned about Jasmine. The Connors of this world rarely see beyond themselves. How did the old saying go? A young mother makes an old daughter. I wished that Marlow would find more than this evening's respite from her role as family caretaker, but I knew that was not going to happen in the Bailey family, now or in the future.

I smiled and nodded. "Jasmine's fun. We'll have a nice evening. You young people get out and forget all of this." I didn't mind taking care of Jasmine and I'd do my best to distract her from George's death, though I imagined she would put it in the category of exciting things that had happened, like Roddy Worrell's fall from the tower and the Gombey dancers.

A string quartet played Cole Porter tunes. I studied Jasmine's bent head. The peppermint-striped ribbon in her blond curls matched her striped blouse. I was puzzled. Instead of her usual bouncy eagerness, she was subdued. She'd scarcely eaten a bite. Perhaps she didn't care for lamb. But the whipped sweet potatoes surely held child appeal.

Our little table was an island of silence in the dining room. None of the guests were boisterous, but there was a current of cheeriness: the clink of silverware, the lilt of the music, low-voiced conversations. Jasmine and I were the only members of our group dining in the hotel. I was glad we'd been placed at a smaller table. I supposed that Steve Jennings had joined either Connor and Lloyd or the youngsters. I'd been prepared to meet and deflect a barrage of questions from Jasmine, expecting that she would give free rein to her curiosity. Instead, when the waiter — Frederick — removed our dinner plates, Jasmine had scarcely said a word and her answers to my questions had been monosyllabic.

I don't particularly pride myself as having great rapport with children, but I can usually get almost anyone to talk.

Frederick brought our desserts. Key lime pie for me and vanilla ice cream drizzled with a mixture of chocolate and raspberry sauces for Jasmine.

She stared at her plate, made no move to pick up her spoon.

I put down my fork. "Jasmine, don't you feel well?"

Slowly she lifted her eyes. Her lips trembled. "I didn't mean for George to die."

I found it hard to breathe.

Her round face was young and unblemished, the skin smooth and pink, but the blue eyes that stared at me were dark and deep with pain.

"Of course you didn't, Jasmine. I know that." But children kill. Even a child could rush up behind a man and push. Oh, dear Lord, why?

"I was so mad at him." She picked up the spoon, pressed it against the tablecloth. "He shouldn't have talked about my mom that way. He —"

"George talked to you about your mother?" I was startled. Yes, George had spread rumors about Connor to Diana and apparently to others on the staff and among the guests. But I was shocked to think he would discuss Connor's behavior with her ten-year-old child.

"Not me. Somebody else. I never saw who he was talking to. I was in the magnolia tree this morning —"

"The one by the cliff?" The tree was at the far edge of the hotel property. Limbs of the huge tree spread over the water on one side. The tree also poked over a wall marking the drop to a road that curled into a parking area for the hotel staff. I'd looked there when scouting out the terrain in search of an explanation for the ghost. There was a thirty-foot drop from the tree to the rocks on one side and the road on the other.

"Yes. I like to climb in the tree. It's a secret place. I go back every year." She turned the spoon over and over in her hands.

I felt a faraway echo of childhood, the delight in finding a niche unseen by the world, whether in a tree or a dim cave or a ridged gully or even a weed-fringed ditch — anywhere that adults would not go, a preserve where magic flourished.

"I slip out real early and climb up the branches and I feel like I'm hanging in the sky and no one knows. This morning I heard footsteps on the road. I heard George talking." Her face crinkled in puzzlement. "I didn't hear anyone else. He said" — she curled her fingers around the spoon — "that my mom was scared. He said maybe she deserved to be scared, maybe she wouldn't chase around after married men again." Jasmine's voice shook. "Mom didn't do that. It made me so mad that I didn't hear for a minute and then it was kind of mixed up. He said, 'I just figured out what happened. I saw her go up in the tower after him. I ought to tell the police.' George sounded like he was scared. He didn't say anything for a minute and kept on walking. I heard his footsteps. His voice was farther away when I heard him again. He said he was going to meet the old lady out on the point and it would take more than five thousand —"

I was the old lady. While Jasmine hung in the magnolia tree and I was picking up the envelope from my floor, George was on a cell phone telling someone he'd figured it all out — the murder of Roddy Worrell? — and he ought to tell the police and it would take more than five thousand for him to keep quiet. Was he willing to keep quiet about murder, or was he talking about the secret of the ghost?

"That's all I heard." Jasmine took a deep breath. "I climbed down and ran to the tower. But it was locked."

I was afraid she was going to say she followed George. I began to relax a little. "Why did you go to the tower?"

Jasmine hunched her shoulders. "The ghost was there last night. I thought maybe Roddy would hear me. Roddy liked my mom." There were tears in her voice. "And Mom liked him. George was wrong about Mom and I thought Roddy wouldn't like what he'd said. I wanted to go up to the top but I couldn't. But I thought a ghost could hear anyway, so I leaned close to the door and I whispered." She dropped the spoon, placed her small plump hands over her mouth.

"You told Roddy what George said." I pictured that small figure of outrage, leaning close to the thick wooden panels of the tower door.

Her blue eyes stared at me unblinkingly.

"And then . . ." I moved my chair, reached over and gently pulled her hands down from her face, held them tight in my own. "You asked Roddy to punish George. Is that it?"

Tears spilled down her face. "I didn't mean for him to die." She gulped back a sob. "I didn't mean —"

"Jasmine, it doesn't matter what you whispered to the door. No one was there.

No one heard. Not a ghost. Not anyone. There is no ghost. There was no ghost. It was a trick that George" — and someone else, someone to whom he spoke that morning — "planned. I know how it was done. Listen closely." I told her about the box kite and the phosphorus. "The kite is locked in the Sports closet right now. Tomorrow I'll show it to the police."

It was like watching sun spill over a dark landscape, chasing away purple shadows, turning water iridescent, creating harmony and peace. "It wasn't me." She breathed the words in a soft little sigh.

"No, darling. It wasn't you." I let loose her hands, smiled. "Now, eat your ice cream before it melts into a huge puddle."

She grabbed up her spoon. "I love chocolate and raspberry."

Chocolate and raspberry, a delectable combination. George and the person to whom he spoke, a deadly combination?

I ate my Key lime pie and waited until Jasmine finished her ice cream before I spoke. "Jasmine."

She was comfortable now, her head bobbing in time with the music. I didn't want to frighten her, but I knew she must be careful. I leaned across the table, held out my hand. "Let's make a pact. We won't tell anyone but the police about your climb in the magnolia tree."

Jasmine's eyes sparkled. She grabbed my hand, shook it so hard I had to catch the tower in the center of the table to keep it from falling. "I promise." Relieved of her sense of guilt, she bounced eagerly in her chair. "I almost followed George down to the shore. I wish I had!"

If she had, she would likely have met a murderer hurrying up the slope in the dusky tunnel.

"But I was hungry." Her tone was regretful.

And so she lived.

When I left Jasmine in her room, I made her promise not to open the door to anyone but Marlow. I waited until I heard the lock click.

Tomorrow I was going to tell Chief Inspector Foster everything.

thirteen

The siren was far away, no more an intrusion into sleep than the rattle of palm fronds or the click of footsteps. Sleep was a weight of darkness, thick and warm. The siren wailed nearer, piercing that cocoon of comfort. I woke, pushed back the light covering. By the time I reached the sliding door, lifted the bar, fumbled with the lock, and stepped out on the balcony, shivering a little in the night breeze, I was wide awake.

I saw no flames, but there was an acrid smell of burning and the whirl of warning lights spangled the darkness beyond the terraces. The terraces . . . I had a sharp, ugly presentiment. It took me only a moment to dress. I tucked my room key into the pocket of my slacks and grabbed a sweater as I plunged out of my room. No one else appeared to have awakened.

As I crossed the upper terrace, the lights were clearly visible, alternating red and white flashes. Men's voices rose above the scuff of boots, the mechanical whir of unreeling hose, and the throaty rumble of the fire engine. Suddenly, water hissed. The smell changed from the dry crackle of fire to charred dankness. By the time I reached the steps to the lower terrace, my nose wrinkled at the stench of doused flame.

The pool area blazed in light, but the snack bar and dressing rooms were dark and shadowy, illuminated by spotlights from the fire trucks. Tendrils of smoke trailed up into the night sky. On the far side of the pool, Mrs. Worrell watched the brisk but controlled efforts of the firemen in their bulky yellow coats and red helmets. The lights in this area shone brightly, obviously on a different line from the electricity for the serving area and dressing rooms. Submerged lighting in the pool cast a green glow upward, turning Mrs. Worrell's pale face the color of a greengage plum. Her gingery hair, cramped close to her head, was uncovered tonight, but she wore the same red corduroy robe and a too-large pair of a man's leather loafers.

I stopped beside her. "What happened?" I watched a knot of firemen near the snack bar.

She shot me a sharp glance, but her reply was civil enough. "A fire in one of the storage areas. Dr. Mackenzie" — she gestured over the hill — "a neighbor, had a late emergency surgery and was coming home.

He smelled smoke. He called nine-one-one, then roused me. I can't imagine . . . There's nothing that could possibly cause a fire there."

A fire in one of the storage areas . . . I knew what the arson experts would find — a broken window at the back of the Sports cupboard, some kind of flammable liquid. I knew everything but who'd done it.

The clump of men by the dressing rooms listened to a big man who gave low-voiced instructions. He gestured toward the Sports closet, then turned and walked toward us, impressive in his shiny white helmet and slick yellow coat. His black boots grated on the pool apron.

Mrs. Worrell took a step forward. "I'm Thelma Worrell, the manager. Is the fire out?"

"Yes, ma'am." He was the kind of man who would stand easily on the deck of a ship or handle a rowdy crowd or make love to a willing woman. Heavy cheeks and a burly build told of many meals well taken. His voice was deep and sure. "Captain Wilson. There's no danger. The fire was localized, confined to the back of a narrow closet. A police constable will be here shortly to secure the area until a thorough investigation can be made in the morning.

There is clear evidence of arson."

"Arson?" Mrs. Worrell scarcely managed the word, a whisper of shock and disbelief.

"Yes, ma'am." He pulled off thick beige gloves. "When we arrived, you said none of the unit was kept locked except for the food service area."

Mrs. Worrell stared past him, one hand tight at her throat. "That's right. In the winter, we lock up the snack bar after tea is finished. In summer, of course, the snack bar is open until ten. But the dressing areas are left open."

The fire captain lifted his gloved hand, pointed. "The long and narrow room just past the men's dressing room —"

Mrs. Worrell nodded. "The Sports cupboard. It's left open. We've not been troubled by petty thievery —"

The fire chief's hand fell. "That door was locked. We axed down the door. That's where the fire was."

Mrs. Worrell wrapped her arms tightly across her front. "That's impossible . . ."

I didn't listen as her voice rose and fell. I didn't follow as she and the fire captain moved toward the burned-out area, picking their way among the hoses. Yes, that door was locked. My fingerprints were on it. Someone else tried the door this night and

227

could not gain access, but the locked door was no ultimate barrier. Now the kite was gone. It scarcely would take one flicker of flame to destroy that flimsy contraption of paper and balsa wood. Quite likely the coating of phosphorescent paint added fuel and brightness to the flame.

How much difference was it going to make that the box kite no longer existed?

I stood in the early-morning quiet on one side of yellow tape strung from a spindly branch of an African tulip tree at the corner of the building to a metal stanchion at the edge of the patio. On the other side of the plastic strip, jumbled boot prints marred the muddy ground. A portion of the back wall of the pool complex bore traces of the night's blaze: a smashed window, scorch marks, traces of soot.

Footsteps clipped on the cement siding of the pool. "Good morning, ma'am. This area is presently closed." The young police constable placed her hands behind her back, waited for me to move on.

I did, but as I climbed the steps to the upper terrace, I knew the smashed window was the means taken by the arsonist to toss some kind of burning material into the Sports closet. I pictured a stealthy figure slipping through the night. Was the window broken with a rock? And then, quite likely, a cloth soaked in gasoline was tossed onto the kite. Did a gloved hand poke through the window with a taper of some sort, hold it until the blaze was well under way?

I was midway across the upper terrace when I saw Chief Inspector Foster standing in the doorway of the hotel. I touched the envelope in my pocket that held the note from George Smith and walked to meet him.

The cardroom was becoming quite familiar to me. I sat opposite the chief inspector. He dropped a lump of sugar into his coffee, slowly stirred. The note from George Smith lay on the desk in front of him. On a legal pad, he'd made a series of notations in tight, neat printing. When I had finished — and I kept nothing back — he turned the pad toward me. "Would you say this is an accurate representation, Mrs. Collins?"

A few feet away, a young detective sergeant held a pen, ready to take down my response. The subordinate was stork-thin with curly black hair, a beaked nose and lantern jaw.

I skimmed the chief inspector's list.

Facts provided by Mrs. Henrietta Collins,

guest at Tower Ridge House:

1. Tuesday of this week: The Drake-Bailey party arrived at Tower Ridge House.

2. Tuesday night: Steve Jennings was awakened by a knock and apparently saw an apparition near the tower.

3. Wednesday afternoon: George Smith snapped a group photo on the headland and claimed to see something white near the tower.

4. Wednesday afternoon: Mrs. Bailey found a broken ceramic tower in her room.

5. Wednesday afternoon: George Smith told Mrs. Collins about the appearances of Roddy Worrell's ghost and (according to Mrs. Collins) insisted that Worrell's fall was not an accident.

6. Wednesday night: The Drake-Bailey party was awakened by screams; a luminous cloud was sighted near top of tower; an investigation found nothing at the tower.

7. Thursday morning: Mrs. Collins received a note, slipped under her door, which requested a meeting at 8 A.M. on the headland. She believed the note to be from George Smith.

8. Thursday morning: Mrs. Collins sighted body of George Smith on the rocks below the headland.

9. Thursday morning: Hotel bartender

suggested Mrs. Collins check the Sports cupboard near the pool.

10. Thursday morning: Mrs. Worrell stated that George Smith said he saw Mrs. Bailey at the tower with Mr. Worrell on the night of his death last year.

11. Thursday morning: Mrs. Collins claimed that she searched the Sports cupboard and found a box kite with evidence of phosphorescent paint. Mrs. Collins placed a call to police.

12. Thursday afternoon: Mrs. Collins locked the door to the Sports cupboard after checking to be certain the kite was still there.

13. Thursday evening: According to Mrs. Collins, Jasmine Bailey claimed to have overheard George Smith early Thursday morning saying that he'd figured out what had happened and he ought to tell the police and that he was going to meet the old lady and it would take more than five thousand dollars.

14. A fire was reported at Tower Ridge House at 1:15 A.M., Friday. Damage was confined to a Sports closet near the pool.

When I finished reading, I looked up to find Chief Inspector Foster gazing at me with the cold, appraising watchfulness of a predator. Cats, wild and domestic, affix their prey with an unblinking regard, alert for the tiniest variation in posture, the most minute shift in attention, ready to jump when weakness is perceived. Foster had that intensity, that stillness.

I watched him with equal care, observing his thick gray hair, bunched eyebrows, long black eyelashes above ink-dark eyes, a tiny half-moon scar above one cheekbone, full lips, a pointed chin, smooth dark skin with only a trace of wrinkles. He might have been any well-dressed businessman in his finely woven green sports coat, dark gray trousers, black socks and shoes, except for his aura of leashed power.

I held tight to the legal pad, struggling to regain my mental equilibrium. I'd told the truth, but truth alone was not going to suffice, not here, not now. The cardroom seemed an odd and unexpected place to stave off attack. The room was small, perhaps sixteen feet by twenty. There were two maple card tables, each with four chairs, a green-and-yellow chintz settee beneath the windows, and bookcases on one wall. Sun speared through the slatted shutters, striping the cedar walls with bars of rich russet and dull brown. Behind the chief inspector, the connecting door to the next room was barely ajar. I felt certain Mrs. Worrell was only a few feet away, ear pressed to that infinitesimal opening. I wondered if she could feel the tension as it built, palpable as a fine mist or a recurring drumbeat or a rocket's fiery trail.

I carefully placed the pad on the table. "Yes. This summary is accurate." I knew as I spoke that my response was irrelevant to Foster.

"Why did you quarrel with George Smith Wednesday afternoon?" Those cold, watchful eyes locked on mine.

"I did not quarrel with him." Granted, I'd been imperious. And, of course, I'd been convinced my talk with him was successful until the ghost rose Wednesday night. "I simply told him that he must not harass Mrs. Bailey and that I wanted all manifestations of the *ghost* to cease." My tone expressed my lack of belief in supernatural creatures.

Foster picked up a sheaf of papers, but he did not look at them. "A witness reports that you and Smith exchanged angry looks."

I'd thought we were alone near the pool after tea. "The witness is mistaken." But yes, I suppose to an observer, we might have appeared angry: I demanding, George considering.

"You admit offering Smith money?" He lifted a long finger, pressed it against his aquiline nose.

"I wanted George to stop the appearances of the ghost so that the wedding could proceed without any more distress for Mrs. Bailey." It sounded lame as I said it.

"A thousand dollars?" His tone was incredulous. Even with the effects of inflation, a thousand dollars isn't pocket change. "Come, Mrs. Collins. Isn't it more likely that you had some personal reason to offer Smith money?"

"Personal?" I was puzzled, unable to imagine what Foster meant.

"You thought your conversation with him would not be repeated." There was smugness in his voice.

"I gave no thought to that. Why should I care?" I didn't like the faint suggestion of a smile on the chief inspector's face.

"In fact, Mrs. Collins" — Foster's tone was almost expansive — "George Smith did repeat your conversation, describing your anger over his attentions to your granddaughter and your insistence that he have no further dealings with Miss Drake."

I understood, of course. Someone had observed at least a portion of my conversation after tea with George and later asked

George why I appeared angry. George came up with a reason that had nothing to do with ghosts and money. Quick. Clever. And damned unfortunate for me.

I suppose I should have been frightened. In fact, I was amused. I leaned back in my chair and laughed. "No, Chief Inspector, I did not warn George away from my granddaughter. Her romantic interests are her own. She doesn't need advice from her grandmother. And should I ever be displeased at her choice, I assure you I would not resort either to money or to pushing the inappropriate suitor from a cliff. But" — and my amusement seeped away — "you are correct that Diana spent a bit more time with George than would be expected of a guest and a hotel staff member. That connection had nothing to do with romance." I described Diana's rather cruel plan for the photo session atop the headland. "You can ask her about it."

He folded his arms. "I will."

He didn't believe me. He had the testimony of someone to whom George had spoken. It was a reminder to me, if I ever needed it, at the possibilities for misdirection when people lie. And people often lie. But I didn't care so much why the chief inspector was suspicious of me; what mattered was the underlying reason. I looked at him gravely. "You think George Smith's death is suspicious."

Foster's eyes narrowed.

"Why?" I meant my query very seriously indeed.

Perhaps my question surprised him. Perhaps he sensed my sincerity despite his suspicions of me. Whichever, whatever, he responded in kind. "As you yourself suggested yesterday morning, Mrs. Collins" — there was the merest suggestion of wryness — "Mr. Smith was young, agile, athletic. Although the postmortem report has not yet been completed, there is no suggestion of illness or inebriation. The day was clear. The terrain was not wet or slick." He came to a full stop. His fingers thumped a tattoo on the tabletop.

There had to be more. There had to be a reason why this experienced police officer suspected murder. I sat very still. The police like to ask questions, not answer them. Would he tell me?

He kept his eyes on my face, skeptical, probing, measuring eyes. Abruptly, he continued. "I spoke with the pathologist this morning. She informed me that the toxicology tests were not yet finished." A pause. "She also informed me of two fist-shaped bruises in the lumbar region."

I pictured the headland and George Smith standing at the edge, the breeze ruffling his hair, pressing his clothes against him. Had he heard footsteps behind him? Over the crash of the waves, quite possibly not.

I nodded, the picture clear in my mind. "Someone came at him from behind, came fast, punched him in the lower back." I made my hands into fists, thrust them forward. "That's what happened."

"You speak as though you were there." His voice was silky.

"No. But the bruises tell the story. That's why you're investigating." I hitched my chair nearer the table. "I knew it was murder. George told too many people that Roddy Worrell was pushed. And Thursday morning he was on the phone with someone, telling them he'd figured out what happened to Roddy and telling his listener he was going to meet me on the headland and he was going to sell what he knew. Don't you see: George was killed because he knew who pushed Roddy Worrell from the tower."

Foster leaned back in his chair, his eyebrows drawn in a thick line over thoughtful eyes. "In the event of unexplained death,

Mrs. Collins, an inquest is conducted in Magistrate's Court to determine the cause of that death. An inquest was duly held after Mr. Worrell's death. After extensive testimony from the police, from forensic authorities and from interested parties, Mr. Worrell's death was adjudged an accident." He threw up his hands as if shooing away troublesome insects. "All this talk about Roddy Worrell — there's no doubt what happened to him. I investigated his death, Mrs. Collins. He'd had too much to drink. And he was careless. Whatever George Smith claimed about Worrell's death is so much nonsense."

I looked at him in surprise. "But last night you asked Mrs. Bailey about the night of his death. You asked her to describe her actions that evening."

He looked irritated. "As Mrs. Bailey must have told you" — he clearly attributed my knowledge of that interview to my connection with the family — "my questions were prompted by a report that she was seen at the tower with Mr. Worrell. Of course, it was necessary to explore the possibility. But Mrs. Bailey reaffirmed her previous statement."

If I'd felt uneasy at the start of our conversation, I felt doubly so now. Obviously

Foster didn't believe there was any truth in George's claim that Worrell was pushed from the tower. That left me as Foster's obvious choice for prime suspect in George's death, thanks to George's creative story about Diana.

"You can't simply dismiss the apparition at the tower. Someone made that happen." I could be just as determined as the chief inspector. "It isn't nonsense that George agreed to lay the ghost for money, took more money to break that promise and came back to me asking for yet more money!"

Foster glanced down at the note lying on the card table, the note I'd found yesterday morning in my room. He pointed at it, carefully not touching the sheet. "You claim that you did not reach the headland in time for your appointment —"

"Not" — and my voice was sharp — "an appointment I sought, Chief Inspector. Don't you see, that note proves that George had spoken to someone else, that someone else had given him money to override my promised thousand and so the ghost floated by the tower Wednesday night. Can't you see what happened?" I was sure I was right. I gripped the edge of the table. "Jasmine heard George tell someone that he was going to meet me on the headland. That person got there before I did and pushed him over the cliff."

"You are the only person known to have gone out on the headland yesterday morning." The words were precise; the accusation clear.

"Jasmine heard —"

"I will speak to the child." He made a note. "Now, Mrs. Collins, about this fire —"

I pushed back my chair, stood. I didn't think he would arrest me. I was sure of it, actually. He was suspicious of me, but there is a big leap between suspicion and arrest.

"I did not set the fire. I did my best to preserve that evidence for you. However, I'm quite sure someone set the fire to prevent anyone from ever knowing for certain who flew the kite. Now we'll never —"

"Wait, Mrs. Collins!" Foster's voice was sharp. He held up a commanding hand. "You claim there was a kite that glowed in the dark. You claim —"

"You can check with James, the bartender." Would James admit that he'd told me? I didn't feel confident of it.

"We will do so, of course. But you left no word about this kite in your telephone message to me last night. The fire makes it impossible to prove or disprove the existence of the kite and, thus, the ghost, as you imagine it. Did you invent this kite to explain your contacts with George Smith?"

I stared at him. Another unspoken question hung in the air:

Did you set the fire?

"No." I kept it short and crisp. I turned away, but at the door, I paused. "Find out who George called on his cell phone yesterday morning. You owe me that much, Chief Inspector."

It was a nice exit line. But I was going to need more than an exit line to convince the chief inspector of my innocence.

fourteen

Thanks to my interview with the chief inspector, I was late for breakfast. Jasmine was the only occupant of our table, diligently spooning whipped cream over a waffle. Curt Patterson's red hair was just visible over the top of *The Royal Gazette* at the table nearest the fireplace. He lowered the newspaper and there was a flicker of disappointment. "Morning, Mrs. Collins," he said, then lifted the paper. Not, obviously, looking for me. I pulled out my chair at the table.

Jasmine looked at me in surprise. "Aren't you going with them?"

It seemed an eternity since I'd felt a part of the Drake-Bailey wedding party and the printed "Programme." Today was Friday. I didn't remember what had been scheduled. I slipped into my chair.

Frederick was there immediately, bringing coffee and juice. "Your regular, Mrs. Collins?"

I have a weakness for bacon and eggs and English muffins when in a hotel. I usually choose applesauce and toast when home. I have a sense of no tomorrow when traveling.

So . . . "Yes, thanks, Frederick."

He poured the steaming coffee and I gratefully picked up my cup. I had the beginnings of a dull headache, as much due to the lateness of coffee as to my session with Chief Inspector Foster.

I smiled at Jasmine. "Where's everyone going?"

She wriggled importantly, enjoying a moment in the limelight. I wondered just how much fun this trip could be for Jasmine, surrounded by adults; her mother at first absorbed in the approaching wedding and now nervous over the nagging reminders of Roddy Worrell; her sister kind but understandably focused on her boyfriend, and the rest of us polite but seldom attentive. "They're going into Hamilton to see about having the wedding in Victoria Park. There's a gazebo there, a really big one —"

I nodded. The park's elegant bandstand was built to commemorate Queen Victoria's Jubilee and was a wrought-iron reminder of another time. The entire park, with its tall and elegant palms and statuesque Norfolk pines, seems like a picture postcard from another era. It would indeed be a much more cheerful site for the wedding than the hotel garden.

"— and it would be fun even though there

isn't a moongate." She frowned, a shadow in her eyes, then continued hurriedly, "Do you know about moongates?" Jasmine eagerly described the romantic associations with the semicircle of stones so often seen in Bermuda. ". . . so Mother and Marlow and Diana have gone to talk to the wedding lady —"

Diana? I suppose my face was revealing.

"— Diana looked grumpy." I didn't doubt Jasmine's appraisal. "She wanted to play golf with Lloyd and Neal and Steve. But Lloyd asked her to go with Mom and Marlow and she said she would."

I was enjoying my bacon and eggs and hoped Jasmine's waffle wasn't getting cold. "So we're the only ones here?"

She lifted her fork with a piece of waffle laden with whipped cream. "Oh, no, Aaron's here. He and I are going to play badminton. He's gone to get the rackets."

I doubted very much indeed that a badminton game was going to occur. The Sports closet would be off limits until the arson investigation was completed. I realized the fire wasn't common knowledge yet. Apparently, I had been the only one curious enough about the sirens to walk down to the pool.

"Didn't Aaron want to play golf?" Had

Marlow asked him to stay at the hotel and keep an eye on Jasmine?

Jasmine's face scrunched into disdain. "Aaron thinks golf's stupid. He says grown men should have something better to do than whack away at a little white ball with fancy metal clubs." She looked thoughtful. "Marlow used to play a lot until she started dating Aaron. He's funny about things."

"How's he funny?" I added marmalade to my second half of English muffin and re-filled my coffee cup.

She picked up her spoon and scraped the last dollop of whipped cream from the plate. "He's always talking about keeping things simple and how he and Marlow are going to live on what he earns after they get married and how you don't need money to be happy, that money just complicates your life. Mother says he's an idiot and he'll outgrow all that. Marlow thinks he's wonderful." Jasmine licked her spoon. "Do you think it would be piggy to ask for more whipped cream?"

"Not the least bit." I raised my hand and Frederick was there. "A little bowl of whipped cream, please."

Jasmine applied herself to the whipped cream, her spoon flicking in and out of the bowl with the regularity of a cat's pink

245

tongue lapping up cream.

I'd almost finished my coffee when Aaron came through the archway. I looked at him curiously. Handsome, confident, charming, he blended well into this enclave of wealth. His polo shirt was new and his khakis crisp. If he didn't like conspicuous consumption, Bermuda was scarcely the right place for him. However, he seemed to have no compunctions about visiting here as the guest of Marlow's family. The island's remote location made everything expensive — land, building, hotels, food. Bermuda had been an elegant playground for the wealthy since Princess Louise, Queen Victoria's daughter, spent several months here in 1883. It was still a holiday destination beyond the reach of the average traveler. Equal beauty could be had for a quarter of the price on the Mexican coast or in the Caribbean. Of course, Bermuda was also famed for its gentility and safety for tourists.

I knew Aaron's presence here surely might not reflect his personal preferences. He obviously had no control over the setting chosen for Marlow's mother's wedding, and perhaps he'd felt that he couldn't refuse the invitation to attend. The year before? Well, love has its power and certainly might cause any young man to compromise his principles to enjoy a beach holiday with his girl-friend. Right now he looked more like a young country dubber than an impecunious graduate student. I rather agreed with Connor. He would very likely change his attitudes with time, slip comfortably into the role of a wealthy young woman's husband. And if he didn't, I was willing to guess, that would be all right with Marlow, too. Although she was always understated in dress and manner, I'd caught her glance upon him several times and there was unmistakable passion there.

Aaron raised a hand in greeting. "Morning, Mrs. Collins. Hey, Jasmine, we can't play badminton after all."

"Oh, Aaron." Her face crumpled.

"There was a fire last night and the Sports closet is messed up. But listen, I was thinking we could go down to the beach and make some boats out of bark. You know that little cove . . ." He crouched beside her chair. They made an appealing picture, the eager young man with tousled chestnut curls and the sweet-faced little girl who obviously adored him.

I wished I could join them. I wished very much that I could walk slowly down the slope to the magnificent beach with its pale pink sand and follow Aaron and Jasmine to the secluded cove and watch as they launched driftwood boats.

But I had other tasks before me.

They scarcely heard me as I left, they were so deep in their plans. Jasmine clapped her hands. "I'm going to call my boat *The Jolly Roger . . .*"

I paused outside the dining room. The main desk was unattended for the moment. I wondered if Foster was still interviewing witnesses and if the door to the adjoining room remained open just a sliver. Mrs. Worrell was keeping a close watch on the chief inspector. I tucked that thought away. Her knowledge might come in handy at some point — not, of course, that she was likely to be readily forthcoming. It would be an interesting contest.

I walked swiftly to my room. I had to discover some fact that would support my arguments to the chief inspector. I stepped out on my balcony, looked first at the tower, looming to my right, then straight ahead, beyond the pool and the gardens, to the headland poking out into the ocean. I looked from one to the other and it seemed so clear to me. Two fatal falls, a year apart. Why did Foster see murder in George Smith's death and accident in Roddy Worrell's? I needed to know more of the facts of Roddy's fall, but it would not do any good to ask Foster.

I shaded my eyes against the warm, soft sunlight and smiled. This was a very small island. The intimacy of Bermuda is perhaps most obvious when riding in a taxi. Often the driver taps his horn, not in warning or irritation but to greet a friend. In effect, all of Bermuda comprises the equivalent of a small town. In a small town, newspaper reporters either know almost everyone or know about almost everyone. I swung back into my room, moved purposefully toward the telephone.

I looked up at the facade of *The Royal Gazette* building. I liked its pale purple hue and the gold crest beneath the newspaper's name. I hurried up the shallow steps and entered the main door. A receptionist looked up from a gray counter and smiled a welcome. Beyond her, accessible through a small half-door to the left, ranged the newsroom, a warren of cubicles. Computer screens glowed a soft green.

I spoke with the receptionist, a pretty young woman with a chartreuse bow in her hair. "Mr. Ellis is expecting you." She pointed to my left. "Please go through the gate and walk to the end of the first corridor.

He will meet you there." She smiled again and picked up a phone.

When I reached the end of the corridor, a plump young man bounded toward me.

"Mrs. Collins? Kevin Ellis. This way, this way." He hustled me right, then left, and right again and ushered me into a narrow work cubicle. He pulled a chair up to his desk and waved me toward it. "So you want to know about the fellow who took a dive out at the Tower Ridge House last year. I punched up the stories and printed out a couple. Here's the one that tells the tale."

"Thanks so much." I sat down and took the computer printout.

Ellis's hazel eyes were bright and curious and I knew some questions were coming. He leaned back in his chair, a small legal pad in one hand, a pen in the other. Around us was the disciplined energy of a news-room, the ring of phones, brisk voices, hurried footsteps. Some things never change.

I read the story quickly:

Proceedings in Magistrate's Court Wednesday resulted in a finding of Death by Misadventure in the fatal late-night fall last month of well-known island entertainer Roderick Worrell from the tower located at Tower Ridge House in Paget.

The small hotel has long belonged to the Palmer family.

Police reported that Worrell, a mellow tenor who often sang with the Coral Reef Trio, lived at the hotel, managed by his wife, Thelma. Mrs. Worrell was distraught on the witness stand as she testified that she had often warned her husband against his custom of sitting on the ledge of the tower, legs dangling outside, and singing.

Worrell's body was found in the early morning of January 20. The autopsy report, also entered in evidence, indicated death resulted from massive trauma consistent with a fall from the top of the tower. Police said the tower was forty feet tall. Worrell was last seen leaving the hotel bar around midnight of the preceding evening . . .

I didn't have to read any more. I understood now why the chief inspector believed Worrell's death to be accidental. The autopsy had, obviously, not revealed bruises similar to those found on George Smith's back. But I wondered if it hadn't at least occurred to Foster that it would take very little force to push a man sitting on a ledge, especially a man who'd had too much whiskey to drink.

"So you are staying at Tower Ridge House?" Ellis was youngish, perhaps mid-thirties, thinning sandy hair, ready smile, but his eyes had the skeptical, inquiring, nothing-you-say-will-surprise-me savvy of an experienced reporter.

"Yes. It's a lovely hotel." I folded the printout, placed it on his desk.

His eyes flickered toward the paper, then back to me. "One of the nicest small hotels on the island. Rather hard times there now. The police are investigating the death of an employee as a possible homicide. You found the body." He didn't have to check his notes. "Why?"

Oh, smart fellow. Damn good question.

I hesitated for an instant. I needed to pick my words with care. Although I didn't expect Chief Inspector Foster to reveal much of the current investigation to me, I didn't want to irritate him. I wanted to be able to ask him a few questions with the hope of receiving answers. And, as a lawyer I knew once observed, there are a great many ways to tell the truth.

"I'd gone out to the headland to meet George." I was rather pleased with the natural sound of my voice, as if I were simply confiding to a friend. "I'd visited with George several times since my arrival about the rumor that Roddy Worrell's ghost had been seen late at night near the top of the tower —"

Ellis's pudgy fingers gripped his pen. His eyes glowed. "Oh, I say. A ghost. Tell me all about it."

Everyone loves a ghost story. Of course, I kept my recital to the information I'd received from George and made no mention of my offer of money to dissuade the ghost from appearing.

"— quite shocking when a shout awakened a number of guests late Wednesday night. Several of us saw the apparition, a luminous glow near the top of the tower, and when we ran to the tower and searched it, we found nothing to explain the appearance."

Ellis hitched his chair closer to mine. "This was Wednesday night, you say. And you found Smith's body Thursday morning. Why were you meeting him on the headland?"

"I had a conviction he knew all about the ghost and who was making it appear and why." There was no need to mention George's note. What I said was true and a nice example of one way of offering truth.

The reporter tapped his pen on his pad. "You don't believe in ghosts?"

"No. I'm convinced it was a hoax of some kind." I waved my hand. "There are always ways to create physical phenomena to dupe people." If only I'd taken the phosphorescent kite out of the closet . . .

He looked down at his notes. "You say that Smith told you the apparition was first seen this past week?" At my nod, he rattled on. "Of course, it could be a prank of some sort. But why would anyone want to do it?"

"Perhaps the idea was to suggest that Roddy Worrell's death wasn't an accident." This was dangerous ground.

Ellis's head jerked up. "Are you suggesting that Worrell was pushed from the tower and Smith knew about it?"

This was farther than I wished to go. I shrugged. "Mr. Ellis, I don't know. But why else would anyone murder George Smith? Have you learned anything that would suggest a reason for his death?"

Ellis's young-old eyes were suddenly wary. Reporters protect their sources. His answer was smooth. "The police have said only that an investigation is under way into the circumstances of Smith's death and there is suspicion of foul play."

If Ellis knew anything more about the investigation, he wasn't going to share it with me. But maybe I could approach it a different way. "Have you learned anything about Smith?"

Ellis hesitated for an instant. I knew he

was reviewing what information he had and whether it mattered if he revealed it to me. His eyes dropped to his notes. Perhaps he appreciated my report of the ghost. That would make a good story. In any event, he swung toward his monitor, clicked on the file folder, clicked on a file and brought it onto the screen. He spoke rapidly, "Canadian. From Toronto. Big family. Parents shocked, said he'd written that he was coming home and planned to go to the university, that he'd saved some money. No bad habits, according to his father. Hard worker. Liked sports. He'd been here for three years. One ticket for speeding on his moped. No other official record. Lived by himself in a basement apartment in Warwick Parish. Landlady said he paid his rent promptly, was a quiet tenant. I haven't found a close friend yet. If he had a girlfriend, nobody's mentioned her." Ellis closed down the file, swung toward me. "Seems like a pretty innocuous chap."

I wanted very much to ask for the address of George's basement apartment, but I didn't want Ellis to know that I might go there. Instead, I murmured, "He does indeed. Well" — I stood, smiled — "I hope the police are successful in their investigation and I appreciate your taking the time to speak with me."

Ellis wasn't going to let me slip away that easily. "Just what is your interest in all of this, Mrs. Collins?" He stood, too.

"I've always been interested in the so-called appearances of ghosts, Mr. Ellis. Usually, there is something in the person's background that accounts for the apparition. So I wanted to find out more about Mr. Worrell."

"I see." His tone was equable, but his gaze was skeptical.

I reached out, shook his hand. "Thanks so much for your time." I smiled and moved briskly away. I glanced back as I turned into a narrow corridor. He was looking after me and I knew he was going to find out everything he could about me and that he was going to wonder a good deal about Roddy Worrell, the ghost, and George Smith.

I like stirring pots. Maybe, if I was patient, this one would begin to boil.

Outside, I took a deep breath. I'd come to *The Royal Gazette* to learn more about Roddy Worrell's fall. Although I'd accomplished that goal, I was discouraged. I hesitated on the sidewalk. That avenue of investigation seemed closed. All that was left was to learn more about George Smith.

I walked down Par-la-Ville Road and

turned left on Front Street, Hamilton's main street, which overlooks the harbor. Hamilton, the capital of Bermuda, is graced with both beauty and charm. Two- and three-story buildings on Front Street glow in delicate shades of lemon, blue, rose, green, and orange. Arches and columns support an overhang that provides shoppers with protection from rain. I wished I could duck into Trimingham's, a department store that wore its one hundred and fifty-plus years comfortably, but I had no time to be a tourist. I was apparently the main suspect in George's murder. I had to know more about George Smith. Somewhere in his life, there had to be a pointer to his death. It was up to me to find it. I lifted my hand, hailed a taxi.

fifteen

My shoes clicked on the wooden floor of the lobby. I reached the front desk. No one was there. I heard the tick of a clock, the soft whisper of blinds rattled by the breeze through an open window, the chirping of birds. I moved a few steps, glanced into the drawing room. A coffee service sat on a butler's table, but the room was empty except for the black cat stretched comfortably on the mantel, one paw resting on the foot of a pink porcelain clock. The cat's golden eyes flicked open, regarded me coolly.

Cats are night creatures. Had the sleek creature been abroad the night Roddy Worrell died? Quite likely, but even if the cat could speak, it likely would not have cared enough to remember.

I walked back to the counter, punched the silver bell.

Footsteps sounded. Rosalind, patting her lips with a napkin, came through the archway from a back office. "Mrs. Collins, how are you today?" Her tone was cheerful, but her eyes had a skittish look. No doubt there was a good deal of gossip among hotel employees. Was there a rumor out that I had quarreled with George? If I'd had any hopes of obtaining George's address from the desk, I relinquished them. Instead, I smiled. "Where is Mrs. Worrell?"

Rosalind brushed a crumb from her sweater. "Uh, she's not in her office this morning." Clearly, Rosalind was reluctant to say where the manager might be found.

"Is Chief Inspector Foster still in the hotel?" If so, I knew where to find Mrs. Worrell.

Rosalind shook her head. "No. He left an hour or so ago."

"I need to speak with Mrs. Worrell, then. Let me see" — I was scrambling to remember that disorganized scene at the foot of the tower Wednesday night and Steve Jennings's comment about a flashlight bobbing up from the lower terrace — "her cottage is the one where the road curves before reaching the hotel entrance." I made it a statement, not a question.

Rosalind looked nervously toward the corridor leading to the upper terrace. "She said she didn't want anyone to bother her. If you like, I'll give her a message."

"Oh, it's no trouble." There is nothing so impossible to combat as obtuseness. I beamed at her. "Thanks, Rosalind. I'll see you later."

"But Mrs. Collins . . ." Her plaintive tone followed me down the corridor.

Once in the sunlight, I walked fast to the stone steps, skirting a spectacular plumeria. Its glossy green leaves glistened in the sun, another of the infinite variations of green that mark the island in January. There weren't many shrubs in bloom now, an occasional hibiscus with a few pink or white flowers, but the subtle shadings of green had their own special magic.

On the lower terrace, I paused just long enough to see that there was little evidence a fire had occurred. The yellow tape was gone. A gardener pushed a roller over the ground marked by the firemen's boots. The door to the Sports closet was open and a sound of hammering echoed out. The Canadian women were stretched out on deck chairs, magazines in hand.

At the base of the second stairway, I looked across the road at a small yellow cottage. The shutters were closed on the landward side. The view over the bay from the front would be magnificent. I was glad Thelma Worrell prized her privacy. She would not see me approach. I stepped up onto the narrow wooden back porch and knocked three times, peremptorily.

When the door opened, I caught a scent of old tobacco smoke and cinnamon potpourri. Mrs. Worrell stood a scant foot away, her white face empty of expression. The door began to close.

"I shall tell the chief inspector you've eavesdropped on his interviews." I don't like to bully. I felt I had no choice.

The door stopped. Thin fingers curled around its edge.

"Please," and I let my voice soften, "let me talk to you."

"I wish you'd never come here. All of you." Her voice was rough.

"I'm sorry." And I was.

In the silence that stretched between us, the persistent, unending boom of the surf was disturbing. George Smith tumbled to his death not forty yards away from where I stood. Surf can mask so many noises — the quick pound of steps on the headland, the soft tiptoe of shoes on the platform of the tower.

The high chirrup of a cell phone startled us both. She pulled the phone from her pocket. "Hello." She listened, her narrow face stony. "It's all right, Rosalind." The manager stared at me. "Mrs. Collins is here now." She spoke distinctly. "She says she needs to speak with me. I will talk to her, then I'll be up to the office in a few minutes."

She clicked off the phone, pushed open the screen door.

I stepped inside. We stood in a narrow, dark kitchen. There was a musty smell, no hint of foods or cooking, only mold and the memory of tobacco smoke. She turned and walked heavily into a short hallway made to look smaller by the wallpaper of huge cabbage roses and a twining ivy.

The hallway opened to a shallow but wide room with four — no, five — windows that looked out to the ocean. These windows were bare to the world below. No shutters, no drapes, no blinds marred the magnificent view of turquoise water, tumbled black rocks, crashing surf and the riffle of white that marked the encircling reef.

The cottage interior was unremarkable: a shabby chintz-covered sofa, an old green armchair, a pair of wing chairs with faded petit-point upholstery. Cast-offs from the hotel? The oriental rug had a discolored fringe. I suspected these were remnants of the days when the Tower Ridge House had been an elegant home. A man's brown leather recliner sat next to a small cedar table. A wooden rack held pipes — big ones, little ones, sleek ones, knobby ones. The smell of old tobacco was stronger here.

Thelma Worrell swung about to face me. The stark light flooding through the windows emphasized the purplish shadows beneath her staring eyes and the deep lines grooved by her thin lips. "Rosalind knows you are here." Her voice was high, uneven.

I realized abruptly that she was afraid of me. She was not simply worried that I might reveal her surreptitious eavesdropping to the chief inspector. She watched me with uneasy eyes, nervously fingered a jade brooch at her throat. She pulled the cell phone from her pocket. "I can call her. If I need to."

"You won't need to call Rosalind, Mrs. Worrell." My tone was dry. "All I want from you is George Smith's address."

"His address?" She spoke the words as if they were in an unknown tongue.

"Where did he live?" I opened my purse, pulled out a notepad and pen.

She dropped the cell phone into her sweater pocket, pushed back a fringe of frizzy hair. "What did George have that you want? What's going on? Did you and George make up this ugly story about Roddy?"

She knew everything I'd told the inspector. I wished I knew what else she'd learned, pressed so quietly against that adjoining door. Obviously, she'd heard nothing to explain more about the ghost.

"I had nothing to do with the ghost." It was like being tangled in an unseen spider's web. "That's what I'm trying to find out more about. You heard me tell the inspector about the kite —"

"There's no proof there was ever a kite in the Sports closet!" Her tone accused me. "I asked James and he said he didn't tell you anything about the closet. He said he didn't tell you anything at all about a ghost, that he doesn't know anything about a ghost."

"James is your employee." I didn't want to get James in trouble. I chose my words carefully. "He doesn't want to lose his job. I don't think he does know much. When he told me to look there, I had the sense that he thought there might be something of interest but that it was a guess. I had no feeling that he was a party to anything George had done. He was afraid George had involved himself in something and it might have to do with his murder."

Her eyes narrowed. She lifted her fingers to one temple, pressed for a moment. "Murder." She repeated the word, shaking her head. "I can't believe it. George — why would anyone kill George? And why do you want to know where he lived?"

"I want to see where he lived. I want to look around. Ask questions." I held her gaze. "Somewhere there has to be a link between George and the person who murdered him. I'm sure George created your husband's ghost. He did it for a reason. When we know that reason, we will know why he died."

"That ghost" — she shuddered — "shiny and white and hanging there." Her voice shook. She took a step toward me. "You think it was a kite? You think George did it? But why, why?" Her voice rose.

"Because he knew who killed your husband. He may have tried blackmail." I was ordering the facts in my mind, clear and cogent and compelling, George talking on the cell phone, telling someone that he should go to the police . . .

Her eyes flared. She clutched at her throat with a shaking hand.

We stared at each other. I couldn't pull my eyes away from hers. I looked at misery so intense, I wanted to turn and run. The memory of a dark and ugly night pulsed between us, raw and painful as an open wound.

"No." Her voice was harsh. "It was her fault. Her fault."

I wondered uneasily then if Thelma Worrell had crept up behind her husband, pushed him from the ledge of the tower. It was possible. Why else was she frightened? Why else was she so insistent that Connor caused Roddy's death? After all, we had only Thelma's word that George had seen Connor at the tower that night. I thought of George's words, on the cell phone yesterday morning — at least the report of them from Jasmine — and yes, George remembered seeing a woman at the tower. He had not said what woman. Yes, he'd been talking about Connor. But what if it was Thelma Worrell he saw that night?

"George didn't —" She stopped, licked dry lips. She fumbled with the brooch, unloosed it. She turned the piece of jewelry over and over in her fingers. "Maybe George tried to get money from her." The sentence wavered uncertainly. Then, more strongly, she said it again. "Maybe that's what happened. Maybe George tried to get money out of her."

I scarcely heard her. My thoughts tumbled. I'd been so certain that George's death was tied to Roddy Worrell's. If I was wrong about that . . . if Thelma Worrell was truly frightened of me, if she thought I'd killed George, then I had to seek George's murderer elsewhere even if she had indeed pushed her husband.

". . . George said he saw her that night. Maybe he saw her push Roddy." Her eyes glittered with an anger that would never be satisfied.

Was Thelma Worrell an actress of great accomplishment? Had she pretended to be afraid of me? Or was it possible that she truly thought I might have murdered George because he'd paid too much attention to Diana? Or indeed for some more obscure reason? What was it she'd asked: "What did George have that you want?"

I couldn't be sure of the truth, but I held fast to one overriding suspicion: Thelma might have murdered her husband. If that was true, it definitely gave her a motive to get rid of George.

"George didn't see Connor." That's all I said.

Her pale blue eyes shifted away from mine. Did she know better than anyone in the world how Roddy died?

I watched her closely. "Nothing happened to George until Roddy's ghost appeared."

"The ghost." She shivered. "Roddy died one year ago this Saturday."

Someone wanted everyone at Tower Ridge House to remember Roddy Worrell.

If I knew who planned the ghost, I would understand everything. I was sure of it. And George had known.

"I want George's address." Once again I held my pen ready. "A basement apartment?" Bermuda has a tight housing crunch, especially for working people. Basement apartments were very popular.

Her mouth shut in a tight line.

"I will tell the chief inspector that you listened to his interviews." I watched as she decided, saw the uncertainty in her eyes. She didn't want the chief inspector to ask why she had eavesdropped. She didn't want him to think again about the night that Roddy Worrell died and perhaps wonder about his wife's anger. On the other hand, she might worry about what I might discover if I gained access to George's living quarters.

She blew out a spurt of angry breath. She turned, was gone for a moment, came back with a sheet in her hand. "A basement apartment in Warwick," she said abruptly. "10 Apple Rose Lane. Half-Crescent Court."

I stepped over the railing from my balcony to Diana's. I pushed on the sliding door and wasn't surprised that it moved. Her helmet and the moped keys were lying on the table. I picked them up, scrawled a note, propped it against the ceramic tower.

I returned to my room, changed into slacks and a sweater. I didn't see anyone on my way to the moped parking area behind the pittosporum shrub near the main entrance. I took time to write another note just in case she noticed that her moped was missing before she went to her room:

Dear Diana,
I've borrowed your moped for a little while.
I'll be back soon.

Grandma

I looked around for something heavy. I walked along the flower bed, pushing on the decorative border of broken bricks. The sixth was loose. I reached down, pulled it free and used the portion of brick to anchor the note on the cement block where the moped was parked.

I'm not much of a helmet wearer, but they are required by law in Bermuda. I adjusted it, snapped the chin strap, and straddled the bike. The key turned smoothly and the motor rumbled. As I'd hoped, riding a motorbike was a quickly remembered skill. I felt fairly wobbly and took my time going down the drive, but the balance came back to me. I drove slowly, of course. Fortunately, the speed limit is 20 miles per hour. That definitely seemed fast enough. I concentrated on keeping to the left.

The curving road — all roads curve and twist in Bermuda — sloped down. At the base of a fairly steep hill, I turned left onto Middle Road. Pastel-painted houses with the distinctive stepped white roofs dotted the hillsides. At the traffic light, I turned onto South Shore Road. I had a hand-drawn map, reluctant courtesy of Mrs. Worrell, tucked in my pocket. I'd studied it carefully before I left. She'd even marked familiar sites. I passed the entrance to Elbow Beach Hotel. So far, so good. A taxi pressed a little too close behind me, but I didn't increase my speed.

At Southcote Avenue, I turned right. The narrow road was bounded by big hedges of Suriname cherry and copper-leaf. The legend is that no two leaves of the copper-leaf, also called matchmacan (match me if you can!), are the same. The red leaves were a cheerful note among all the greenery. Happily, I had this stretch of narrow road to myself.

I turned left on Ord Road. As I passed the bright green of Paget Primary School, I came up behind a battered little car traveling even slower than I. That was fine with me. When we crossed into Warwick Parish, there was a patch of more modest homes. I slowed to turn on a rough dirt track that angled up the hillside. A field to my left was filled with cabbage, beans and lettuce. I slowed at a low wall that bounded a small square lot. A wooden sign read Half-Crescent Court. It is the custom for houses to have names in addition to the formal address.

I stopped in front of the two-story gray house with lime shutters. Masses of pink and purple petunias bloomed in front beds. Norfolk pines flanked each end of the house. The main entrance was directly before me. A flagstone path branched off the main walk, curved around the east side of the house. I guessed the basement apartment would be at the side of the house or perhaps in back.

The house was in good repair, the paint bright, the flower beds well tended, the front steps swept clean. I hurried up the steps, knocked. I wasn't certain what I would say. Should I inquire about the vacant apartment, say I'd heard from a friend it might be available? Should I claim acquaintance with George's parents, say I was there to look over his belongings to see what should be returned to Canada?

I always move at too fast a pace. I had lifted my hand, ready to knock again, when the door swung in. An imposing woman — six feet tall, dark hair in an untidy chignon, a faded pink turtleneck and purple slacks, a two-strand necklace of amber beads — looked at me politely. She had fine dark eyes and a magenta-bright mouth. The blue mixing bowl in the crook of her arm was half full of smooth, yellow batter. I smelled the rich cream of butter and a hint of nutmeg.

I made a quick decision. Sometimes the truth works better than a clever ploy. "Hello. I'm Henrietta Collins, a guest at Tower Ridge House. I found George's body Wednesday morning. I'd like to talk to you about him, if I may."

Her expressive face mirrored surprise, sadness, curiosity, uncertainty. "I don't know . . ." she began hesitantly.

"I won't take up much of your time." I pointed at the bowl. "Not many people bake these days."

She looked at the batter, her dark brows drawing together. "I love to bake. I always put a plate on George's kitchen table." She shook her head. "I still can't believe he's gone. I took him a piece of pie Tuesday afternoon. He was so cheerful. He gave me a thumbs-up, said everything was coming up roses for him."

I felt the old familiar tingle, the heightened sense a reporter develops. I was close to a discovery, so close I could taste it. But I needed to be careful not to shut her down, not to alarm her. "Do you have any idea what he was talking about?"

She frowned and rubbed her thumb along the rim of the bowl. "Why do you want to know?"

"I am convinced that George was involved in what he believed to be a practical joke. I think he accepted money to create the appearance of a ghost at the hotel." I looked at her soberly. "I think that 'joke' caused George's murder. I want to find out who hired him."

Her eyes flashed. "George was a nice boy."

"Yes. But he may have been foolish. Please, if you know anything at all that can help me . . ."

"I don't see what business it is of yours." Her face was puzzled, her eyes questioning.

I turned my hands palms-up. "It isn't any of my business. Not in the sense you mean. But it is important to me because I don't want to feel I might have been a cause of his

273

death. I offered George money not to do the ghost trick. Instead, the ghost — a shiny white cloud — appeared Wednesday night near the tower on the hotel grounds. The next morning — the morning he died — I found a note pushed under my door. It was from George. He asked me to meet him on the headland and he wanted more money to tell me about the ghost. I went to the headland. I found his body."

"Mrs." — she paused — "Collins?"

I nodded.

"I'm Joan Abbott." It was a murmur as she thought. Finally, she gave a decided nod of her head, said briskly, "Even if someone killed George to keep him from revealing information to you, it was George's decision to ask you for money."

"Still . . ." And my voice was weary.

"George was a good boy." She gave me a level stare. "But he thought everyone who stayed at Tower Ridge House was rich." Her smile was wry. "I guess that's true enough. I suppose he thought people there spent money so easily, why not some for him? He wanted to go home, you know. He missed the snow, missed the seasons. Missed his family. Tuesday afternoon, when I talked to him, he was excited. He said" — she turned her face up, squeezed her eyes shut as if re-creating a picture in her mind, cupped the blue bowl in her hands — "he was having fun, that Americans were all nuts, and especially about weddings, and this was going to be his lucky weekend. He was going to pick up enough on the side to go home and get back in school." Her eyes snapped open, deep and dark and sad. She lifted her shoulders in a hopeless shrug. "I don't know what wedding he meant . . ."

Unfortunately, I did. I didn't want to talk about that. "Mrs. Abbott, would you show me George's apartment?" George was pinning his hopes for money to a wedding. There was only one wedding party staying at the hotel. Who in that group — that very small group — wanted Roddy Worrell's ghost to walk? I would have to think about that.

"His apartment?" She looked at me steadily. "Why?"

"Maybe he kept a diary." I knew that wasn't likely. "Or if he had a computer . . ."

Mrs. Abbott waved a hand in dismissal. "No, he couldn't afford a computer. There's a café downtown. He used to go there, get soccer scores on the Internet. I don't think he read much. I offered him books, but he liked television. He had a little black-and-white set."

I'd not really hoped for a diary. I lifted my shoulders. "I don't know. There may be nothing there to help. But I'd like to look."

"The police have already been through the apartment." Her judgment was clear. The police knew what to look for. If there had been anything there, they would have found it.

But what had they looked for? Perhaps I would see something they'd missed.

She frowned. "The inspector said he would be in touch with George's family. I need to know where to send his things." She studied me. "All right. I'll show you." She glanced at the stairs near the door. "The baby's asleep. But it shouldn't take us long. If you'll wait a moment, I'll get the key."

I nodded.

The door closed. She had not invited me in. That was all right. She might be fairly convinced I meant well, but she wasn't a woman to invite a stranger into her home.

It was several moments before she returned. I rather imagined she had called the police. But that, too, was all right. The chief inspector might not be pleased at my presence, but I was breaking no law.

When the door opened, she held a key in one hand and a small plastic object in the other. "The baby monitor. Just in case

Jeremy wakes up. My daughter and her husband live with me." She hesitated in the doorway. "I spoke with the chief inspector."

"That's fine." I kept my tone pleasant.

"He asked that we not remove anything from the apartment." As she came down the steps, she motioned toward the flagstones. "This way. The entrance is at the side."

She moved quickly. I was right behind her.

A red wooden railing marked the steps down to an equally red door.

She gave me a brief smile. "I usually rent to young people. They like the door." She stepped inside, clicked on the light, held the door for me.

The studio apartment was simply furnished. Everything was shabby, well-used. Even though the yellowish-brown linoleum curled at the edges and the chairs had worn upholstery, the long room was cheerful, with bright posters adorning the pine walls and everything in order and quite clean, despite the musty smell.

She wrinkled her nose. "You can't get rid of the mold. No matter how often you mop."

I circled the room. The single bed in one corner was neatly made, the spread a light gray with red squares. On the dresser was a tray with cuff links, coins. An airline ticket lay to one side. I picked it up, flipped it open. A one-way ticket to Toronto for next Wednesday.

Joan Abbott was murmuring behind me, ". . . why, there are his suitcases! He must have got them out of the storage shed. And everything is quite bare. He'd got rid of a lot of his things."

George had definitely intended to go home. He'd come into money. I was certain I knew why. He was being paid for the appearance of the ghost. That had been easy money. And he'd hoped for more easy money, five thousand from me for information about the ghost. Had he asked someone for even more money to keep quiet about the ghost? Or had he asked Thelma Worrell for money to keep quiet about her husband's fall? Whichever, someone reached the headland before me on Thursday morning and that person brought death, not money.

The kitchenette was tidy, a single rinsed-out coffee mug in the sink.

I opened the cupboards. Assorted tins — coffee, peanuts, cocoa mix, Spam. A loaf of bread.

". . . George ate most of his meals at the hotel. Cheaper that way."

I felt a wave of fatigue. I reached out, held

on to the countertop. I fought off the bone-tiredness, a remnant of the pneumonia. Or was I feeling the effect of hopelessness, my inability to scratch out a connection between George and his murderer? I knew that connection existed. Somewhere. But if not here, where?

I was turning away from the little kitchenette when I saw the calendar hanging from a nail. A tarpon arched above blue water on a sunny day. The month — January — was in bright red paint, the days in black. The block of space for each date was perhaps two inches square. Many of the blocks held notations. I stepped closer. George apparently made it a practice to mark down appointments — the dentist, haircut, Rugby training — in small square printing. I scanned the month and felt a flicker of excitement:

Thursday, January 6: BUEI — ghost???
Monday, January 10: Kite ready. Practice tonight.
Tuesday, January 18: Ghost
Wednesday, January 19: Ghost
Thursday, January 20: The Point 8 A.M. Ghost tonight?

The notation for January 6 — in blue ink,

as were all the notes — had an addendum in pencil: $500 for Roddy's ghost / $250 now / $250 January 22.

I read it to mean that George met with someone at the Bermuda Underwater Exploration Institute and was offered $500, with half up front if he agreed to arrange for Roddy's ghost to appear the week that our group arrived. Mrs. Abbott understood that George's "prank" was connected to a wedding. The Drake-Bailey wedding was set for tomorrow, January 22. If anyone checked — and perhaps the chief inspector would do so now — perhaps it could be proved that George bought a kite and phosphorescent paint between January 6 and January 10. Steve Jennings saw the ghost the night of January 18. Many of us saw the luminous white cloud the night of January 19. The question mark following "tonight" in the January 20 block suggested that George's meeting with me on the headland Thursday morning would determine whether the kite flew Thursday night. But George was dead when I came to the headland. Someone made certain the ghost would never rise again.

Who met with George at the BUEI on January 6?

sixteen

I sat on the balcony of my room, a mug of hot coffee cradled in my hands, and looked out at slate-blue water. The wind was up, gusting to twenty knots. Water spumed over the ever-dangerous reef. Whitecaps rippled as far as I could see. The surf boomed. Palmetto fronds rattled like stiletto heels on uncarpeted stairs. Wispy needles of the tall casuarina pines rustled like a petticoat dropping to the floor. The leaden sky was the color of a Norman castle and just as foreboding. I huddled in my thick turtleneck sweater and felt rooted to the chair, my mind sluggish, my body heavy and lumpy.

I was tired, so tired, but I had to think. I was convinced there were answers if only I could find them. I also faced the discouraging realization that I'd raised more questions than I'd answered with my foray to *The Royal Gazette*, my startling interview with Mrs. Worrell — Was I wrong in suspecting her of her husband's death? Had I mistaken grief for guilt? — and my visit to Half-Crescent Court, where a plane ticket to Toronto lay on George's dresser.

281

I thought I'd sensed guilt in Mrs. Worrell. But I could not be absolutely certain she had killed her husband. In fact, I couldn't be certain that his fall was murder. It could easily have been an accident, given the entertainer's penchant for sitting on the tower ledge. A cocky man, cocky to his end. Who would want to kill him? There were certainly possible suspects:

His wife might have reached the end of her patience with his flirtations.

Connor Bailey left the bar in search of Roddy. What if she followed him to the top of the tower and he turned ugly, called her names, turned his back to her in contempt? Could Connor have run forward and shoved him in anger?

Steve Jennings could have gone up to the tower, worried about Connor. I rather thought Steve was in love with Connor and would go to any lengths to protect her.

Lloyd Drake was on the periphery of that night, but he was falling in love with Connor. He could have followed Roddy to the top of the tower. If he was jealous enough, would he come up behind an unsuspecting man and push him to his death?

Marlow was very protective of her mother. Surely that protection would not extend to murder.

Aaron Reed . . . I shook my head. Aaron loved Marlow. I didn't see that as a bridge to Roddy's murder. I didn't really know his private judgment of Connor. It would be interesting to know.

Thelma Worrell blamed Connor for Roddy's death, but Thelma's eyes glittered with fear. Why should she be afraid?

I sipped my tea. All right, I couldn't say whether Roddy's fall was accident or murder. Not yet. But there was another question that had to be answered. Why was the ghost created?

There were several possibilities:

Assuming Roddy was murdered, was the ghost created to frighten the murderer?

It didn't seem likely to me. The ghost, after all, wasn't going about waving a placard with the guilty person's name. Unless the ghostly visitations resulted in a reopening of the investigation, the appearance of the ghost was nothing more than an annoyance.

Was the ghost created to upset Thelma Worrell?

It was a good deal of money to spend in a pointless harassment, unless the plan was to injure the hotel by frightening away guests. Or perhaps the hope was to use the ghost to drive Thelma to a confession. Certainly

Thelma was distraught, but I doubted that guilt would ever drive her to confess.

Was the ghost created to distress Connor by bringing back memories of Roddy's death?

Assuredly, the appearances bothered Connor. But once again, the effort scarcely seemed worth the making. Who would want to upset Connor?

Admittedly, Diana had made several efforts to annoy Connor, but Diana was not in Bermuda on January 6 of this year. Moreover, I didn't see how she could have learned enough about the circumstances of last year's accident to be the creator of the ghost. Of course, so far as I knew, no one in the Drake-Bailey wedding party was in Bermuda on January 6 to meet with George at the BUEI. However, Thelma Worrell was on the island on that date and she would obviously take great pleasure in deviling Connor. But why would Thelma meet George at the BUEI when she could visit with him at the hotel any day of the week at any time of day convenient for her?

I sighed. None of it jelled. If I was right in suspecting Thelma of her husband's murder, then certainly she would do nothing to bring back memories of his fall, no matter how much she disliked Connor.

I was right back where I started from, still not knowing who planned the ghost or why.

All right, then, who paid George? Try it from that angle. Thelma seemed unlikely. Then who? As for our group, no one was here then unless . . . I pushed up from my chair, moved slowly into the room. What if one of our group had been here?

I ran over the names in my mind, all of them: Lloyd Drake, Diana Drake, Neal Drake, Connor Bailey, Marlow Bailey, Jasmine Bailey, Aaron Reed, Steve Jennings. Could one of them have been at the BUEI on January 6? Not Jasmine, obviously, but one of the others?

Immigration records would reveal if one of them had flown to Bermuda that day. Could I convince the chief inspector to check those records?

Ultimately, though, the critical question remained. Why did George die?

Because he knew the truth behind the ghost? Or because he knew and threatened the murderer of Roddy Worrell?

I frowned, moved restlessly in my chair. Knowing about the ghost certainly didn't seem to warrant murder. As for the possibility that George knew something about Roddy's death, that could well be. But if he'd had information from the outset, why would he wait until now to take advantage of it?

Blackmail. Such an ugly word. I thought about George. Yes, he was ready to pick up easy money. He saw money freely spent by people who, from his perspective, were very rich. He saw nothing wrong in chivying what must have seemed like rather grand sums if people were dumb enough to pay him to float or not float a shiny kite. But blackmail? Hiding facts about murder?

"I don't think so." I said it aloud, that oh-so-trite smart-ass reply. But I truly didn't think so. I had the feeling that I was close to discovering something important. If I could just push my tired mind to understand. But I was too tired. Perhaps I'd fix another cup of coffee.

I moved toward the coffeemaker, checking the clock as I passed. Almost four. Surely the others would be back soon, the wedding planners and the golfers. We'd gather for tea and later for dinner and hopefully they'd have spent a happy day. We'd compare notes and worry about the weather. But the wedding could occur here as well as at Victoria Park, I had no doubt. The wedding was at one o'clock tomorrow afternoon. Perhaps my involvement in the search for the ghost and George's death would perforce recede to an academic puzzle in my mind. All of us were flying home Sunday, except for the newlyweds. I picked up the coffeemaker.

A swift knock at the door was followed by a call. "Grandma, are you there?"

I put down the coffeemaker. Some of my fatigue ebbed. It's amazing how the voice of someone you love can lift you. I was smiling as I opened the door.

Diana stood in the hallway, hands on her hips. "Grandma, I can't believe you'd take the moped. It's so windy! Where did you go?"

"Oh" — my tone was airy — "I just took a little outing." So many ways to tell the truth. "The wind came up after I got back." I held the door wide. "Come in. How did your morning go?"

"Interminable." She drawled the word with a heavy sigh and flung herself onto my chaise longue. "What a bore. Now the wedding's all set for the park and the weather's turning lousy. They said gale-force winds tomorrow."

I closed the door and settled in a chair by the table.

"Connor's talking to Mrs. Worrell to see about having the wedding here. I'd say the manager's into passive resistance. She doesn't like Connor. But if it rains, it sure can't be in the park. It's a mess." Diana couldn't quite hide a flicker of pleasure.

January in Bermuda can be lovely and it can also be rainy and cool, the weather reflecting winter storms along the American East Coast. The temperature since our arrival had been in the low sixties, too cool for the tiny tree frogs whose chirp was so much a part of my memories of the island.

I didn't say anything. I simply looked at Diana.

Her eyes slipped away from mine. She brushed back a tangle of reddish-golden hair. "Oh, I'll be good, Grandma. But everything really is in a mess. Connor's a complete wreck. She called Dad on the golf course twice to ask him to check into getting the tickets changed to go home tomorrow afternoon." She sat up, tucked her knees beneath her chin, looked at me soberly. "Actually, I think Dad should listen. I mean, if he's going to marry her, he's going to have to deal with her neuroses. She honestly thought that stupid cloud at the top of the tower was this Roddy guy coming back to haunt her. Trust Connor to be sure he's haunting *her*. She has to be the center of any universe. Did it ever occur to her that a ghost might want to impress someone else?

Anyway, she ended up screeching at Dad and hanging up. The deal is, she's never given a thought to what Dad's like. I mean, he can be pretty stubborn. He got so mad, he quit playing. They're all back, too, but Dad's sitting in the bar, drinking and watching ESPN. She doesn't understand that he's got it in his head that this is a big romantic deal and he wants —"

In the hall, a door crashed against the wall. "Steve. Steve, come quick." Connor's cry was high and desperate.

Diana reached the door first, flung it open. I was right behind her. We ran up the hall. Connor huddled near her open doorway. She stared at us wildly, her mouth trembling, her Dresden-china face a pasty gray.

I reached out, took her arm. "What's wrong, Connor?"

Trembling, she pointed inside the room.

"Mother," I heard Marlow cry behind me. "What's happened?"

I stepped into Connor's room warily. My gaze moved back and forth. The bed was neatly made. The furniture was in place, with no sign of disarray. My eyes reached the curtain drawn across the glass door to the balcony. The cloth rippled.

Steve Jennings thudded to a stop beside

me. "What the hell's going on?"

I pointed at the moving curtain.

In three strides, he was across the room and yanking the curtain wide. The sliding glass door was open. He stepped onto the balcony. "Nobody here. Must have been the wind."

I didn't answer. I stopped beside the circular table where once the ceramic tower had stood and looked down at reddish smears. The streaks formed uneven letters. The message was short:

I'm coming for you

The words might have been written by a finger dipped in blood. I bent nearer. The strokes that made the letters were ill-formed but smooth, perhaps drawn by a finger sheathed in a plastic or vinyl glove. The last word trailed downward.

Jennings came up behind me. He caught his breath as he stared at the streaked words. "Jesus!"

I reached out, lightly touched the sticky moist *y*. My index finger looked as though it had a bloody tip. I held the finger close to my nose, smelled. Then I delicately touched my finger to my tongue.

"My God, what are you doing?" There

was a curl of disgust in his voice.

"Not real blood," I said quietly. "A nice peppermint flavor. Stage blood."

"Stage blood." There was a wealth of relief in his voice.

"Definitely." I'm no Dracula. I'd been pretty certain before I tasted the liquid, even though the streaks looked real. But there had been no sour, unmistakable odor when I smelled my fingertip. "Stage blood can be bought in any costume shop." In small bottles. I was willing to bet that the container would never be found, not with the Atlantic Ocean only steps away.

Jennings's deep voice boomed. "It's all right, Connor. It's stage blood."

Connor stood in the doorway, clinging to the jamb. "All right? You tell me it's all right? It's hideous. What does it mean?" She shuddered, her body quivering. "Was that Roddy we saw that night? Does it mean he's coming for me?"

Marlow slipped her arm around her mother. "Don't be silly —"

"Silly?" She pushed Marlow roughly away. "Don't tell me I'm silly." Connor's voice wobbled. "That's what Lloyd keeps saying. No one cares. Roddy hates me and he's going to come for me and I shall die of fright. I'm so frightened. I have to get out of here. I have to. Steve." She darted toward the lawyer, clutched his arm. "Call now. Get us on the plane." Hysteria lifted her voice.

Steve spoke even louder, a courtroom voice intended to impress a judge. "Connor, get a grip on yourself. Look at the time." He pointed at the clock. "The last plane for Atlanta's already left."

Marlow said over and over, "Don't be scared, Mother, we're all here. Don't be scared . . ."

From the hallway, Jasmine's little-girl voice demanded, "Mom, what's wrong? What's wrong? What's . . ."

I heard their voices. I felt Connor's fear, but I was drawn back to the table. I stared at the cruel, mocking message. Damnit, there was no ghost. This was a vicious attempt to frighten Connor.

Jasmine poked her head around my elbow. "Golly, look at that. Is it blood? It looks like blood!"

I glanced around the room, from the now closed balcony door to the open door to the hallway. The balcony door had been open. No doubt the intruder came that way, slipped into Connor's room while she and the girls were in Hamilton. Or the open balcony door could be a clever ploy. Mrs.

Worrell would have a key to the room, of course. She could easily have entered the wing, hurried up the empty corridor, opened the hall door, and, in only a moment, have left the message. A few more quick steps and the balcony door could be pulled ajar.

Connor rushed to the telephone, reached down to grab the receiver, thrust it toward Jennings. "Here, Steve. If it's too late today, we'll leave tomorrow. Oh, God, if only I hadn't gone into town today, if only I'd gone out to the airport this morning. I knew I should, I knew it. Steve, call now and see about a plane tomorrow. I have to get out of here!" She pushed the receiver into his hand.

I'd always thought Connor's strikingly blue eyes were hard. Now they were pools of terror. There was no trace of her arrogant veneer. Her lovely face was pitiable. She gave a low moan. "Steve, you've got to help me." She jerked her head toward Marlow. "Let's start packing now."

Steve took the receiver. "I'll call, Connor, but you need to talk to Lloyd."

Jasmine reached out toward the table.

I lifted my hand. "Please don't touch it, Jasmine. We should call the police."

"The police." Marlow stared at me. "But

what can they do?"

"Investigate. Someone —"

Connor gave a ragged cry. "They can't catch ghosts. It's Roddy. You saw him —"

I took three quick steps, stood close enough that she had to look into my eyes.

"Listen, Connor. There is no ghost." I paused, said it loudly again. "There is no ghost. George Smith flew a kite painted with phosphorescent paint. That was what Steve saw" — I looked toward him. He still held the phone, his long face somber — "Tuesday night. That's what we all saw Wednesday night."

Connor's breaths were light and shallow. She clutched her throat with a shaking hand.

"Connor, I found the kite that was used." I couldn't prove that, but I was certain in my own mind. "It was hidden at the back of the Sports closet down near the pool." I was so intent on reaching her, on trying to restore a gleam of reason to those frantic eyes, that I blocked out the rest of the room. "Someone set the closet on fire so that the police would not see that kite. That must be the person who scrawled those words on the table."

Connor's head moved slowly toward the table, then jerked away. She shuddered. "If it isn't Roddy, then someone hates me. Someone hates me and wants me to die!"

"Oh, now, Connor." Steve's tone was hearty. "That's not true. It's nasty but —"

"I'm frightened, damn you. Damn you all." Her voice was high and shrill, "I tell you I'm —"

"My God, there's enough noise in this hall to wake the dead!" Lloyd filled the doorway, his face red and heavy, his voice truculent. "What the hell's going on?"

Connor reached out her hands. "Lloyd, get me out of here. Someone hates me." She hurried toward him. "Steve's going to call now and get our tickets changed. I want to go home tomorrow."

"Go home!" Lloyd's glazed eyes looked at her in dismay and with a hot flicker of anger. His always reddish face was an unhealthy plum color, too much whiskey or uncontrolled hypertension. His red-blond hair straggled over his forehead. He looked disheveled and belligerent. He folded his arms, rocked back on his heels. "So Steve's gonna call. Hell, I bought those tickets. I spent a fortune on this whole frigging trip. And all you do is act like an idiot — when you aren't chasing after that clown from Texas. What's the matter, hasn't the cowboy been sniffing around? You need for Steve to dance attendance —"

Connor lifted her arm. Her hand flashed through the air. The sound of the slap was followed by a stricken silence. No one moved or spoke for an instant.

Marlow hurried forward, slipped her arm around her mother's trembling shoulders. Connor squeezed her eyes shut. Tears streaked down her ashen cheeks. Steve slammed the phone down. "Wait a minute, Lloyd —"

"Make your goddamn call, Steve. What the hell do I care?" Lloyd touched the splotchy imprint on his cheek.

Marlow pulled her mother away from Lloyd, shepherded her into the bathroom. Jasmine cried, "Wait for me, wait for me." The little girl squeezed inside and the door slammed shut.

Lloyd stared at the closed bathroom door, lunged forward and knocked.

Diana darted toward him. She reached up, grabbed his wrist. "Dad, wait a minute."

"No." He shook free, pounded again. "We better get this straight," he shouted. "Connor, do you want to get married or not?" He leaned toward the door. "I want to know. We have a wedding tomorrow. If you're not too busy, of course." The sarcasm was heavy.

Steve came up behind him. "Drop it for now, Lloyd. Why don't you —"

Lloyd swung heavily around. "Take a walk? Play golf?" He cocked his head toward the balcony. "Pretty lousy weather out there. The whole day's gone to hell. I go out for a little golf and the cell phone squawks like a hustler at a flea market. Connor's supposed to be putting the finishing touches on our day and all she wants to do is go home. That's pretty swell, isn't it?" His jaw jutted out, but his eyes were bright with pain. "I don't know what's going on."

I slipped in front of Steve. "Lloyd, you haven't seen the warning Connor received." I took his arm, tugged. "Come over here."

Steve stepped out of our way, his face uneasy.

Lloyd glared at me. "Warning? Is Connor moaning about that stupid ghost again? That's dumb —"

We reached the table.

He broke off, his eyes blinked. "Some kind of hoax, obviously." He leaned forward. "That looks like blood."

"It's supposed to look that way. Stage blood. Somebody put it there to upset Connor." I looked at the uneven letters. "We ought to call the police."

"The police." Lloyd faced me. "But that

inspector talked to Connor . . ." He didn't finish.

I wondered suddenly if he had been thinking about that night a year ago and if he had been thinking about what might have happened after Connor left the bar in pursuit of Roddy.

"Let's not get the police involved." Steve moved quickly toward the table, a clump of tissue in his hand.

"Oh, no —" I reached out to stop him.

A long arm poked past me and in three swipes the sticky letters were obliterated. Reddish smears were all that remained.

I frowned. "That may have been done by George's murderer."

"George's murderer?" The lawyer looked at me blankly. "What do you mean?"

"Murder?" Diana reached out, gripped my arm. "Grandma, what are you talking about? I thought George fell. I thought it was an accident."

"No. The chief inspector told me there were fist-shaped bruises on his lower back." I closed my hand over hers. "Someone came up behind George — ran, probably — and struck him, knocked him over the edge."

Lloyd kneaded a fist against one cheek. "That's crazy."

"It may be crazy." I was crisp. "It's true."

Lloyd shook his head. "I don't believe it. Why would anybody kill the kid?"

Diana's voice shook. "George was telling everyone that Roddy was murdered. Is that why, Grandma?"

Lloyd looked at his daughter, his eyes shocked. Slowly his gaze moved to the closed door of the bathroom. He moved heavily across the room, rattled the knob of the bathroom door. "Connor, come out."

The door opened. Marlow slipped through and closed the panel behind her. "She wants everyone to leave except Steve."

"Steve." Lloyd shrugged. "Sure. Let Steve take care of everything. Why not? Why the hell not?" He ducked his head, blundered toward the hall door.

I've seen wounded animals move in the same blind, hurtful way.

"Dad, oh, Dad!" Diana darted after her father.

I looked from Marlow to Steve. "Call the police."

But I knew they wouldn't.

seventeen

So I called Chief Inspector Foster.

I sat on the edge of the bed in my room, looked through the balcony door at the wind-whipped palmettos and casuarinas, and waited for the connection to be made. The wind rattled the window, made a high singing sound in the eaves.

"Chief Inspector Foster." His voice held just a hint of impatience. I glanced at the clock. Almost five. Was he ready to leave for the day and irritated at the delay, or was he immersed in work and resented the interruption?

"Henrietta Collins, Inspector. There's been" — I hesitated for an instant, searching for the right word — "an ugly incident here at the hotel affecting Mrs. Bailey. I thought you should know."

Foster listened without comment as I described the message and Connor's reaction and Steve's swift swipe of the table. When I finished, he was silent for a moment.

"Nasty," he said finally. "But why call me?"

"I think it is connected to George Smith's

murder." It was only as I spoke that I clearly understood why I had called Foster. "Yes." I picked up steam. "That's why it matters. George's murder isn't the end of it."

"The end of what, Mrs. Collins?" He wasn't rude or dismissive. He spoke as a man who understands that he is in strange terrain without a map.

It was my turn to be silent. I didn't know. I took a deep breath, tried to be clear. "George's death has to be linked to Roddy Worrell's death." I spoke fast before he could challenge me. "I know, Inspector. Roddy's fall was adjudged an accident. I went to *The Royal Gazette* and saw the report of the inquest. Roddy liked to sit on the ledge of the tower. But for some reason we don't understand, George was hired to create an apparition —"

"Hired?" His tone was sharp. "How can you be certain George didn't create Worrell's ghost for his own purposes, if indeed he had any connection to the apparition? For that matter, someone who dislikes Mrs. Bailey may simply be taking advantage of her fear of the ghost."

"Money." A simple, clear answer. "I went to Half-Crescent Court today."

"I know." The answer was uninflected.

"George had a ticket to Toronto for next

301

week. He'd told Mrs. Abbott that he was" — I paused, remembered her exact words — "that he was picking up enough money this week to be able to go home. Somebody paid George extra. He was paid to fly the kite and create that luminous cloud by the tower." I told Foster about the notation on George's calendar, about the BUEI on January 6 and the addendum in pencil, outlining payments for the ghost. "I think George believed it was a joke having to do with the wedding. The ghost wasn't for George's purposes. I believe the prime motive behind the ghost was to upset Connor. If that is true, the person who left the stage blood message in Connor's room was very likely the person who paid George."

He didn't answer.

"And the person who paid George killed George." I felt more and more confident this was true.

Foster's reply was equable. "Possibly. But equally well not. You have to remember your own thesis, Mrs. Collins. George might have created the ghost and he might also have learned something that convinced him Roddy Worrell was murdered. You claim George was quick to ask for money, money from the person who wanted the ghost, money from you to reveal that information. What if George asked for money to keep quiet about Worrell's death?"

"I don't think so." I was back where I'd started, pinning my response on my contacts, admittedly few, with George. I thought he could be hired. I didn't think he could be bought. There is a world of difference.

"And, of course, Mrs. Collins, all of this may be a smoke screen created by you." His tone wasn't unpleasant, merely brisk. "You may be offering an alternative to the information received about your quarrel with Smith."

"False information, Inspector. Falsified by George." I was brisk, too.

His reply was quick and pointed. "Whom you decline to view as a blackmailer, but paint as a liar?"

"I didn't say George was perfect, Inspector."

He was silent. I hoped he was smiling.

No, George hadn't been perfect. But I didn't think he was a blackmailer. "Inspector, we must find out who met with George at the BUEI."

"To what purpose?" His voice was irritated. "Even if you're right, even if George was hired to create the ghost, what does that have to do with his murder? The ghost is nonsense. Even if it upsets people —"

I wanted this to be clear. "Not people, Chief Inspector. A specific person. Connor Bailey."

He paused. "Not just Mrs. Bailey. Mrs. Worrell can't be pleased."

"No. Certainly she isn't pleased. But the message in Connor's room proves that the point of the campaign is to harass Connor." Rain pelted against the balcony door.

"It seems a great deal of effort merely to upset a spoiled rich woman. And murder, Mrs. Collins?" His disbelief was clear.

I didn't answer directly. "Connor is in a state of hysteria about the warning. She is terrified. She wants to go home as soon as possible. Lloyd is offended. They've quarreled. The wedding is very likely off."

"I see." There was a considering tone in his voice. "Have you thought through what you are saying?"

I rubbed my thumb along the receiver. I knew where he was headed. Yes, I'd thought it out. I sighed. "Have I considered who might want the wedding canceled? And whether that would be worth murder? The first answer is clear, Inspector. Unfortunately, scarcely anyone in either family is happy about the wedding. That includes both of my grandchildren as well as Connor's older daughter. Steve Jennings is no fan of Lloyd's. Aaron Reed, Marlow's boyfriend, supports Marlow. And let's not forget Mrs. Worrell. She would do anything in her power to make Connor unhappy. But the question becomes whether canceling Connor and Lloyd's wedding is worth murder. I hope not, Inspector, but I very much fear that is what happened."

I'd tugged the problem every which way in my mind, but each time I'd come back to this conclusion. If I was right, the suspects in George's murder were limited to a very short list:

Diana, Neal, Marlow, Jasmine, Aaron, and Steve.

"Not Diana or Neal." I didn't say it combatively, I didn't have to. I had no doubt in either my mind or my heart, and, thank God, I had good reason to exclude them. "Neither Diana nor Neal was in the group at the hotel last year, when Roddy Worrell fell from the tower. They knew nothing about Roddy until they arrived here this week. Moreover, neither of them had ever met George Smith. There is no way they could have originated the plan for the ghost and contacted George. No, Diana and Neal are out of it. The choices come down to

Marlow, Aaron, Steve, or Mrs. Worrell —
not Jasmine, of course."

"A very serious accusation, Mrs. Collins."
Foster wasn't convinced, but I definitely
had his attention.

"And," I was reluctant to say it, "I don't
believe it's Mrs. Worrell. She would like to
make Connor unhappy, she may even truly
believe Connor is responsible for her husband's death, but I can't see any reason for
her to meet George at the BUEI. She could
speak to him privately here whenever she
chose. Why meet him in a public place, even
though it's unlikely that anyone would ever
remember or identify them?"

"You want to drop Mrs. Worrell from
your list and you won't include your grandchildren or Jasmine. The possibilities grow
fewer and fewer." His tone was dry.

"Marlow. Aaron. Steve. One of them
came to Bermuda to meet with George.
That meeting is critical." I pinned all my
hopes there.

Foster's retort was quick. "Critical to *your*
theory, Mrs. Collins."

"Will you check with Immigration, see if
Marlow Bailey, Steve Jennings, or Aaron
Reed came to Bermuda on January sixth?"
I scarcely breathed as I waited for his
reply.

His chair creaked. Finally, slowly, he said, "I can do that."

"And, Chief Inspector?" I wondered if I was pushing my luck.

"Yes?" Now he was impatient.

"Who did George call on his cell phone Thursday morning, the conversation Jasmine overheard? George told someone he was going to the headland to meet me."

"No call was made on his cell phone that morning."

I was sure Jasmine's report was accurate. I frowned. "Then someone called him."

"Yes. From the pay phone in the side hall of the hotel." He reported it without fanfare.

"I see." And I did. Someone was determined not to be linked in any way to George. The pay phone. I'd noticed it when I slipped up that side hallway to join Mrs. Worrell as an eavesdropper. It had taken an extra bit of effort for the chief inspector to trace that call. He must have had an assistant check all of the hotel lines for calls to George's cell phone. "Thank you."

"My job."

"It could have been anyone in the hotel, including Mrs. Worrell." I couldn't resist making the point.

"About the message in Mrs. Bailey's room" — his chair creaked again and I knew

he was ready to end this conversation —
"I'll get in touch with her, though there's
not much to be done, since the lawyer wiped
the table. However, I appreciate your call,
Mrs. Collins."

"You'll let me know when you've checked
with Immigration?" Marlow or Aaron or
Steve; one of them, I was sure of it.

There was a pause. "You are scheduled to
fly home on Sunday."

Of course, he knew our plans. "Yes. Neal
and Diana and I fly out Sunday. Possibly
Lloyd, too. There's no point in his staying if the
wedding is canceled — as it appears to be."
There was no way for the one-o'clock wedding
to take place if Connor and her daughters and
Aaron and Steve flew out tomorrow afternoon
on the one-fifty flight to Atlanta.

I felt a wave of sadness mixed with anger.
Damnit, there should be something that
could be done to salvage two lives and
avenge at least one death, perhaps two.
"What are you going to do, Inspector?"

"What can I do?" His voice was tight with
frustration. "It takes proof to arrest a murderer, Mrs. Collins. Something tangible —
physical evidence, a witness. All I have are
two bruises on the back of a body."

"Dad won't let Neal in." Diana paced up

and down next to the balcony door. It was dusk outside now, but the wind still gusted and rain slapped against the glass. "Oh, Grandma, what are we going to do?"

I rested on the chaise longue and wished I had a good answer. I didn't. I temporized. "Your dad needs time." Lloyd was struggling with anger and jealousy and loss and humiliation. There was little that any of us could do to help. "I'd try to convince him that Connor is terrified, that she simply isn't responsible for her actions at this point."

Diana flung herself into a chair, looked at me mournfully. "Grandma, I don't want him to marry her, but I hate this, I simply hate it. He's so" — tears glistened in her eyes — "hurt. Oh damn her, why is she such a fool?" Diana pressed her hands against her cheeks, let them fall. "But she doesn't love Dad, not really, or she'd cling to him. Not that old lawyer."

"She's known Steve for many years." I spoke quietly, hoping Diana would understand. "Connor can't help herself, Diana. She's unstable and she's scared."

Diana impatiently pushed back a strand of red-gold hair. "That's dumb. What does she have to be scared about?"

I wasn't sure. Perhaps Connor had memories of Roddy Worrell that she could not bear to face.

Diana pushed up from the chair. "We've got to help Dad. Grandma, will you call him? See about going out to dinner. There's no way we can eat here tonight. You know she had that special dinner planned . . ."

Going out to dinner would scarcely serve as a panacea. But Diana was right. The dinner to celebrate the coming wedding wouldn't do at all. "You call, Diana." This was not the time for Lloyd's former mother-in-law to take charge.

She hesitated, then strode to the telephone. As she picked up the receiver, I said, "Suggest Flanagan's. It's loud, lots of excitement. There's a reggae band tonight." I'd found that announcement in *The Royal Gazette*. Flanagan's also had a terrific sports bar. Richard and I had been here in summer and we'd gone several evenings to catch the telecast of the Yankees. "There will be plenty of soccer and lots of noise."

Diana punched Lloyd's room number. Her hand gripped the receiver so tightly I turned my head away. There was too much pain on this night that should have been a happy night prefacing a new beginning. In Connor's "Programme," a series of entwined hearts circled the menu planned for this evening. I would have spoken with Lloyd if I thought it would help, but I was not the right person. I would have tried to see Connor but, again, I wasn't the right person.

"Dad." Diana's voice was hearty. "Listen, Neal and I thought it might be fun to go into Hamilton tonight. There's a neat sports bar" — she glanced toward me and I nodded — "yes, Flanagan's." She checked her watch. "How about seven? I'll call for a taxi. Oh, that's okay, I can call" — she paused, nodded. "Okay. See you then."

She put down the phone, squeezed her eyes shut. Tears slipped down her cheeks.

I reached out for a tissue, rose. I gently touched her cheeks, then held her in my arms. "I know, honey."

"He's trying to sound" — she gulped back a sob — "like it's any old Friday night and Neal and I are in town and we're going out. He said he'd call for the taxi. You know, he's Dad and he's in charge. Oh, damn that woman."

۰ A string quartet played Debussy, a nice complement to the elegance of the dining room, the rich amber of the cedar walls, the fresh-cut flowers, the shiny damask tablecloths. I touched the pearl choker at my throat as I paused in the wide entryway. Only four tables were occupied, most of them with two or four guests, and these tables were near the main entrance. The far reaches of the room drowsed in darkness. I'd half expected to have our table to myself.

Steve and Aaron pushed back their chairs, stood as I approached.

I nodded. "Good evening."

Steve almost managed a smile, but it drooped into a tired frown. "Hello." Aaron's voice was subdued.

I hesitated, then took a chair next to Aaron, not the seating we'd followed since our arrival.

Aaron looked surprised, then dropped into his chair.

Steve sat down heavily. "Goddamn mess, isn't it?" He was talking to me.

"A shame." I unfolded my napkin, placed it in my lap.

Aaron glanced toward the archway. "Anybody else coming? Marlow and Jasmine are with Connor." He nodded toward Steve. "So it's just us."

"Lloyd and the children have gone into Hamilton." I picked up the water goblet. "I understand you are flying back to Atlanta tomorrow."

Aaron looked at Steve.

The lawyer's face tightened. "It seemed the best way to handle everything." His eyes dared me to disagree. "Connor should be at home."

We spoke in jerky half-sentences, talked about the weather, carefully did not talk about the gourmet dinner: green chili gazpacho, Caesar salad, roast rack of lamb, whipped potatoes with garlic, grilled vegetables, miniature cheese ravioli, and, finally, a heart-shaped serving of watermelon sorbet laced with raspberry-and-peach syrup and a glacé of brown sugar.

Aaron moved restively in his seat as the waiter replenished our coffee cups. No doubt Aaron was eager to be free of the dining room and the oh-so-cheerless meal. Free to do what? The wind still howled around the building and occasional bursts of rain spattered the windows.

"Ugly night." Steve stared toward the dark windows.

"A very ugly night." I meant every word. I looked from Aaron to Steve. "Maybe we can make it better. You've both figured it out, haven't you?"

They looked at me blankly.

I put down my coffee cup with a sharp clink. "It's obvious that the message was put on the table in Connor's room to upset her, to encourage her to fight with Lloyd." I paused, spoke deliberately. "Someone wanted to stop the wedding. We need to figure out who did it. We need to tell Connor —"

Steve flung down his napkin, pushed back his chair, stood. "Mrs. Collins, you don't know what the hell you're talking about." He looked down at me with steely dislike. "Connor's a sensitive creature. She can't handle stress. Lloyd's acted like an ass. No way should she marry a man who can't give her support. Damn good thing this happened."

As he walked away, I called after him, "Support you are quite willing to provide?"

Steve kept right on going.

"Sheesh." Aaron stared at me, his eyes wide.

I caught his gaze, held it, knew my own eyes blazed with a hot anger. "True or false?" I demanded.

Aaron blinked, studied me with quizzical blue eyes. Then he grinned, a lopsided, charming smile. "Hey, I'm just an innocent bystander." He stuck out a strong brown hand. "Truce?" His unruly hair tumbled down on his face. His eyes had a friendly-spaniel uncertainty.

I took his hand, gave it a firm shake.

"Sure." But I wasn't above taking advantage of Aaron's youth, if I could. "I'll bet you'd like a little more substantial dessert than the sorbet, right?"

His eyes lighted. "Do you think I could?"

"For what our hosts are paying for these dinners, I certainly think so." I lifted my hand. William, our waiter, a slender blond with a serious face, was there in an instant.

"There's a dessert cart, isn't there, William?"

"Oh, yes, ma'am. I'll bring it over." In a moment, he'd trundled the cart to the table. "Key lime pie. Trifle. Raspberry cheesecake. Burnt-sugar cake. Chocolate mousse with peppermint."

Aaron surveyed the offerings. "The burnt-sugar cake, I'll have that."

William looked toward me.

I shook my head. "No, thanks. But I'll have more coffee, please."

Aaron forked a bite of the cake. "Mmm."

"A favorite of yours?" I sipped my coffee.

"You bet." He picked up another bite, frowned. "Seems kind of mean to be enjoying dinner so much. Poor Connor's a wreck. But it will probably work out for the best. Old Steve's been waiting in the wings all along." He gave me a stricken look. "Sorry. Lloyd's a good guy."

315

"Do you think Steve is interested in Connor?" I tried to sound only mildly interested.

Aaron swept up a curl of brown icing. "Oh, big time. Steve played it cool for a while after his wife died. But last year, until Lloyd showed up, Connor was paying a lot of attention to Steve. I don't think there was anything going on before his wife died. Connor's not like that." He spoke faster. "I don't want you to get the wrong idea. See, Connor" — and he planted his elbow on the table, looked at me seriously — "is kind of nuts about guys. Marlow explained it to me. Connor needs lots of attention —"

Yes, I remembered Marlow's apologia quite well. Aaron had it down pat.

"— but she doesn't mean anything by it. That's what caused the trouble with that Roddy guy. That's why she's so spooked by this ghost business." He finished the cake, absently pushed the plate back. "Are you serious about thinking somebody planned this stuff to scare Connor and cancel the wedding?" He shook his head, didn't give me a chance to answer. "Aw no, that can't be. The only people unhappy about the wedding . . ." It was obviously a new and unwelcome thought. "No." The word fell between us. He stared at me with suddenly anxious eyes. "Oh, hey, that can't be right. Anyway, Steve's a good guy. He wasn't happy about Lloyd, but hey, he was handling it real well." As we walked out of the dining room, I felt Aaron's gaze on me. I'd worried him, no doubt about that.

Maybe in the morning, Chief Inspector Foster would call. Marlow, Aaron, or Steve, one of them.

eighteen

I finished dressing — navy blouse, white corduroy slacks, well-worn sneakers — and debated whether to make a pot of coffee. The dining room would open for breakfast in a quarter hour. I decided instead to go to the gardens for a walk. I'd left the curtain open last night and this morning the sun poured, rich as a river of gold, through the glass door to the balcony. A lovely day awaited us, as if the scudding clouds and gale-force winds of yesterday had never occurred. The wedding could have proceeded as planned in Victoria Park. Had anyone called, canceled the decoration of the bandstand? But that wasn't my responsibility. I frowned, the loveliness of the morning receding before the reality of the day.

I stopped at the closet for a sweater. As I slipped it off the hanger, I heard a thudding sound. I remained with my arm raised, the sweater dangling from my hand, listening. There was urgency in that pounding. I moved fast, yanking open my door and stepping into the hall.

Marlow stood at the door to her mother's room. "Mother! Mother!" She rattled the knob, knocked again, knocked hard, as if she'd knocked many times before. "Mother, answer the door!" Her voice was high and frightened. Her dark hair flowed loose, vivid against the crimson of her dressing gown.

Jasmine darted into the hall, golden hair tousled, rubbing sleepy eyes. "Marlow, what's wrong?"

Doors opened up and down the hall. Steve swiped his half-shaven face with a hand towel. Chest bare, he held the waist of silver-gray silk pajama pants. "What's going on?" Aaron, wearing only green-and-black-plaid boxers, reached Marlow in two quick strides. "Doesn't your mom answer? Maybe she's sick." He lifted a well-muscled arm, battered the wooden panel.

The door to the next room banged open. "What's all the noise?" Lloyd, unshaven, glowered and pressed his hands against his head. "Who the hell's making so much noise?"

Aaron ignored him, struck the door again and again.

Marlow cried, "Mother doesn't answer. I've knocked and knocked."

Lloyd rubbed his eyes. His red-blond hair was limp, his face an unhealthy grayish white, his eyes bloodshot. He fumbled with faded blue jeans, ineffectually tried to push his wrinkled T-shirt into the waistband. "What do you mean? How come she doesn't answer?"

Neal poked his head out of his room. "Is something wrong?" He was neatly dressed in a polo and khaki shorts, but his dark hair was damp and unruly. He held a brush in his hand. Diana hurried from her room, pulling on a gray sweatshirt. She skidded to a stop by me. "Grandma, what's happening?"

"They can't rouse Connor." There was no response behind that door. "Diana, go to the desk. Get a key. Quick."

Without a word, she jerked around and ran down the hall, long legs swift.

I walked purposefully toward Lloyd.

Aaron had stopped pounding. He used both hands to rattle the knob. "Connor. Connor, wake up!" Steve stood beside him, leaned against the door, shouted, "Connor, Connor!"

Lloyd gripped the doorjamb, looked wildly up and down the hall. "She's gone for a walk. That has to be it. Or for breakfast . . ." The words trailed away. Connor had breakfasted in her room every morning. She was rarely finished with coffee and the newspaper before nine. It was not quite seven.

I reached Lloyd, smelled stale whiskey.

"The connecting door, Lloyd." I pointed into his room.

Lloyd stared at the floor. "That's no good." His voice could scarcely be heard. "She locked it last night. Damnit, she locked it."

Steve pushed roughly past Lloyd. "We can try." Aaron was on Steve's heels. Aaron fumbled with the light switch. The light came on, revealing tightly drawn curtains, rumpled bed, clothes thrown in a heap on the floor. On the table sat a bottle of whiskey and a half-full tumbler.

"Won't do any good," Lloyd mumbled. He glowered at Steve and Aaron. The rest of us gathered outside his doorway. Marlow watched Steve and Aaron. Jasmine clung to her sister's robe. Aaron looked over his shoulder at me. "Stay with them." Neal squeezed past me to stand by his father. Lloyd slumped against the wall, face drooping, his arms crossed tightly over his chest.

Steve reached the connecting door. He grabbed the knob, turned, and the door swung in. "Hey, Connor," his voice rising with relief, "Steve here, honey. Connor —" He stopped, frozen, rigid, as if he'd slammed into a wall. "Oh God, oh God."

Aaron came up behind Steve. He looked

past the lawyer and his face emptied with shock.

Lloyd pushed away from the wall, peered toward the two men.

Steve swung around. He took a deep breath, another. "Get back, all of you." His face was twisted in shock. "Get out —"

Lloyd squinted. "Connor?" His voice was uncertain, frightened. "Is something wrong with Connor?"

Steve stood in the doorway, looked at Lloyd as if he didn't know him, as if they were strangers. "You said the door was locked." His tone was accusatory.

"Locked? Yeah, it was locked." Lloyd looked bewildered. "How did you open it? Where's Connor? Why doesn't she answer?" He moved heavily toward Steve. "Where's Connor?"

"Get back, Lloyd." Steve blocked the doorway.

"Connor?" Lloyd reached Steve, grabbed his arm, poked his head into the room. He gave a deep, harsh grunt. "Con-nor — oh, no, no, no . . ." Lloyd's face had the sheen of wax.

Steve shoved him roughly away, slammed the connecting door. "We've got to call the police."

"Mother?" Marlow's voice was a thin whisper.

I slipped my arm around her shoulders, pulled her gently into the hallway. I reached down and gripped Jasmine's small hand.

Marlow tried to get free. She squirmed and twisted, struggling to get back to Lloyd's room.

"No." I held tight. "Come with me." The horror in Steve's voice, the shock in Aaron's gaze, the sickly pallor of Lloyd's face warned me that Connor's daughters must not look into that room.

Aaron came up beside us, his chest heaving as if he had run a long distance. He tried to talk. "Your room, Marlow. Go there. Now."

"Mother." Marlow's face crumpled. "What's happened to Mother?" Jasmine trembled.

Aaron blinked. "Somebody . . . Somebody hurt her. Marlow, oh, Marlow, I'm so sorry." His voice wavered. He pulled Marlow into his embrace, pressed his face against the top of her head. Marlow clung to him.

Jasmine began to cry. I slipped my arm around her. "We're going to your room. Come on, honey."

The door to Marlow and Jasmine's room was open as Jasmine had left it when she followed her sister into the hall, seeking their mother. I settled the girls on the sofa and stood in the doorway so that I could intercept Diana when she returned with the key. "Call nine-one-one, Aaron."

Aaron punched the numbers. "I want to report a murder." His eyes were wide with remembered horror.

Footsteps thudded in the hallway. Diana saw me in the doorway, held up a key. She looked at my face and stumbled to a stop. "Grandma?"

"Connor's dead." I reached out my hand.

Diana shook her head. "She can't be dead. She can't be!"

Behind me, I heard Aaron, his voice unnaturally high, ". . . that's right, a murder. Tower Ridge House. Room thirty-two. Mrs. Connor Bailey. Yes, yes, I'm sure she's dead. She was" — his face anguished, he looked at Marlow — "she was strangled."

The long narrow conference room, comfortably furnished with several sofas and easy chairs, overlooked the upper terrace through French windows. A sideboard held an assortment of pastries, a bowl of fruit, and a coffee service. Mrs. Worrell had arranged for breakfast in these private quarters after the police closed off our wing.

Marlow, staring stonily out the windows, cuddled Jasmine on a far sofa. Marlow had pulled on a crumpled pink blouse, black slacks. Her hair was pulled back in a ponytail. Her face was white, her eyes red-rimmed. Jasmine's hair hadn't been brushed. There was a chocolate stain on her white blouse and her shorts were sandy. She pressed her face against her sister's shoulder. Aaron perched on the sofa arm, one hand on Marlow's shoulder. Occasionally, he gave a deep sigh, brushed a hand through his curly hair, looked around the room as if seeking help. Steve stood at an open window, facing toward the sea, his back to all of us. His head was bent forward. His hands hung at his sides. Occasionally, a shudder rippled through the muscles of his shoulders.

At the opposite end of the room, the Drake family slumped on another sofa, this one facing the door to the hall. Lloyd was still unshaven. One hand plucked nervously at a worn place on his jeans. Diana had pulled off her sweatshirt, crumpled it in a ball. She stared at the door but every so often her eyes jerked toward her father. Neal stared blankly at the floor.

A young policewoman stood near the hall door.

No one spoke. The silence was oppressive. I felt, too, that the division between the families was deliberate, marked, and, on the part of Connor's family, hostile. I don't know when that became apparent to Neal and Diana, but slowly the realization had come. Neal and Steve exchanged angry stares. Diana reached out, gripped her father's arm. Lloyd slowly lifted his face, looked at her, eyes burning with tears.

It seemed that we'd been together, yet each of us so separate, for many hours, but it was only a few minutes past eleven when the door opened and Chief Inspector Foster stepped inside. He spoke in a low tone, too low to be overheard, to the constable, then surveyed the room.

Marlow hugged Jasmine, then slowly stood. Her eyes burned with questions. She walked toward Foster. They met near a shining mahogany table in the center of the room. A huge cut-glass vase with daffodils and birds-of-paradise sat on the table.

"Miss Bailey, you have my deepest sympathy." The inspector's face was somber.

Marlow pushed back a strand of dark hair, managed to retain her composure though her hand shook. "Thank you, Chief Inspector. Please, tell me what happened to my mother."

Slowly, as if drawn to that place, we all

rose and gathered near enough to listen as Foster spoke.

He spoke quickly. "The time of death is estimated to have been between midnight and three A.M." Foster rocked forward a little on his feet. Sometimes the task of a policeman is grim indeed. "She was strangled. The autopsy will determine whether the cause of death was asphyxia or a broken neck. From the color of her skin, the ruling likely will be asphyxia."

Marlow pressed her hands to her cheeks. Jasmine clung to her sister. Aaron said thickly. "Maybe that's enough, Inspector."

"Was she able to —" I hesitated. I'd intended to ask whether Connor had been able to claw her attacker. Instead, I said, "Resist in any fashion?"

His glance at me was quick and appraising. "That will be determined during the autopsy procedures, Mrs. Collins."

I met his stare. "How was she strangled?" I heard Marlow's quick-drawn breath and I was sorry, but the answer mattered.

Steve jerked toward me, glared. I understood his repugnance. But I asked for a purpose.

Foster said blandly, "These matters are under investigation."

I felt stymied. Foster was speaking, but not communicating. Was Connor strangled manually? Or had a rope or cord of some sort been used? But obviously. Foster didn't intend to reveal any fact which might be of use to him in his interviews.

Foster's eyes moved from person to person.

Lloyd wavered unsteadily, his face sagging. His bristly face puffy and pale, he'd never managed to tuck the rest of the T-shirt into his blue jeans and he looked disheveled and disreputable. Diana, her face bare of makeup, clutched her father's arm. Neal gave a deep sigh. Marlow hugged her little sister and leaned against Aaron. Steve, his face hard and suspicious, watched Lloyd.

"Oh God." Lloyd's moan was deep and agonized. "Oh God, it's my fault."

The stillness was abrupt.

Steve took an angry step toward Lloyd.

Foster held up his hand. "Wait, Mr. Jennings." There was absolute authority in his voice.

The lawyer jolted to a stop, though his hands balled into fists. He'd dressed hurriedly, a wrinkled shirt and trousers from yesterday and sand-stained boat shoes. His half-shaven face looked lopsided, but he was still an imposing man, a dangerous enemy.

Lloyd was unaware of the circle of watching faces, the pain and fear in the eyes of his children, the anger and dislike in the glares of Marlow and Aaron and Steve. Lloyd's lips trembled. His breaths were labored. "I got mad at her." The words came in uneven spurts, as if he pulled them from deep within.

The silence was cold and hostile, sharp and ugly as barbs on a gaff.

Lloyd touched his head as if every strand of hair hurt, as if his skin flamed in agony. "She was so scared. That message — 'I'm coming for you' — somebody put it on the table in her room and it scared her and she wanted to go home. She acted like the wedding was just something we could forget about, that all that mattered was to leave. I got mad. Oh God, I got mad! I didn't listen. And somebody did come for her, somebody came and killed her" — Lloyd was sobbing now — "and it's my fault. I should have listened. I should have taken her in my arms and held her and told her it was all right. Oh, God, I was supposed to take care of her" — Lloyd turned away, burying his face in his hands. He stumbled blindly toward a sofa, flung himself down.

Diana followed her father, dropping to her knees beside the sofa. She gripped his hand. "Dad, it's not your fault. Dad, nobody could have known —"

"Oh, yeah." Steve's voice grated. He stared at Lloyd with loathing and a deep, pulsing anger. "Somebody knew. I think Lloyd knew. He's the murderer. He killed Connor. He got mad at her and he killed her because he was eaten up with jealousy. Ask him how he yelled at her, accused her of chasing another man. Ask him how mad he got when she begged me to help her go home. Connor realized what kind of man he was and she called off the wedding. So he killed her. Damn him to hell, he killed her!"

"And he lied about the door!" Aaron paced toward Foster. "That's important." Aaron swung toward the lawyer. "Steve, tell him." Aaron pointed at the chief inspector. "Tell him about the door."

Lloyd's hands fell away from his face. He looked at Steve, then at Aaron. Slowly, he began to shake his head. Awkwardly, as if it took every ounce of energy he possessed, he pushed himself to his feet, leaned forward as if to hear better. "Wait a minute, what are you talking about? What door are you talking about?"

"The connecting door." Aaron's tone was urgent.

Marlow's voice was high and shrill.

"That's what must have happened. Oh my God."

Lloyd turned toward her, his face stricken. "Marlow, you can't believe that."

"Quiet, please." Foster's sharp tone threw them back into silence, a silence that quivered with anger and fear. "I will interview everyone in turn and we will determine all of the facts in due order. Miss Bailey, I will speak with you first." His gaze slid over us. "I am requesting that the rest of you remain here until you are summoned." He nodded toward the uniformed policewoman. "Police Constable Phillips will be on duty."

Steve moved quickly to Marlow's side. "I will accompany Miss Bailey." He didn't ask; he announced. "I am both a longtime family friend and the lawyer for Mrs. Bailey's estate."

Chief Inspector Foster nodded gravely. "I'm sure Miss Bailey appreciates your support, Mr. Jennings. However, I will first speak with each witness privately. Miss Bailey is not a suspect in her mother's death and is not in need of counsel."

"Nonetheless, Inspector" — Steve's voice was combative — "she has a right to have counsel present and I am going to insist upon that right."

Aaron reached out toward Marlow. "Miss

Bailey is my fiancée. I want to be with her."

Marlow shook her head impatiently. "I don't need anyone with me. Let's not slow things down." Her eyes touched Lloyd's face, jerked away as if she couldn't bear to see him. "Besides, Steve, I want you and Aaron to stay with Jasmine." She bent down, kissed her sister's blond curls, whispered.

Jasmine nodded twice. "Okay." She rubbed at her eyes. She looked toward Lloyd, took a step in his direction. "Lloyd, you didn't hurt Mom. Did you?"

"No, never. I never did. Jasmine, honey, I loved your mother." Tears brimmed in his eyes. "You know that, don't you?"

Jasmine reached out, grabbed her sister's hand. "See, Lloyd didn't do it."

Marlow shuddered. "Baby, please, we'll talk later. You stay with Steve and Aaron. Okay?"

For an instant, Jasmine resisted, then she moved away, with Steve's hand on her shoulder.

As the door closed behind Foster and Marlow, the occupants of the room were divided again, Steve and Aaron standing near the windows by Jasmine, Neal and Diana following their father back to the sofa.

The breeze through the open French

window ruffled Aaron's hair. He leaned forward. "Hey, Jasmine, take a look. Way out there." He pointed. "Can you see the ship?"

She tumbled to her feet, ran to the window. "Where? I don't see it!"

Aaron knelt beside her. "This way." He lifted her hand, held it to the south. "Look straight —"

The policewoman was watching Jasmine and Aaron.

I drifted casually closer to Lloyd and the children. My back was to the policewoman. "Lloyd, don't talk to Chief Inspector Foster without a lawyer present." I spoke softly.

Diana and Neal looked at me with scared, sick eyes.

Lloyd's head jerked up. "Henrie, you don't believe Steve, do you? You can't think I would hurt Connor?" His eyes were stricken and desperate.

I looked deep into his eyes, saw pain and despair and misery. But if he had killed Connor, that would be precisely what I should expect to see. I didn't answer him directly. I hoped he was innocent. I wanted him to be innocent. I would do everything possible to help him establish his innocence. But, at this moment, I didn't know who had murdered Connor. I did know this was the father of my grandchildren and I would give him the advice anyone in his situation should follow. "It doesn't matter what any of us think, Lloyd. Insist on counsel before you answer questions. That should keep you free from questioning until late today, possibly until Monday."

Lloyd got up, faced me. "Hell, no. I don't need a lawyer." He glared at me and, beyond me, at Steve and Aaron. "Goddamn, I didn't kill Connor. I can talk to the police. I'm not —"

The policewoman moved quickly toward us, her shoes clicking on the wooden floor. "If you please, sir." She was soft-voiced but firm. "I will ask you to remain calm and not to speak until your interview with the chief inspector is concluded."

Perhaps only a lawyer would have the arrogance to think that the advice common to all in a criminal investigation need not apply to himself. Of course, Lloyd was not a criminal lawyer.

"Grandma!" Diana's voice wobbled.

"It will work out," I said briskly, but I didn't look directly at Diana or Neal. I turned away. I'd done my best. I walked toward the young policewoman and murmured, "There's a rest room in the hallway near the desk. I'll be back in a moment."

"Yes, ma'am." She followed me toward

the door, resumed her patient stance by the entrance.

In an instant, I was in the hall. I walked swiftly toward the main lobby, my goal the short hallway that contained the telephones, rest rooms, and, of course, the cardroom where Chief Inspector Foster was interviewing Marlow.

nineteen

I reached the short hallway and was relieved to find it empty. I slipped past the cardroom and reached the second door. I turned the knob, moved the door quietly and slipped inside. The light was off, but sunlight slanted through the partially open wooden blinds. It came as no surprise that Mrs. Worrell stood near the connecting door, which, once again, was ajar the merest sliver, not enough to attract notice but quite adequate to overhear the conversation. Moreover, as I recalled the cardroom, Chief Inspector Foster sat with his back to this door.

Thelma Worrell's mossy-green dress sagged against her, emphasizing her height. She was a big woman. She hunched beside the connecting door, her bony face intent. One hand clutched the double-strand carnelian necklace that echoed the dull orange of her hair. She darted an angry yet defensive look toward me.

I tiptoed across the floor, came up beside her, and bent my head to listen.

". . . Mother was terrified. I tried to convince her she shouldn't be afraid, that the silly message was just an ugly prank, but she insisted we fly home immediately. Of course, that infuriated Lloyd. She didn't even seem to focus on the fact that the wedding was canceled. All she could think about was getting away from here." Marlow's voice wavered. "If only we could have flown out yesterday."

Chief Inspector Foster's chair creaked. "Did Mr. Drake make any threats against your mother?"

Her reply was slow in coming. Finally, doubtfully, she said, "No. No, he was really mad, but it was the red-faced, shouting kind of mad. I never thought he would hurt Mother. None of us thought that or we would have stayed all night with her."

"You've said she was frightened. Exactly what did she fear?" The chief inspector sounded puzzled.

Marlow sighed. "Oh, it's all so stupid. She thought Roddy Worrell was a ghost and he was going to come back and kill her."

"A ghost." He was silent for a moment, then said briskly, "I understand there were sightings of some kind of phenomena near the tower. Why should your mother believe that Mr. Worrell — or his ghost — would intend to harm her?"

"Oh, it isn't rational. But Mother felt

guilty about his death," Marlow said reluctantly.

Thelma Worrell drew her breath in sharply.

"And why is that?" Foster was polite but insistent.

Marlow didn't answer.

Foster waited a moment. "Miss Bailey?" Clearly he wanted an answer.

"It's very complicated, Chief Inspector. Mother was very attractive to men and she loved attention. But she didn't expect men to take her seriously. Unfortunately, Mr. Worrell became very upset when she made it clear she wasn't looking for any kind of long-term relationship." Marlow cleared her throat. "I think Mother was afraid he jumped from the tower because he was upset and had been drinking heavily. She felt guilty."

"Yes." The whisper was so faint I might have imagined it, but I didn't imagine the burning hatred in Mrs. Worrell's tortured eyes.

The chief inspector rustled a paper. "So your mother saw the message on the table and she thought Mr. Worrell's ghost was going to come for her."

"It's so terrible. She was afraid she was going to die — and she did." Marlow clapped her hands together. "If only I had stayed with her."

"Why didn't you?" He said it quietly.

"I thought it was all nonsense." There was a sharpness in her reply. "And, of course, it was. She wasn't killed by a ghost. We spent the evening with her. Jasmine and I had dinner in her room. I helped her pack. Steve had taken care of getting the tickets changed. He came up after dinner. We had her calmed down and almost cheerful. Before we left — oh, I think it was about ten — Steve checked the sliding door to the balcony. I saw him swing shut the metal rod that prevents the door from opening. Mother locked the door to Lloyd's room. Out in the hall, I waited until I heard the chain in place. There was no way anyone could get into that room."

Marlow was right. At that moment, no one could have entered Connor's room. Obviously, Connor later opened either the hall door or the connecting door to Lloyd's room or opened the balcony door. Finding out which could make the difference between life and death for Lloyd Drake.

Foster tapped a pen on the card table. "The chain was in place when we arrived this morning."

The muscles in my throat tightened. If the

chain was in place this morning . . .

Marlow saw it at once. "That means who-ever killed Mother came through Lloyd's room." A quick-drawn breath. "So it must have been Lloyd." There was a faint uncer-tainty in her voice.

"Not necessarily, Miss Bailey." He spoke matter-of-factly. "Your mother might have admitted her killer through the hall door and the chain could have been hooked after her death. She might have opened the sliding door to the balcony. The only fact of which we can be positive is that the murderer exited from her room through the connecting door to Mr. Drake's room, since the hall door was chained and the bar was in place at the bal-cony door when her body was found this morning. Of course, the murderer also could have been admitted through the connecting door." Foster clearly under-stood the possibilities.

"Lloyd's room . . ." There was horror in Marlow's voice. "Mother thought Lloyd was wonderful. Even as upset as she was, if he'd called to her, apologized, she was al-ways so hungry for love. Oh, God, she would have opened that door . . ."

Foster said quickly, "Do you think Mr. Drake was responsible for the message which presumably was left by Mr. Worrell's ghost?"

"Oh, no." Her surprise was evident. "Why would he do that?"

Foster waited.

"That message . . ." Marlow thought out loud. "Somebody who hated Mother left it. And the only person —" She broke off.

"The only person . . ." The chief inspector repeated her words.

Marlow's tone was reluctant. "Mrs. Worrell. She must have left that message. She looks at Mother — looked at Mother — as though she'd like to push her out of the tower."

Mrs. Worrell twisted the beads in her fingers, hunched her head between her shoulders like a turtle drawing into its shell.

I looked at the manager's rigid face, willing her to lift her eyes, to meet my gaze.

She remained as still as a snake poised to strike, emanating malignancy.

"Chief Inspector?" Marlow's voice was breathless. "Do you think Mrs. Worrell —"

A knock sounded. A door opened. "Chief Inspector, excuse me, please." The musical voice was strained.

"What is it, Constable?" His voice was patient.

"The older lady, sir. Among the witnesses

341

still to be seen. She asked to be excused to go to the ladies' room and she hasn't returned. I checked the rest room and she isn't there. Apparently, she is still in the hotel or on the grounds. There has been no call for a taxi and . . ."

I was already at the hall door, pulling it open, peeking out. I stepped into the hall, closed the door behind me, and lightly ran to the exit, propped it open, hurried outside, turned about, and reentered the hall just as the door to the cardroom opened. I let the outer door slam behind me.

The young policewoman looked toward the exit. "Ma'am!"

I smiled and strolled toward her. "Yes, officer?"

"You did not return." Her tone was sharp.

"Return?" I looked blank. "Oh, I'm sorry. I didn't know it mattered. I've just been out for some air. Do you need me?" I picked up my pace.

Chief Inspector Foster came to the doorway.

I strode toward him. "Are you ready for me, Chief Inspector?" If I was lucky, he'd agree to speak with me now, then I would be free to discover what I could and hope the damning facts against Lloyd could be explained away. However, I looked at the chief inspector with only casual inquiry, as if his decision were of little moment.

He hesitated, shrugged. "If you'll wait here in the hallway for a moment, Mrs. Collins?"

"Of course."

He nodded at the policewoman, said, "Thank you, Constable," and shut the door.

I sat down on an upholstered bench near the pay phone. I had learned a very important — and sobering — fact through my eavesdropping: Connor's hall door had been chained. I wanted to talk to Lloyd. Would he claim to have slept so heavily, so deeply that someone might have moved through his room? But how had access to his room been obtained? Yes, I needed to talk to Lloyd. He had either lied about the connecting door's being locked or he'd meant that it was locked on Connor's side, not his. But whichever, facts consistent with his guilt were stacking up, much like scraps of timber that could flame into a devouring fire.

I pushed away thoughts of Diana and Neal. Their father . . . If he was guilty, that would be a burden on them throughout their lives. But, even worse, if Lloyd was innocent yet falsely accused, the pain would be even greater. I wanted Lloyd to be innocent, but deep inside I could not swear that he was.

I wished I were still crouched next to Mrs. Worrell. However, I could imagine much of the rest of the chief inspector's inquiry. Was Marlow on good terms with her mother? Had Connor approved of Marlow's engagement? Whom might Foster contact in Atlanta for information about Connor's estate? What was Steve Jennings's attitude toward Connor's planned marriage? Was Jennings hostile to or jealous of Lloyd Drake?

The door opened. Marlow didn't notice me on the bench. She walked back toward the main lobby, shoulders slumped, gait leaden.

I looked after her for a moment. She was in such pain. Whatever I could do to help, however little it might be, I would do. I walked toward Foster.

The chief inspector held the door for me, closed it behind us.

I took the chair that faced the card table and the connecting door, my gaze sliding over the slight opening.

Foster stopped beside the card table, jingled some coins in his pocket. "Where were you, Mrs. Collins?"

I looked at him steadily. "I stepped outside. I wanted to think." It was true as far as it went.

Foster drew out his chair, dropped into it with athletic grace. He nodded toward a corner where a young man with rather long dark hair and a tweedy jacket sat on a straight chair, pad of paper on his knee, pen in hand. "Detective Sergeant Barnes will transcribe our interview. If you have no objection."

I wondered if an objection would result in detention? But I had no objection. "That's fine, Chief Inspector."

He eased back in his chair, placed his fingertips together, and regarded me thoughtfully. I was reminded of the old children's rhyme. If only he could turn his fingers and out would come a murderer. "When did you last see Mrs. Bailey?"

The question surprised me. I'd expected to be queried about the message found yesterday afternoon and Connor's response and Lloyd's anger. But, of course, I'd already described that episode to him. He was not going to cover old ground.

"Shortly before I called you. Marlow took her mother into the bathroom because she was angry" — I wished I could change the words, but it was too late — "with Lloyd."

"Mrs. Bailey slapped Mr. Drake." Foster's eyes were half closed.

"Yes." I didn't elaborate.

"You didn't see her again?"

"No. I went to my room, called you. My granddaughter came and we had a brief visit. She and her father and brother went out to dinner. I had dinner here with Steve Jennings and Aaron Reed." I remembered Steve's angry departure. "You might ask Aaron whether Steve Jennings was in love with Connor."

Foster dropped his hands to the table. "Are you suggesting that Mr. Jennings would kill Mrs. Bailey rather than see her marry Mr. Drake?"

I massaged my temple, a headache created by tension and lack of food. "I know that sounds absurd. But there could be other reasons. Perhaps Steve has embezzled funds from Connor. She didn't strike me as a sophisticated woman about money. But I'm quite sure he didn't want to see her marry Lloyd." I spoke with confidence. "And if he isn't a thwarted lover, why should it matter to him?"

"Perhaps" — and the chief inspector's tone was dry — "as a longtime friend of the family, Mr. Jennings didn't trust Mr. Drake." He cleared his throat. "In any event, you didn't see Mrs. Bailey after the incident of the message. To your knowledge" — he emphasized the last word —

"had anyone at any time threatened harm to Mrs. Bailey?"

Marlow and Steve didn't want Connor to marry Lloyd and both Diana and Neal opposed the marriage, but that certainly had no relevance here. I looked at Foster bleakly. "I don't know of any threat to Connor." It was an admission that I didn't have any idea who might want to kill Connor. And I saw no correlation between the murder of George Smith and the murder of Connor Bailey. "Except . . . Mrs. Worrell. She blamed Connor for her husband's death."

"I understand that is so. I will speak with Mrs. Worrell." I wondered that he didn't feel the anger pulsing so near him behind that slightly open door. He stood. "Very well, Mrs. Collins. I appreciate your cooperation."

Our interview was at an end. I rose, moved toward the door, then looked back at him. "Chief Inspector, Mr. Drake is my former son-in-law."

Foster's face was impassive.

Pictures of Lloyd through the years fluttered in my mind: Emily and Lloyd hand in hand as they left their wedding reception; Lloyd bending down to scoop up the baby Diana; Lloyd at his mother's funeral; serious, intense Lloyd only days ago looking at me earnestly and saying, "Yes, it was love at first sight."

"Chief Inspector." I knew my words would not help, but I felt impelled to say them. "Lloyd is not a violent man. Oh, he can explode" — I remembered years ago when a car rear-ended Lloyd's and Emily had clamped her hand on his arm to keep him in the car until his temper was under control — "but he is genuinely kind and decent and serious." He'd won the heart of a little girl as well as that of her mother. "The idea that he would strangle a woman . . ." I took a deep breath, forced myself to ask, "Was Connor bruised?" I was thinking of a man torn by jealousy and heartbreak, losing control, grabbing a woman by her arms, gripping painfully tight, and those hands plunging toward her throat, squeezing until her face turned purple and her body sagged into death.

Foster stood very still, a man deep in thought. I knew suddenly that the question worried him. Finally, his voice expressionless, he said, "The autopsy report, of course, is not complete."

"Chief Inspector, please." I looked at him eagerly. "Tell me —"

"The investigation is continuing, Mrs. Collins." He was abrupt. "Detective Sergeant Barnes, summon Mr. Jennings."

And I was out in the hall. But as I walked away, I had the beginnings of hope that Lloyd might be innocent. Some fact about the manner of Connor's death puzzled Chief Inspector Foster. Maybe it was a stretch to take his apparent concern to be a pointer toward Lloyd's innocence, but we were talking about Lloyd and violence and the trauma suffered by Connor when Foster took refuge in blandness and diversion.

I reached the main lobby and hesitated for a moment, uncertain which direction to go, and realized that was true in every respect. Still, no matter what happened, I was determined to look at the facts as they existed, unswayed by my longing to protect my grandchildren. If Lloyd had committed murder, I wanted him caught and tried and convicted. If he hadn't, I wanted to do everything I could to help Chief Inspector Foster discover the guilty person.

First and foremost, I needed to talk to Lloyd. I glanced toward the door where Lloyd and the others awaited their summons. It wouldn't do any good to go in there. The police constable had her instructions. In fact, it might be difficult for me to obtain any moment alone with Lloyd. No, to discover what Lloyd knew and perhaps gain a better picture of the chief inspector's suspicions, my best bet was to try once again to slip unobserved into the room next to the interviews. That was treading on dangerous ground. But, frankly, what could — or would — the chief inspector do, even if I was discovered there? In fact, if I hurried, I might catch part of Foster's interrogation of Steve Jennings.

I moved casually toward an open door to the terrace. I kept my pace slow until I was out of sight of both the drawing room and the conference room so starkly divided between Lloyd's and Connor's families. As soon as I rounded the corner of the hotel, I picked up speed. Or tried to. I realized I was desperately tired, a combination of weakness and lack of food as well as stress. I took a moment to root in my purse. When traveling, I always have a candy bar available. Chocolate, sugar and peanuts can work miracles. I pulled out the Baby Ruth, and hurrying once again, stripped the paper and carefully bit around the central core of sweetness — I save that for last — and welcomed the instant surge of energy.

At the end of the short wing, I looked carefully about. A gardener pruned a pittosporum bush. There was no evidence of police presence — if the gardener was what he seemed — on this side of the hotel. I opened the door, poked in my head. The hallway was deserted. I moved fast, taking the last bite of candy as I turned the knob and slipped inside the room.

Mrs. Worrell's head jerked toward the door. When she saw me, the tension eased out of her body. She once again bent near the sliver of light that marked the narrow space between the connecting door and jamb.

I eased across the room. She and I stood no more than inches apart. I smelled a faint scent of geranium. I tilted my head to listen.

"... don't understand why you haven't arrested him." Steve's chair scraped. "What more do you need?" His voice was nearer and I knew he stood over Foster's card table, glaring down at him. The lawyer spoke fast and hard, a prosecuting attorney lining up his facts. "Drake and Connor argued. She struck him. The marriage was off. He stormed away. Connor had dinner with her family. She packed to go home. We said good night and she was safe in her room, the balcony door locked, the connecting door to Drake's room locked, the hall door locked and chained. Don't forget that chain, Chief Inspector." Ladies and gentlemen of the jury ... "That chain means no one entered her room from the hall. We know the balcony door was barred. That leaves only the connecting door to Drake's room. The next morning, Drake claims that door is locked. It was not locked. I opened it and we found Connor dead, strangled with the belt to a hotel bathrobe. I'll tell you my question, Chief Inspector. Where is the belt to Lloyd Drake's bathrobe?"

The belt to a bathrobe — I understood now why Foster hadn't answered my question. He had questions of his own. Using the belt of a bathrobe argued premeditation, not a crime of uncontrolled passion.

"Our investigation will address that question, Mr. Jennings." Foster's tone was mild. I pictured him watching the lawyer, eyes half closed, face impassive, his mind toying with the puzzle: If Lloyd wore the bathrobe into Connor's room, was it likely, if they quarreled, that he would pull the belt free and use it to strangle her? Possible, yes. Likely, no. If he entered her room carrying the belt, that meant there was no quarrel, that he came with murder in his heart.

"You can test the belt for DNA. If Lloyd held it in his hands" — Steve's voice shook — "pulled it tight around Connor's neck, it will have traces of his sweat, the moisture from his hands. And if the belt that was used to kill Connor has Lloyd's DNA, what more would you need, Chief Inspector?" It was a harsh demand.

A chair creaked. Foster spoke briskly. "I appreciate your suggestions, Mr. Jennings. And your cooperation. Sergeant Barnes, please summon Mr. Reed." The door opened. "Mr. Jennings, I trust you and the rest of your party will remain on the island until Mrs. Bailey's body is released."

"We aren't going anywhere, Chief Inspector, until justice is done."

Substitute "Sheriff" for "Chief Inspector" and it was the kind of exit line that would have been delivered well by Gary Cooper in an old Western flick. I was afraid that all the good lines in the upcoming scenes belonged to Connor Bailey's retinue. It was time, if I could figure out a way, that the posse rode over the hill to save Lloyd.

twenty

I moved quickly to the hall door, opened it. I waited until the sound of Steve's brisk footsteps ceased, peered cautiously out and stepped into the empty hall. Again, I moved fast, and I succeeded in reaching the exit before Detective Sergeant Barnes returned with Aaron Reed. I doubted Aaron would contribute anything new. It was Steve who had opened the connecting door in Lloyd's room and discovered Connor's body. I'd already heard Marlow's report of that last evening. Aaron knew no more than Marlow or Steve about Connor's quarrel with Lloyd. Aaron would simply confirm the accusations already made against Lloyd.

I reached the terrace and entered a side door into the drawing room. I stopped just inside the door, next to a tall vase with flaming birds-of-paradise, and watched as Marlow and Jasmine came out of the room where the Drake family waited.

Jasmine tried to wriggle free of her sister's grasp. "I want to say good-bye to Lloyd." I couldn't hear Marlow's murmured reply. Jasmine leaned back on her heels. "I don't want to go to the beach." Marlow smoothed her little sister's hair in a forlorn, hopeless gesture. "Later, Jasmine. We'll talk later. I've got to . . . There are things I have to do. Come on." She managed a brisk tone. "We haven't had lunch. Let's go down to the pool and get something to eat." She took Jasmine's arm in a firm grip and tugged her toward the terrace. Jasmine gave a final worried look back at the closed door. "Lloyd hasn't had anything to eat . . ."

Jasmine either didn't understand or refused to understand. I'd tried to be a character witness for Lloyd, and here was another one. But kind words and good thoughts were not enough. I probably had at least ten or fifteen minutes before the sergeant returned for Neal or Diana. I felt rather certain the chief inspector would leave Lloyd for last.

Just for an instant, I thought about Lloyd — unshaven, haphazardly dressed, and, if innocent, struggling with terrible pain and guilt. Oh, yes, he would feel guilt, not that he had caused Connor's death but that he had not listened, that he had been angry, that he had turned away from her when she needed him. Nothing would ever lessen that ugly, searing, irremediable truth. Just for an instant, I reached out and held on to the rim of the big blue vase.

I understood guilt. Years ago it was I who insisted on a trip on a narrow twisting mountain road that ended in a car smash and the death of my son. My hand tightened on the pottery rim, held so hard I felt the edge crease my palm. Nothing can change the past. Lloyd — and I — would always live with our own sins of commission and omission. But sometimes the future can be changed.

I darted a glance toward the closed door. Neal and Diana and Lloyd waited, but time was running out for Lloyd. I'd known when I heard Steve's description of the thick terry-cloth belt used to strangle Connor. I knew precisely what the belt looked like. Every room in the hotel had two of the comfortable white robes with the Tower Ridge House crest on the lapel. I'd worn the robe in my room. I remembered the thickness of the white belt.

I dropped into a wing chair near the blue vase and pulled a small notebook and pen from my purse. Old reporters never travel without paper and pen. I wrote a quick note for Neal and Diana, instructing them to call the American Consulate and request a list of criminal defense lawyers. They were then to contact the lawyers until someone agreed to represent Lloyd and come either to the hotel or, if such was the case, to the police station. I frowned. If I had time, I'd call Kevin Ellis, get his recommendation, but there was so little time. However — I scrawled Kevin's name at the top of the page. He had covered plenty of stories in Magistrate's Court and would very likely have a savvy view of the local bar.

Shoes clicked on the wooden floor. Detective Sergeant Barnes strode toward the door.

I added beside Kevin's name: "Reporter. *The Royal Gazette.* Use my name, try him first for suggestions in re lawyers. Don't worry about me. I'll check with you later this afternoon." I folded the note and was almost to the door when it opened.

Detective Sergeant Barnes followed Neal into the lobby. I glimpsed Lloyd sagging on the sofa, chin on his chest, hands hanging limply. His face sagged too, gray and empty, hopeless and despairing. Diana looked after her brother, her eyes bright with fear.

I stepped in front of Neal and the sergeant. "Neal, I'm going to rest for a while on the terrace." I looked at the sergeant, held his gaze, "I'm just recovering from pneumonia, officer. I wanted to let my grandson know where to find me." I'd turned so that my left hand with the note was hidden from view by my body. I tucked the note into Neal's hand. Neal's fingers closed around the piece of paper. His expression didn't change. "I will see you later," and I moved toward the terrace.

I settled in a white wooden chair over-looking the lower terrace, the pool and, beyond the cottages and the dark green of the headland, the ever-changing ocean. The surf was a dull roar today, the turquoise water placid with only a faint ripple marking the dangerous reef. No clouds marred the perfect blue of the sky. I gave myself twenty minutes to rest. I leaned back, closed my eyes, welcomed the warmth of the sun on my face, let my thoughts range. I'd told the chief inspector that Lloyd was not a man to commit murder. My witness, of course, would not weigh against the facts, and the facts were grim: Lloyd's jealousy, the quarrel between Lloyd and Connor, the cancellation of the wedding, the unlocked connecting door between Lloyd's room and Connor's, Lloyd's assertion that the door was locked, the chained door to the hall, the barred balcony door.

If the belt used to strangle Connor proved to belong to Lloyd's robe, his arrest would be almost certain.

And there was the insidious, dreadful, inescapable question: If not Lloyd, then who?

I sat up straight, turned to look toward the hotel wing. Quite likely the police investigation of the site was complete. After all, these were hotel rooms with standard furnishings. The only additions were belongings brought by guests. The search in this instance would be confined to the room where Connor died and Lloyd's room.

Lloyd. Everything came back to Lloyd.

I swung my eyes away from the wing. It did no good to stare at the smooth yellow stucco exterior walls and the balconies with their big pots of flowers and webbed chairs. I knew the process of careful exploration that had occurred since the police forensic team arrived this morning. I needed to know what had happened last night. The chief inspector estimated that Connor died between midnight and 3 A.M.

Surely Connor was asleep at that hour. She'd said good night to Marlow and Jasmine and Steve about ten. Marlow insisted the balcony was barred, the connecting door locked, and that she heard Connor chain the hall door.

What happened then?

I'd had one late-evening talk with

Connor, a frightened and worried Connor who'd been drinking. I'd ask the chief inspector about the autopsy results. I thought it very likely that last night, after her family left, Connor had hurried to the wet bar, opened one of the small bottles of whiskey. Perhaps she'd drunk it as she made a final check of her luggage, making certain everything was packed, ready for departure the next day.

I had a sudden sad vision of Connor in her room and Lloyd in his, beset by loneliness and hurt, drinking to dull their pain, both finally curling into a restless sleep. Did Connor wake and, restless and edgy, seek comfort? Did she knock on Lloyd's door? That would presume that he came at her invitation and a quarrel ensued. Or did Lloyd knock on her door? Did she wake, admit him? Connor, after all, might have been angry with Lloyd, but she was not afraid of him. She was afraid of Roddy Worrell. She would not have hesitated to open the connecting door to Lloyd. Did they quarrel again and did this quarrel end in murder?

No. My conclusion was as quick and hard as the slam of a door. There had been no late-night quarrel. A screaming match between them would surely have been heard. Marlow and Jasmine were in room 30,

Connor in 32, Lloyd in 34. Had the furniture been disarranged in Connor's room? Was there evidence of a struggle? The chief inspector indicated that Connor had not resisted her attacker. Why?

All right. There was no quarrel. If Lloyd committed the murder, he had done so quietly, moving with deliberation and stealth. Wasn't that at odds with his apparent motive? Were stealth and deliberation the attributes of a man deviled by jealousy, trembling with anger?

But once again came the stiletto-sharp question: If not Lloyd, then who?

The answer was simple. If Lloyd was innocent, there were two possibilities. Connor had awakened and contacted someone or someone knocked on her door. Whichever, Connor unfastened the chain and admitted the visitor. Whom would Connor call upon in the middle of the night? Her daughter Marlow or Steve Jennings. Whom would she admit to her room in the middle of the night? Marlow, Jasmine, Steve, Aaron. Why would she open her door at that late hour? That was the easiest answer of all. All that would be needed was the urgent message that Jasmine was sick and needed her mother. That was a message no mother would resist or question. Even if the caller at the door was Thelma Worrell, Connor, be-fuddled by sleep, perceptions likely dulled by alcohol, would no doubt open her door.

All right, I had no trouble figuring out how the murderer got access to Connor. But that was only half the equation. What motive did anyone have? So far as I'd been able to determine, Connor was on excellent terms with both her daughters. I had no suspicion of Jasmine. Yes, children sometimes kill, but a young child could not strangle a parent. That simply couldn't be. Not Jasmine. Marlow? Her attitude throughout this journey had been one of caring and concern for her mother. I'd never spotted a trace of anger or dislike. If they had any quarrel, it was well hidden.

That left money, always a possibility when great sums are involved. I didn't know how much of Connor's fortune might be diverted through her marriage to Lloyd. But that marriage was already canceled. Could the thought have been to make certain that Connor and Lloyd didn't patch up their problems? Connor's fortune was now permanently out of Lloyd's reach. It was also now under the control of Steve Jennings as executor of Connor's estate. Had that been imperative for Steve? Had he made financial transactions that wouldn't have borne the scrutiny of Connor's new husband, also a lawyer?

As for Aaron, he professed to have little interest in money, yet he fitted into Marlow's expensive world quite well.

Finally there was revenge. Thelma Worrell loathed Connor Bailey. But would that dislike, that sense of grievance over the death of her husband, be enough to propel Thelma Worrell to murder?

I rather thought it possible that Thelma had climbed the tower last year and found her drunken husband sitting on the ledge and that she'd pushed him to his death. She blamed Connor because Connor had enticed Roddy and humiliated Thelma. If Thelma pushed Roddy and George threatened to tell the police something that would reopen the investigation, that was motive enough to explain George Smith's murder. But Connor posed no threat to Thelma. And I didn't see that I could have it both ways. Actually three ways: Thelma guilty of her husband's death, Thelma killing George Smith in a desperate move to hush him, and Thelma strangling Connor in revenge. Moreover, I always came back to George's January 6 meeting at the BUEI. Why would Thelma meet him there when she could easily speak to him privately here at the hotel?

I sighed and pushed up from the chair, walked slowly across the terrace. I judged that Chief Inspector Foster had likely finished talking with both Neal and Diana. It would be Lloyd's turn.

I wanted to hear what Lloyd would say, not only about his own actions, about the connecting door and the bathrobe tie and his feelings about the quarrel with Connor; I wanted to hear what he said about Marlow and Jasmine and Steve and Aaron and Mrs. Worrell. Lloyd was shaken, distraught and despondent, but he must by now realize his peril. Surely he was thinking, and thinking hard. Who wanted Connor dead?

The short hall was empty. I quietly opened the door to the room adjacent to the cardroom and slipped inside. I had the room to myself. Had Mrs. Worrell lost interest, or learned everything she needed to know? It might be useful to find out what she had overheard that I had missed. But I was eager to overhear Lloyd's interview. I somehow felt that if I heard his answers to Foster's questions, I would know whether Lloyd was innocent or guilty. That judgment would be grounded on instinct, but it is instinct that we follow when we fall in love, when we trust, when we fear and when we dislike. Instinct can be a faulty barometer, but we ignore it at our peril.

I eased across the wooden floor. The connecting door was closed. Carefully I turned the knob, opened it a sliver. The door opened to darkness and silence. My breath caught in my throat. I had the same startled, shocked feeling I'd once felt during the onset of an earthquake in Mexico City: the expected, orderly world suddenly shaken. Where was Chief Inspector Foster? Where, for God's sake, was Lloyd?

I pushed the door wide, stepped inside. The room might never have held a living creature on this day. The chairs were drawn up to the card tables. There was no trace of occupancy — no papers, no disarray, nothing to reflect the emotions that had pulsed in this small room, the sorrow and fear and anger.

I hurried across the room to the hall door, making no effort to be quiet, and yanked it open. In the hall, my shoes clipped against the wooden floor. I darted out of the wing, past the counter, where Rosalind's round face was still and watchful, and into the main lobby.

Footsteps clattered up the outside steps. Diana burst through the open front door. "Grandma, where have you been? We've looked everywhere. Oh, Grandma, they've taken Daddy away." Diana's voice trembled. Her eyes were huge, her features taut with strain.

Neal gripped his sister's arm. "Take it easy, Dinny. We'll handle this." But his eyes, too, were frightened.

I held out my hands. "Tell me."

They tumbled into speech, one interrupting the other.

"We were in the main lobby" — Diana pointed at chairs on either side of a wrought-iron table where crimson poinsettias bloomed in a blue pottery planter — "because we thought they would take Dad to the room where the chief inspector talked to us, but —"

"Instead of the guy that came for us" — Neal looked toward the room where they all had waited — "here came the chief inspector. He went into the conference room. I guess Dad was the only one left, Dad and the policewoman. The inspector was in there for a little while; then he came out with Dad. They walked straight across the lobby toward the door. Dad saw us and —"

Diana pressed her hands against her cheeks. "Dad kind of stumbled to a stop. He looked at us like we were on the other side of a canyon, like he was never going to see us again. He said, 'Stay with your grandmother. She'll take care of you. I'm going into town for a while.' "

Neal's broad face was suddenly combative. "The policewoman was walking right behind him. I got up and went straight to the chief inspector and I asked him where he was taking Dad."

"He was so smooth and pleasant." Diana's tone was bitter. "And he looked at me with those cold eyes even though his voice was nice. He said something like the investigation was continuing into the death of Mrs. Bailey and Mr. Drake had been invited to the Hamilton Police Station to assist with the inquiries."

Yes, they put it politely in Bermuda, but the message was clear: Lloyd Drake was to be interrogated as the number one suspect in Connor's murder. Chief Inspector Foster was focusing on his quarry. Given the facts, I certainly wasn't surprised. But, if Lloyd was innocent, there had to be other facts.

And there was no time to lose.

"Diana, Neal." It was a call to arms.

They looked at me in relief, sudden hope in their eyes, welling eagerness in their faces.

I maintained a confident composure, though my heart ached. Oh, children, this isn't a moment that Grandmother can make right simply because she loves you and will always fight for you. But perhaps it was as well that they invested me with power far greater than I possessed. It's amazing what faith can achieve. "I want you to get on the phone, contact Kevin Ellis at *The Royal Gazette*, get the name of a criminal lawyer —"

Neal nodded, pulled my earlier note from his pocket.

"And I will —" Oh, Lord, what would I do? Quick, quick, I needed definite objectives for all of us. "— determine how the actual murderer got into Connor's room." I didn't give them time to ask what difference that could make or how I could possibly discover that information. "Use the phone in your room. Get some help from the consulate if you need it. They must have a list of lawyers. Call around. Get a lawyer. Then go to the police station —"

"Where's that?" Neal was all business, poised to begin.

"Parliament Street. Right up the hill from Front Street." I didn't know that it would help, but I didn't think it would hurt for Lloyd's family to appear at the police station. In any event, they needed to talk to the lawyer and surely the lawyer would agree to meet them there.

Diana was impatient. "That doesn't

matter right now, Neal. Let's go call."

They were halfway across the lobby when Marlow and Aaron and Jasmine, carrying luggage and backpacks, came in the side door.

Diana stopped, glared at them. "I hope you're satisfied, all of you. You've said horrid things about my father. He didn't hurt your mother. He never would have" — her voice rose — "not in a million years."

Neal grabbed his sister's arm. "Come on, Dinny. They don't care."

Marlow jerked her head toward Aaron. "Go on upstairs with Jasmine. Get our stuff into the new rooms."

Aaron nudged Jasmine toward the curving staircase, just past the counter.

Jasmine wrapped her arms around her backpack. The head of a teddy bear poked out of the opened pack. "I haven't said anything bad about Lloyd." Tears welled, spilled down her cheeks. "See, Lloyd gave me Teddy and he told me he'd always be here for me. I want to tell Lloyd I think everybody's wrong. I don't think Lloyd hurt Mom."

"Jasmine, shut up." Marlow's voice was sharp. "You don't know anything! Go on with Aaron —"

Jasmine pulled away from Aaron. She

whirled and darted toward the French doors to the terrace, the head of the stuffed bear bobbing up and down in the backpack.

"Jasmine!" Marlow's cry was ragged.

Aaron took a step toward the terrace, then shook his head. "Let her go, Marlow. Let her be alone for a while. Maybe out in the sun . . ."

"She knows Dad's innocent." Diana's voice was triumphant.

"Innocent!" Marlow cried. "If he's innocent, then who killed my mom? Tell me that, damn you. Who killed my mom?" She buried her face in her hands, her shoulders heaving.

Aaron dropped the suitcases, pulled Marlow into his arms. His face was hard as he met Diana's gaze. "Leave us alone. Okay? You've done enough, all of you. Just, for God's sake, leave us alone." His handsome features twisted with misery. "We're stuck here for now. Don't make it any harder than it has to be." Awkwardly, he turned Marlow toward the stairs, scrambled to pick up the cases.

Neal took two strides. "I'll get them. You go on ahead with Marlow." He glanced at his sister. "I'll meet you in your room. Get started on the phone." He hoisted several pieces of luggage, turned away from Marlow and Aaron, moving toward the stairs. "I'll put them in the hall up there."

Aaron didn't answer, his look startled, uncomfortable, grudgingly accepting. "Come on, Marlow."

Diana watched them leave, face slack. She lifted trembling fingers to her lips.

I patted her shoulder. "Go on to your room, honey, and make those calls. We need to hurry. Your dad needs help." I wanted to pull her back from the no-man's-land opening in her mind, the cold and stricken realization that Connor's murderer had to be someone Connor knew and knew well.

Diana stepped toward me. "What Marlow said . . ." Her voice was uneven.

I understood. "Yes, that's the point, isn't it? If your father is innocent, then who killed Connor? She would never have opened her door to a stranger. It had to be someone she knew" — I ticked the names off on my fingers — "Marlow, Jasmine, Aaron, Steve, you, Neal, me, and, less likely but still possible, Mrs. Worrell or a hotel employee or a guest that she'd met." The only hotel guest who might qualify was Curt Patterson, the big redhead from Fort Worth who had been so assiduous in his attentions to Connor.

It was, obviously, the first moment that Diana had moved beyond her father's danger to grapple with the reality that someone she knew — almost certainly someone with whom she had spoken, someone whose face she would recognize — had committed a brutal and violent murder. Clearly, she found the possibilities almost beyond belief.

"One of them . . ." Her voice trailed away. "But, Grandma, why?"

Why, indeed?

Neal's footsteps clattered down the stairs. He reached us, frowning. "Hey, Dinny, why haven't you gotten started? Come on." He jerked his head toward the door.

As they moved away, I looked after them, glad they were going to be busy, glad they faced a task that required concentration and effort. And now it was time for me to look for answers to questions nobody had yet asked.

twenty-one

No one was behind the front desk. I looked to my left at the pigeonhole cabinet attached to the wall in the hotel office, within easy reach for a desk clerk, just beyond the grasp of anyone on this side of the counter. Tower Ridge House was an old-fashioned hotel with actual room keys, not electronic cards. The last crimson splash of the setting sun slanted through open blinds, falling across the lower rows of pigeon-holes, glinting on the shiny metal tower that served as a tag for each key. Most of the compartments held two keys because so few of the rooms were occupied.

There was one key in the slot for room 32, one in the slot for room 34. I made up my mind in an instant. At the far end, to my right, a portion of the counter was hinged and could be raised. I stepped quietly in that direction. I gave one swift glance around the lobby and the entrance to the drawing room and the hallways branching off. There was utter quiet, no voices, no movement.

I lifted the counter, stepped into the small office. My shoes clicked on the uncarpeted floor as I moved toward the cabinet. I reached for the keys.

"Mrs. Collins." Thelma Worrell hurried through the archway from the back room. She strode across the small space, stood so near I could see the glisten of her mascara, the deep indentations on either side of her mouth and the flicker of anger in her eyes. I realized once again how big and strong she was. "It is not our policy to have guests in this area. If you will step beyond the counter, I will be glad to assist you."

I didn't answer. Instead, I plucked the keys from the slots for rooms 32 and 34.

A bony hand gripped my wrist, hard and tight and painful.

We stood close together, two women, each of us determined to prevail.

"I shall call the police." Her voice was thin, but determined.

I closed my fingers tightly around the keys. "Let go of me." I stared into her eyes.

Slowly, her grip eased, her hand dropped away. She folded her lips together, continued to block my way. "I shall call the police."

"I don't think so." I put the keys in my pocket, met her angry gaze with calm. "You are going to move out of my way and you aren't going to call anyone."

"You can't walk in here, take keys to other

rooms." Her long fingers curled into tight balls. "This is private property." She whirled away, walked toward the desk, grabbed a telephone.

"Do you want the police to question you again about the night Roddy died?" I spoke to her back.

Her shoulders hunched. She leaned against the desk, slowly returned the receiver to its cradle.

"That's going to happen, you know." I stared at her angular body, motionless as a threatened crab. "Just because the police have arrested Lloyd Drake" — I knew arrest was coming even if at this point Lloyd was simply being questioned — "that won't end the investigation into George's murder. Who had a motive to kill George? Certainly not Lloyd." I was working it out in my mind as I spoke and I knew this was what puzzled me about the murder of Connor Bailey. In a reasonable world, whoever strangled Connor should have been the person who pushed George off the cliff. Otherwise, two different murderers had claimed victims within a matter of days. That didn't seem reasonable, but that definitely had to be the case if Lloyd was guilty. There was simply no way to link Lloyd to George. Of course, the world is often a jumbled, irrational swirl of chaos. There were other reasons to assume the deaths were separate and distinct. George died from a push. Connor was strangled. Repeat murderers have a well-known tendency to use the same method — firearms, knives, poison, blunt force, strangulation. The deaths of George Smith and Roddy Worrell were clearly similar. The death of Connor Bailey did not follow that pattern. Although Connor's murder apparently resulted from the turmoil created by Roddy's ghost, her death could not be considered sequential.

As I came to that realization, I understood just how difficult Lloyd's situation was. The police analysis — and my late-come understanding — of Connor's murder made all kinds of sense:

The wedding party arrived on the eve of the anniversary of the death of Roddy Worrell in a fall from the tower. Connor Bailey was reluctant to return to the site of Roddy's death. Her fiancé, Lloyd Drake, had insisted. Other members of the wedding party opposed the upcoming marriage. Someone hostile to the wedding hired George Smith to create Roddy's ghost. The ghost terrified Connor. Connor insisted upon returning home, regardless of the wedding. Lloyd was infuriated. The objective had been accomplished: the wedding was off. Last night either Connor and Lloyd quarreled and he killed her or, furious at the ruin of his plans, willing to see her dead rather than lose her, Lloyd woke Connor, gained access to her room, and killed her. I felt sure that these were the facts that seemed apparent to the police.

Everything depended upon the reason for Connor's murder. Why was Connor killed? The wedding was off. That had obviously been the plan behind the ghost. It certainly wasn't necessary to kill Connor to prevent the marriage.

Why did Connor die? And who killed George? That brought me back to this room, back to the woman who braced herself against an old wooden desk as if her body had no strength.

"You hated Connor." I walked slowly toward that defeated, weary figure. I moved past the desk, turned to face her. "You were jealous —"

"It was her fault." Her eyes were dull and empty, as if no matter how long she looked, she would never see. "If she hadn't chased after Roddy . . ."

"There were always women with Roddy, weren't there?" I knew that kind of man, the cocky bantam rooster strutting his masculinity, always seeking a conquest.

"I loved Roddy." It wasn't an answer. Or maybe it was the most complete answer of all. "If only . . ."

"If only you'd not been so angry that night." I spoke quietly. Her eyes closed, her sandy lashes light against her freckled skin.

"You went up to the tower." I could see the moonlit platform, Roddy sitting on the ledge, legs dangling on the outside. He must have heard the footsteps coming up the stone stairs. He was just a little drunk, maybe sliding toward the maudlin, singing something old-fashioned, one of the songs so popular with the guests, maybe "Smoke Gets in Your Eyes" or "Paper Doll," his husky voice soft as velvet. A cocky guy, used to wowing the ladies. "Did he think you were Connor, coming to say she was sorry? That's what happened, isn't it? He didn't even look around, did he?" He didn't need to. Let the woman come to him.

Thelma's eyes opened. But she wasn't looking at me. She was looking into a grave.

"He thought you were Connor. What did he say? Something sweet? Something crude?" Or was it worse than that? "Did he ask about his ticket to Atlanta, and you knew that this time he really was walking out?"

Her lined face drooped, the slack skin flaccid as a punctured balloon. She moved like a sleepwalker toward the counter, lifted the hinged section.

I followed, a hound on the heels of a wounded fox, pleasing to a dog, sickening to me. But if the fox had bloodied fangs . . . "Was it you George saw that night at the tower? You claimed he saw Connor. You made that up, didn't you?"

She opened the door to her office. "Get away from me." She was almost in command of herself, her voice once again cold and hard. "I don't have to talk to you." The door slammed in my face.

I turned on my heel and moved swiftly across the lobby and out onto the side terrace. I moved fast just in case Mrs. Worrell decided to call the police. It wouldn't take me long to do what I needed to do. My fingers tightened on the keys in my pocket.

When I stepped into the long shadowy hall of our floor, I was shaken by the utter quiet. But perhaps it was the very ordinariness of the hall which shocked me most. There was no trace here of drama. Investigators had walked here, carrying their paraphernalia — lights, cameras, sketchbooks, fingerprint powders. A pathologist had knelt beside Connor's body, examined the trauma, made observations and came to conclusions. I walked on tiled floors which might possibly, here or there, show a scuff. But that was all. The doors along the corridor were closed, as mute as the doors to anonymous hotel rooms around the world. This could be a hallway in Bangkok. This could be a hallway in Paris. There was nothing in this hallway to mark the murder of a woman.

I hesitated outside Neal's door, glanced from it to my own and on to Diana's. The doors were closed. It didn't matter which room they occupied. All that mattered was their search for help.

I walked on, then stopped, listened, every fiber of my being alert and wary.

The sound came again, a click and a rattle. I realized there was a break in that long series of closed panels. The door to Connor's room was open. There was no police tape, no sealing of the room. The investigation was done, the forensic team departed, the body removed.

I eased ahead as carefully as a cat burglar in the bedroom of a sleeping socialite, jewels casually tumbled on a nightstand.

The last ten feet I heard no sound, no movement. Why was the door to Connor's room open? I reached the doorway, looked into the room.

Steve Jennings was a big man, but he looked old and shrunken leaning against one of the sliding doors to the closet. His head rested on his crooked arm. In one hand dangled a red silk dress. His face burrowed into the soft folds.

I looked past him, at the suitcases ranged along the wall, the unmade bed, the half-open door to the bath.

They'd packed for Connor last night. But, of course, that would not include the things she would need for today. Now Steve was readying Connor's belongings for return to the United States. "Where was she lying, Steve?" It was a hard question. I made my voice gentle.

Steve jerked toward me, the dress crumpled in his big hand. He had finally completed shaving, but his face looked like old leather swollen by rain, baked by sun, puffy, a sickly shade of ocher. He studied me like a man spotting something particularly nasty, a bloated corpse, a bloodsucking leech, a crow picking at a carcass. "Goddamn ghoul. That's what you are." He pushed away from the closet door, blocked my view into the room. "I'll be goddamned if I'll satisfy your curiosity."

I didn't look at him. I looked at the red

dress, so enduringly feminine in his huge hand. "Was that what Connor was going to wear home today?"

A spasm of grief rippled over his face. He tried to speak, closed his eyes, once again buried his face in the crook of his arm.

"I'm sorry, Steve." And I was, desperately sorry. Life should never end this way. Never.

"Sorry." His voice was muffled. He tried to control his ragged breathing.

"Steve, you cared for Connor. You don't want to let the person who killed her get away with it, do you?" I forced myself to speak quietly, to be patient. I needed to get in that room. More than that, I needed this man's help.

His head jerked up. Eyes bright with tears glazed into hard, bright anger. "They've got him. They've taken Drake into Hamilton. I never liked him, prissy, humorless, selfish bastard. I tried to tell Connor. Oh God, if she'd only listened to me."

"You didn't want her to marry him." This was a man who could think and plan. He'd been here last year. He knew all about Roddy. He could have flown to Bermuda, met with George at the BUEI. Steve knew Connor Bailey better than perhaps any of the others. He'd known her for years, her insecurities and uncertainties. He could have foreseen the results of the ghostly visitations — vulnerable Connor frightened, unimaginative Lloyd dismissive. Had Steve hoped to be there to pick up the pieces? But once again I slammed into a dead end. He wanted Connor's love. Why would he want Connor dead? The only possible reason would be mismanagement of Connor's money. And then, to save himself, would he kill the woman he loved? He might still press the soft folds of her dress to his face, breathe in the scent that would never exist again.

He glared at me. "I knew he was wrong for Connor. But I never thought he would hurt her."

I met his gaze directly. "Lloyd says he didn't kill Connor."

Steve's look was contemptuous. "What else would he say?"

I smoothed back a strand of hair, taking an instant to fashion my answer. "I have known Lloyd for almost a quarter century, Steve. Yes, he is a far cry from macho, definitely humorless, serious. And yes, he has a temper and he can be selfish. The fact that he pressed for the wedding to be here is an example of that, but do you know, it is also an example of a sweet side of Lloyd, a romantic sensitive desire to wed the woman he loved where he first saw her." I could hear his voice — "Yes, it was love at first sight" — as he'd replied to my joking query. Serious, sensitive Lloyd.

I took a deep breath. "I won't tell you that I know Lloyd is innocent. I don't know that. I can see the facts. But I will tell you that the man I've known for twenty-five years would not strangle anyone and certainly not the woman he loved. And he did love Connor. Maybe they weren't well suited" — I waved my hand in dismissal — "but their love was genuine." I took a step toward Steve. "I want you to think for a moment, Steve, about this man, now at the police station in Hamilton, facing question after question after question, and I want you to believe that he is innocent. Just for an instant, imagine how he feels. He isn't young. He came to the most romantic island in the world to marry a woman he adored. They quarreled and he was jealous — jealous of you, jealous of the big Texan. His dreams crash into nothing — the wedding off, Connor turning to you for support. But there is worse to come, much worse. Connor is strangled and now he is at the police station, and they are accusing him. If he is innocent, he is torn by the anguish of loss and the helpless terror that he is going to be jailed for a crime he did not commit, would never have committed. And Steve, if you don't care about Lloyd, if in one way or another you still blame him for everything that happened, think about Connor. Do you want her murderer brought to justice?" I held his gaze. "No matter who it is?"

"That's where your pipe dream turns to nothing, Mrs. Collins." He leaned forward and now his eyes were thoughtful, calculating, intelligent. He was a lawyer looking at a problem. "Because who are you going to cast as your killer? Who the hell had any reason to kill Connor? Cops always look at family first. You've got Marlow and Jasmine. Marlow took care of her mother. Marlow loved her mother. They had no fight. Connor was proud of Marlow though she always laughed that she could have a daughter who never gave a thought to fashion. And Jasmine's just a kid. Aaron? He's a throwback to the old hippie days, you know: money's the root of all evil, green the earth, that kind of stuff. But Connor liked him. No problem there. Who does that leave? Me?" He didn't bother to make a denial. He simply shook his head. "I'm sorry, Mrs. Collins. I understand you want to help your grandkids, but the truth can't be changed."

"You've forgotten one name, Steve — the person who hated Connor." I left it at that, watched as his face changed.

"Oh." He rubbed his face. "Mrs. Worrell."

"So you will admit there is one possibility." I made it a statement, not a question. "And as long as there is even the most remote chance that Lloyd is innocent, I have to keep looking." I gazed straight into his intelligent, grieving eyes. "You can help me."

Steve looked down at the red dress, carefully folded it. He walked slowly toward the open suitcase on a luggage rack, gently placed the dress on the top. He closed the lid and, finally, faced me. "What do you want to know?" His face was grim, his voice remote.

"Where was Connor lying?" So much depended upon his answer.

He stood just past the hallway that ran between the door to the bathroom and the sliding doors to the closet. The luggage rack sat between the closet and a dresser. The bed was opposite the dresser. There was a generous amount of space on the far side of the bed, room enough to accommodate two easy chairs and the round table with two straight chairs. The connecting door to Lloyd's room was at the far end of the dresser. It was closed.

Steve's tired, swollen face turned toward the dresser. He swallowed jerkily and pointed. "There. She was lying on the floor between the dresser and the bed."

On the floor between the dresser and the bed. Not lying in bed or sitting in a chair. She must have been standing when she was attacked. But which direction had she faced? "Where was her head?"

He pointed again. "Her head was toward the balcony, her feet toward the hall door. Her face" — his voice wavered — "was pressed against the floor. When I opened the door" — he nodded toward the connecting door to Lloyd's room — "I saw the top of her head and the side of one cheek, all purple and bloated, and the thick white terry-cloth belt to one of those robes. It was crossed behind her neck."

Connor's killer came up behind her, looped the tie over her head, pulled it tight.

I moved past Steve and that's when I saw a twisted and crushed pair of wire-rim glasses poking out from beneath the dresser. "Are those Connor's glasses?"

"Yes. Usually she wore contacts. She was terribly nearsighted. But she didn't like glasses." He almost managed to smile. "She thought they made her look frumpy. She only wore the glasses when she wasn't using her contacts."

Now those glasses, crumpled by the force of her fall, poked from beneath the dresser. Obviously, the police had left everything in the room as they'd found it. Clearing up the room was the responsibility of the family.

Connor fell forward holding her glasses . . . I looked back toward the open door into the hallway and a picture formed in my mind. She had answered the door last night, admitted a visitor. She'd been awakened and she needed her glasses to see. She turned and started toward the dresser, picked up her glasses.

That's when the belt of the robe was looped over her head.

I pointed at the open doorway to the hall. "The murderer came through that door. Connor went to get her glasses. That must mean she'd just been awakened. Did she see so poorly she would have had her glasses on if she was awake?"

"Yeah. That's right." Steve rubbed his cheek, stared down at the glasses.

"The attack came from behind. If she was walking toward the dresser, it definitely indicates the murderer came in from the hall." I pointed at the connecting door to Lloyd's room. "But that's how the murderer left — after putting up the chain on the hall door."

Steve frowned, folded his arms across his front.

"Think about it, Steve." I gave the room one last swift glance. "Why would Lloyd knock on the hall door? That makes no sense."

I left Steve, face bent forward, chin on his chest, thinking.

I was damn glad there was something to think about. For the first time, I didn't simply have to hope that Lloyd was innocent. For the first time, I didn't have to say that violence was not characteristic of Lloyd. For the first time, there was a specific physical fact — Connor's crumpled glasses — that pointed toward Lloyd's innocence. Yes, the reasoning was based solely on the glasses and the orientation of her body, but that reasoning worked for me. I was certain that if the murderer came in from the hall, Lloyd was innocent.

Now, if only I could make that evidence work for Chief Inspector Foster.

I hurried up the hall, glancing at my watch. The day was dwindling down. A few minutes before six. I realized as I reached the door to the terrace that I was almost lightheaded from lack of food. But that could wait. And I didn't take time to check on the kids. I trusted them to get the job done. They might well have contacted a lawyer by this point and be on their way to Hamilton to meet him at the police station.

The setting sun had slipped behind the hills to the west. The water was nothing more than an impenetrable swath of darkness except for faraway lights that marked the slow passage of a freighter. Lampposts glowed at either end of the wall on the upper terrace. Tiny white lights spangled the occasional bay grape tree. I paused for a moment to let my eyes adjust to the darkness. I walked carefully on the flagstones, the light in the hotel grounds sufficient for a romantic evening, inadequate for serious illumination.

I was midway across the terrace, marshaling arguments in my mind, planning peripherally to resort once again to the candy machine in the short hallway for a meal substitute, when I saw the shadowy form sitting on the terrace wall. A face was turned toward me, a pale indistinguishable blob. There was movement and the sitter swung about, stood. "Mrs. Collins."

I was surprised. If I couldn't see in the darkness, how had the person sitting on the terrace wall recognized me? I realized that I had been clearly visible in the hall light when I opened the door to come outside.

After the initial greeting, Aaron simply stood by the wall, looking my way.

I walked toward him.

He lifted his hand, swung it toward the steps leading down to the parking lot. "I saw Neal and Diana. They left a few minutes ago on the mopeds." He cleared his throat. "I've been out here for a while. Marlow's got a migraine. She's really sick. I got her some medicine and an ice pack, but she just wants to be left alone. I don't blame her. Maybe she can get some sleep. I looked around for Steve but I didn't find him. I've just been sitting here. Diana and Neal were in a hurry." He paced back and forth, glanced out at the darkness of the ocean. "I thought Diana saw me, but she didn't say anything. I guess they don't want to talk to any of us." He sounded forlorn and tired. "I'm sorry, sorry about the whole thing. Their dad . . . God, it's tough, isn't it?"

Impulsively, I reached out, touched his arm. "Lloyd's innocent, Aaron. Please tell Marlow. I've found proof. I'm on my way to see the chief inspector."

"Proof!" He bent toward me. "Hey, really? What's up?"

I explained about the location of

Connor's body, turned away from the hall door, and the crushed glasses.

"Yeah." His tone was considering. "Well, yeah, maybe. It's something, I guess. But how about Lloyd came through the connecting door, they fussed around and he started for the hall door and . . ." His words trailed off.

I felt vindicated. There was hardly a reasonable way to place Lloyd on the hall side of Connor.

Aaron shoved a hand through his thick curls. "If it was someone who came in from the hall . . . But who would she let in?"

I didn't answer, but I didn't need to. Aaron stepped back from me, jammed his hands in the pockets of his trousers. "Oh, no. That can't be, Mrs. Collins."

"She opened the door to someone she trusted, Aaron." I felt his resistance. I understood. I refused to list that short, oh so short, tally of names. I held the picture of those crushed glasses in my mind like a talisman and flung my parting words at Aaron. "You can tell everyone. Lloyd is innocent."

But would anyone ever believe me?

twenty-two

The Central Division Police Station at 42 Parliament Street was a pale gray stone building. Blue iron bars added a somber note to blue-trimmed windows. I paid the taxi driver and walked up the sloping sidewalk to a worn wooden door. Two flags — the red flag of Bermuda with the Union Jack in the upper left corner and the Bermudian coat of arms in the lower right, and the blue police standard — hung on either side of a small blue awning at the entrance.

I opened the door and stepped into a small alcove with pale blue walls. The office was to the left, behind plate glass and a wooden counter. I walked to an opening in the plate glass.

The station officer, a middle-aged woman, looked up from her desk. "May I help you?"

"I must talk to Chief Inspector Foster." I spoke courteously, but firmly. If I was turned down, sent away . . . "Please tell him that Mrs. Collins wishes to see him and that I have important information about the murder of Mrs. Connor Bailey." Would that be enough to win me an audience? Truth to tell, this was not new information for Foster. I must persuade him to think about Connor's twisted glasses and what they told us.

Her dark face betrayed no curiosity, though her eyes studied me for perhaps an instant longer than usual. "Yes, ma'am." She lifted her telephone receiver, punched an extension. "Chief Inspector, a Mrs. Collins is here to speak to you in regard to the Bailey investigation."

I braced myself against the counter, fighting off a wave of dizziness. Although I'd retrieved another Baby Ruth from the coin machine in the short hallway while waiting for the taxi, I'd not yet eaten it.

"Yes, sir. I will tell her." She replaced the receiver and looked at me in concern. "Are you all right, ma'am?"

"Yes, thank you. Just a little tired." I pushed away from the counter, managed a smile.

She looked at me doubtfully. "The CID section is on the third floor. You will have to climb the stairs."

I was past the first hurdle. I would have climbed ten flights of stairs to reach the chief inspector. "That's fine."

She gestured toward a door opposite the

entrance. "Press the buzzer and it will open."

I was still a little dizzy, but I walked without faltering, pressed the button, heard the buzz. In a moment, I turned the knob. As the door closed behind me and I started up the worn wooden stairs, I opened my purse, pulled out the candy bar, unwrapped it. Every bite was elixir. I stopped at each landing to rest. The air was stale and musty in the enclosed stairwell. It was eerily quiet and I found the eggshell-blue walls dingy and cheerless. I finished the snack as I reached the glass door to the third floor. I pressed another buzzer.

A young man with protuberant blue eyes and scant brown hair opened the door, stood aside. I looked over a work area of cubicles with desks and computers. The screens glowed sea-green. Only two cubicles were occupied, but it was seven o'clock on a Saturday night.

"Chief Inspector Foster?" My voice sounded overly loud in the almost deserted room.

The young detective gestured to a corridor. "The chief inspector's office is the fourth door on the left."

"Thank you." As I moved briskly, thanks to the infusion of sugar, up the corridor, I realized my left hand, tucked in my sweater pocket, was tightly gripping the keys to rooms 32 and 34 at Tower Ridge House. I doubted Chief Inspector Foster would approve. I unclenched my fingers, pulled my hand free. At the fourth door, I knocked firmly.

The door swung open. "Come in, Mrs. Collins." Although his voice was as polite as usual, Foster looked weary, the muscles in his face a little slack, his eyes somber, his dark navy suit wrinkled.

The square office was plain vanilla, with several metal filing cabinets along one wall, a rank of bookcases behind the gray metal desk, shuttered windows, a bare floor. There was one surprising, refreshing burst of color, a Cézanne poster blazing with orange, yellow and red. The legend at the bottom informed: CHICAGO ART INSTITUTE. Foster's worn green leather chair creaked as he sat down. On his desk was a paperweight of a mountain scene, several folders, and a double picture frame with studio photographs of a smiling, confident woman and a fresh-faced, eager teenage girl.

Two wooden straight chairs faced the desk. I settled in the near chair, scooted it closer to the desk. "Thank you for seeing me, Chief Inspector. Is Lloyd Drake under arrest?"

Foster's voice was brisk, but his eyes were troubled. "Mr. Drake is being held on suspicion of a felony. He has been read his rights and has been given access to a lawyer. He and his lawyer are presently conferring."

If Diana and Neal had been here, I would have given them a thumbs-up.

Almost as if he'd read my mind, Foster's tired face softened with a brief smile. "Mr. Drake's children arrived here with the lawyer. They left a few minutes ago to return to the hotel. I understand the lawyer will meet with them there later this evening. Now" — he rested his arms on his desk — "you wished to see me. You have some information?"

"If you don't mind, Chief Inspector, I have a question. I saw Connor's room." He shot me a sharp look but didn't interrupt. After all, the police investigation there had been completed. "It appears that she was walking toward her dresser and reached for her glasses when she was attacked. This morning you said that Connor did not resist her murderer. This suggests to me that she was attacked without warning. Is this true? Was she attacked from behind?"

He picked up a pen, tapped it softly on the

metal desk, an erratic beat. "That appears to be the case."

"Was the belt from the bathrobe looped over her head, drawn tight?" I pictured Connor, sleepy, nearsighted, hand outstretched to pluck her glasses from the dresser. She could not have been angry or fearful. She was reaching for her glasses . . .

The tiny clicking sound continued as the pen struck the desktop. Foster was silent for one moment, another.

I sat on the edge of my chair. There was some fact here that worried him.

Finally, he pointed at a closed folder. "The preliminary examination by the pathologist" — he tapped the folder — "revealed that Mrs. Bailey had a large bruise in the middle of her back."

I understood. Connor opened the hall door. The visitor entered. Connor turned to find her glasses. The attacker moved fast, throwing the garrote over her head, driving a knee into her back. Quick, efficient, ruthless, brutal.

I stared into Foster's intelligent eyes, alive with imagination and reason. "Chief Inspector, do you honestly believe Lloyd Drake killed Connor that way? That was no crime of passion. That was an execution." Now I knew why Foster was troubled.

Foster understood the significance of Connor's body lying with her head toward the balcony. Obviously, the murderer stood between the hall door and the dresser, not between the connecting door and the dresser. There was no reason why Lloyd should have knocked on the hall door. Moreover, nothing in Lloyd Drake's character or manner would suggest a planned crime of this nature. Yes, it was reasonable to believe that Lloyd might strangle Connor in the midst of a violent quarrel. But I did not believe — would never believe — that Lloyd planned in advance to kill Connor. It seemed equally obvious that Connor's murder was the result of a careful, well-thought-out plan . . .

I reached out, gripped the edges of the chief inspector's desk. The coolness of the metal seemed in odd contrast to the hot torrent of thought in my mind.

A careful, well-thought-out plan . . .

I almost caroled my question. "Chief Inspector, why is Lloyd a suspect?"

"I beg your pardon, Mrs. Collins." Foster blinked. He looked both disconcerted and irritated, a tired man dealing with irrationality.

I had the answer for him, the answer that I was certain would lead us to a clever and cruel murderer. "Lloyd is a suspect because it was planned from the very first moment that Lloyd should be arrested for Connor's murder. Lloyd is a suspect," I spoke slowly, "because he quarreled with Connor and the wedding was canceled. It is essential to understand why that quarrel occurred." I ticked off the reasons, one by one: "Lloyd quarreled with Connor because she believed the message in stage blood was written by the ghost of Roddy Worrell. She believed Roddy's ghost had returned because of the apparitions near the tower. This is the critical point, Chief Inspector: the ghost appeared at the tower specifically to frighten Connor. I am as sure of that as I've ever been of anything. When I talked to you after that message was found, I thought someone had mounted a campaign to derail the wedding. But it was more than that, much more, Chief Inspector. The point of the ghost was to frighten Connor. Anyone who knew the circumstances of Roddy's death the year before could be reasonably certain Connor would panic and insist upon returning home, wedding be damned. That, as expected, led to a quarrel between Connor and Lloyd. But the ultimate point of the plan was not to derail the wedding, it was to kill Connor and see Lloyd blamed for the crime. As for the physical evidence against Lloyd, that was easy." I pulled out the keys to rooms 32 and 34, jangled them. "It's quite simple to slip behind the desk and get room keys from the pigeonhole cabinet. Yes, this was part of a meticulously planned crime, Chief Inspector. That's why George Smith was pushed off the cliff. George knew the identity of the person who hired him to create the ghost. George had to die so that he could never expose that person. Connor's murder — and George's, too — were planned long before the wedding party ever came to Bermuda. Someone met with George at the BUEI on January sixth to make the arrangements for Roddy's appearances. That person, Chief Inspector, strangled Connor last night." I was so confident. "Have you checked with Immigration?"

The answer was so near. All it would take was one quick phone call . . .

I was puzzled by the expression on Foster's face, a mixture of pity and sadness.

"I checked, Mrs. Collins." His slim hand reached out, touched a blue folder.

For an instant, I simply didn't understand. "Yes?"

He spoke without inflection. "On January sixth none of the following persons entered

Bermuda: Connor Bailey, Marlow Bailey, Aaron Reed, Steven Jennings, Lloyd Drake, Diana Drake, Neal Drake, Henrietta Collins."

He had checked, looking beyond even my suspicions. I'd limited the list to those who were present on the island when Roddy Worrell died. But the chief inspector wasn't missing any possibilities. "You are sure . . ." My voice trailed away. There could be no question of a mistake. Every person entering Bermuda shows a passport and fills out an immigration form. My voice was almost a whisper. "But, Chief Inspector . . ."

"I'm sorry, Mrs. Collins." He pushed back his chair, rose.

Slowly, I stood. I was bewildered. I'd been so certain. This was the only theory that explained the deaths of both George Smith and Connor Bailey. But if no one on my list or the chief inspector's list had been in Bermuda on January 6, I had to be wrong.

I walked toward the door slowly, wearily, all my energy and hope gone. I gripped the knob, looked back at Foster. "There is no reason why Lloyd would knock on Connor's hall door."

He was tidying his stack of folders, clicking off the desk lamp. His evening's work was done. He came around the desk, held the door for me. "There are always inconsistencies, Mrs. Collins. I have to go by facts. We've sent the belt of the robe used to strangle Mrs. Bailey to the RCMP lab in Canada. The belt to one of the robes in Mr. Drake's room is missing. If the lab matches the belt we sent to Drake's DNA" — he clicked off the wall switch and the office was plunged into darkness. He didn't finish his sentence. He didn't have to finish. "Good night, Mrs. Collins." The chief inspector gave me a weary nod, turned away. I walked back the way I'd come. I was almost to the big open room when I stopped and called out, "Chief Inspector!"

He paused at the far end of the hall.

"Mrs. Worrell is a big woman." If no one in the wedding party had been in Bermuda on January 6, certainly Mrs. Worrell had very likely been present. That could be confirmed. Thelma Worrell hated Connor Bailey and Thelma Worrell had access to every room in the hotel. Getting the tie to Lloyd's robe would have been so easy for her.

"Good night, Mrs. Collins."

I walked up the hill to Reid Street, turned left, hurried past the closed stores, turned down Burnaby Street to the Hog Penny. I had to have food and I was in no hurry to return to the hotel. Diana and Neal would be eager to talk to me, to tell me about the lawyer, and they would look to me for hope. Right now I had no hope to give to them.

I was still confident of their father's innocence, but I had no idea how we could save him from a murder charge and conviction.

The hostess seated me at a dark wooden table along the north wall. The Hog Penny hadn't changed in the years since I'd last been there: white-painted ceiling, exposed beams, brick walls with dark wood half-paneling, red carpet with black-and-gray squares. The menu was the same, lots of pub favorites such as bangers and mash and fish and chips. As an unreconstructed and very tired American, I ordered a hamburger with fries. The food was hot and good, the chunky fries a salty delight.

I looked at the hard facts:

Connor would not have opened her door to a stranger.

Connor was not afraid of the visitor whom she admitted.

Connor turned her back on that person and walked to the dresser.

Connor was garroted with the belt to Lloyd's robe.

Either Lloyd yanked the belt off in anger

404

and murdered Connor or someone had stolen the belt from Lloyd's room.

If the latter was true, the crime was planned in advance.

If the murder was planned far in advance, that explained the apparent lack of motive on the part of the others in the wedding group. A murderer knowing a crime would occur would be careful indeed to appear on good terms with Connor.

Indications of prior planning:

George's meeting at the BUEI on January 6.
The appearance of Roddy's ghost.
The possession of stage blood and the message on Connor's table.

Then, as earlier, I smashed hard against the unalterable fact that no one in the wedding party had passed through Bermuda Immigration on January 6.

That brought me full circle to Mrs. Worrell.

I took my last sip of coffee, paid my check. By the time I hailed a taxi on Front Street to return to the hotel, I had the beginnings of a plan.

"Finished, Dinny?" Neal stared at Diana's plate, only a bite or two gone from the club sandwich, the beet salad untouched.

Diana flung down her napkin, jumped up. "I can't eat." She paced up and down beside the table. "Grandma, I know you mean well but she'll just laugh at you."

I pressed my fingers against my temple. Despite the food at the Hog Penny, I was terribly tired. I'd pushed myself close to exhaustion. But Lloyd was in jail and time was running out. Tonight was the moment to act.

Neal slipped the cover atop Diana's plate, picked up the dishes from the table and placed them on the room service tray. "Let me put this stuff out in the hall."

I waited until he returned. "It's worth a try."

Neal nodded, his young face pale and tired.

I spoke to Diana's back. She stood at the balcony door, staring out into the night, fingers twisting a strand of her red-gold hair.

"Look at it this way. There is simply no other explanation. Either your father's guilty" — the silence in Diana's room was as heavy and cold as sodden snow — "or Mrs. Worrell killed Connor." I'd told them everything I knew and I needed their help.

Neal rubbed his nose. "Okay, we'll give it a try. You want to wait until midnight, go down to her cottage, wake her up —"

I would bully myself inside, no matter what it took. I was sure I could do it. "She'll let me in when I tell her I have a note from George and he describes seeing her follow Roddy up the tower steps —"

"Wait a minute." Diana waved her hand toward us. She bent forward. "Something's going on out there." She slid open the balcony door, stepped outside.

With the door open, there came the sound of faint shouts, running footsteps.

In four quick strides, Neal was across the room and out on the balcony. "Hey, those must be flashlights!"

"What do you suppose is going on?" Diana and Neal stood at the railing.

I came up behind them. Neal was right, the swoop and dance of lights had to be the beams of flashlights, several in the gardens, at least two others glinting like faraway fireflies among the tangle of shrubs and trees near the rugged shore. I leaned forward, listened. "They are calling for Jasmine!"

"I've rung nine-one-one." Mrs. Worrell's bony fingers clutched the carnelian beads at her throat. "Surely one of the boys will find her. They know the grounds . . ." Her voice trailed away. She stood by the front desk, her tired face creased with worry.

Marlow sagged in one of the green tapestry oversize chairs near the center table. "Oh God, oh God, oh God." She looked desperately ill, her eyes glazed with pain, her face bleached white. She tried to get up, wavered, fell back. "I'm so sick. My head . . . I've got to look for Jasmine."

Aaron thudded down the stairs from the second floor. He carried a small towel bunched in his hands. "I've got some ice here. Hold it to your head, Marlow. Listen, you've got to rest. We'll look for Jasmine. Maybe she fell asleep down on the beach. Don't worry. We'll find her. You come back upstairs."

I remembered then that Marlow had a migraine, the devastating headache that makes thought and action impossible.

Steve came through the front door carrying an armful of flashlights. He nodded toward Mrs. Worrell. "I found these in the storeroom off the drive like you said." He looked at Diana and Neal and me. "Can you help? The staff's out looking."

I took a big plastic flash. "How long has she been missing?" It could not be as simple as Aaron suggested. This was January and the nighttime temperature often fell to the mid-fifties. With the darkness and the onshore breeze, it would be far too cold to sleep on the beach even if Jasmine had worn a sweater.

Hands outstretched, Neal and Diana hurried toward Steve. They each took a flashlight, headed for the terrace. "Dinny, be careful on the cliffs." Neal was the younger sibling, but he had the protective instinct of all good brothers. "Sometimes the ground's soft at the edges . . ."

Marlow touched the tips of her fingers against her temples.

Steve, his face grim, was almost to the terrace door. "Nobody's quite sure how long she's been gone. She went out this afternoon late —"

I remembered now — Aaron and Marlow moving their belongings into the main hotel and Jasmine darting out the French windows. She'd had her backpack with her, so surely she did have a jacket, perhaps even some crackers or cookies.

"— and nobody's seen her since."

Marlow shuddered. "I should have gone after her."

If Marlow lost both her mother and her sister . . . The thought slid through my mind as cold and dark as an eel easing along the ocean floor. Her mother and her sister. I moved slowly after the others. By the time I reached the wall at the end of the terrace, the others were far ahead, the bobbing lights marking their progress.

I thought Aaron's shout came from near the top of the sloping green tunnel that led down to the sea. His voice was loud enough to carry over the ever-present roar of the ocean and the rattle of the palm fronds in the onshore breeze. He called out, "I'll check the caves on the headland. Diana, there's a picnic grove that branches off from the walk down to the beach. Neal, you go to that natural pool . . ." Aaron's voice faded. He must already be running down the leafy passageway toward the beach.

I shivered in the sharpening breeze and buttoned my sweater as I walked. The lights on the garden paths blazed, but they made little impress on the heavy shadows, the swaths of light surrounded by impenetrable splotches of darkness. Yes, the tower loomed white on its high ridge, but most of the garden was hidden, the shrubbery and trees mysterious and sinister shapes. Cloud cover hid the moon and stars. Somewhere out there a little girl was hidden or lost. Or dead.

I was swept by an atavistic awareness of evil, like a dimly seen but hideously realized specter in a nightmare — slimy poison-tipped tentacles quivering, seeking, ready to destroy. I breathed deeply, trying to force the image from my mind. I was overtired. This was no time to be frightened. Yes, we'd been surrounded by evil these past few days, but tonight was nothing more than a search for a girl distraught by her mother's death. That was all that had happened. Jasmine had run away from sorrow she couldn't bear. And she'd fought against the idea that Lloyd was involved. She'd been terribly angry with Marlow and Aaron and Steve. She'd left the hotel behind. My head jerked up. What was it Jasmine had told me? She loved the magnolia tree. Perhaps she was there, hunkered between a big branch and the trunk, listening to the crash of the waves below and hearing the frantic calls. Would Jasmine box her ears with her hands and be very quiet, afraid she was in trouble?

It was going to be all right. I realized that I'd said the last words aloud to myself . . . *all right.* I blinked against tears. Damnit, Jasmine with her curly blond hair and pug nose and saucy smile was not at risk.

Still, I had that sense of sickening evil.

Her mother and her sister. That phrase lodged in my mind. Oh God, no one would want to hurt a little girl.

I reached the stairs to the lower terrace, looked down at the pool area, barely glimpsed the figure of a young man in a white polo shirt and chino slacks and then he was gone, lost in the darkness by the arbor. "Neal?" But I realized as I called that, of course, I'd not seen Neal. He was down at the beach by now, his flashlight beam poking into the dark crannies of rock, sweeping along the pale pink sand. One young man was so like another that it was easy, even for a grandmother, to make a mistake.

I was halfway down the stairs when I stopped. All the thoughts and feelings, the little pieces of knowledge and the presence of evil swirled and coalesced. I thought of the planning to create a perfect murder, perfect in that the murderer was never to be a suspect, in that another man was cleverly placed in utter peril. I thought of the meeting with George at the BUEI, the appearances of Roddy's ghost, George's murder, the destruction of the Sports closet, the vial of stage blood brought from the United States and used to write the message that terrified Connor, the theft of the belt from Lloyd's robe, the knock on Connor's door and the message — *Jasmine's sick, can you come?* Or perhaps *Marlow sent me. She needs help* — something on that order, the entry into Connor's room, her turn to get her glasses, the swift and brutal garrote, the chaining of the hall door, the unlocking of the connecting door to Lloyd's room and a stealthy exit. And I thought of the sense of evil and the knowledge that it would be to only one person's advantage for Jasmine to die. If Jasmine was dead, all of Connor's fortune would belong to Marlow, every last penny of it.

But the planning had started long before Connor's murder. I turned and hurried up the steps, ran across the terrace, burst into the drawing room. Mrs. Worrell pressed her hand against her chest. Marlow lifted her head, struggled to her feet. "Oh my God, what —"

"There's no time. Marlow, tell me. When you met Aaron, you said he'd taken his friend's place to come here during spring break." I looked into dazed, pain-filled eyes, willed her to answer, now, now, now.

"Aaron." Her voice was dull. "I don't know . . ."

I gripped her arm, my fingers gouging. "Tell me. You must. Did he use his friend's passport?"

"Passport?" Her voice was thick, either from the exploding pulses of agony in her skull or from drugs for the headache. Marlow squeezed her eyes almost shut, struggling against the pain, against my question. "That's a secret. Aaron said we'd never tell anyone. Paul might get in trouble."

Paul. Paul's passport. Did Paul and Aaron look alike? Enough so, I was sure, that there'd been no question at Immigration. The chief inspector could discover Paul's last name. And I knew Paul's passport carried an entry-date stamp for January 6.

Paul didn't matter now. Even Aaron didn't matter now. All that mattered was Jasmine. I swung away from Marlow, ran to Mrs. Worrell. "Tell the chief inspector when he comes. The big magnolia tree by the cliff. That's where Jasmine must be. We've got to get to her before Aaron does."

twenty three

I was breathing hard by the time I reached the garden. The lights in the trees illuminated the flagstone path that curved in a lazy, summery meander among the cultivated beds. The blooms, mostly pansies and poinsettias in January, were invisible in the darkness. I almost struck out across the dark grounds, ignoring the walk, the quicker to reach the far end of the garden where the huge magnolia loomed at the cliff's edge. I had a flashlight, but I didn't want to use it. I wanted to come up quietly in the darkness, just in case. I took some comfort in the fact that Aaron had led the sally toward the beach. But as I remembered his shouted directions, I realized that in only a moment more, he and Diana and Neal would have gone their separate ways — Diana to the picnic area, Neal up the beach to the natural pool in a small cove, and Aaron to the caves.

I was midway through the gardens now. I saw the occasional dart of a flashlight, heard shouts over the boom of the surf.

"Jasmine . . . Jasmine . . . Jasmine . . ."

These would be legitimate searchers,

moving openly and loudly.

If Aaron was coming to the magnolia tree, he would slip silently through the darkness, carrying death in his heart. My only hope was that Aaron didn't know of Jasmine's passion for the magnolia tree. But Aaron had made it a point to charm Jasmine, to play with her, to pay attention to her. I was terribly, desperately, sickeningly certain he knew about the magnolia tree. And, if he knew, he'd kept quiet about that knowledge. There would be only one reason not to tell everyone — not to lead the searchers to the tree. If he killed Connor to keep her from marrying Lloyd and funneling away part of the Bailey fortune, he would kill Jasmine to secure even greater money for the woman he intended to marry. And when would he ever have an easier opportunity than now? It would seem such a tragedy, Marlow's little sister, distraught over their mother's death, flinging herself out of the hotel, running to sanctuary in a big tree, but a tree with limbs that hung over the edge of the cliff, and far below were the sharp and deadly rocks and the water. A terribly sad accident and Marlow left all alone, with only Aaron to comfort and care for her.

Aaron had professed to spurn the life of the wealthy — big homes, fine cars, expensive clothes, elegant resorts. So why did he first come to Bermuda? It was the playground — had always been the playground — of the very wealthy. Only well-heeled college students chose Bermuda for their spring break. Aaron claimed to love the simple, the homespun, but his clothes were expensive.

Ostensibly, Aaron's spring break in Bermuda was happenstance, a free ticket not to be used by his roommate and the decision not to waste it. I rather doubted any of it was happenstance. The Aaron we all thought we knew, carefree, smiling, easygoing, charming, was a mask, and behind that mask lay cunning and greed and evil. Aaron had planned far in advance, and I was sure he'd planned his meeting with Marlow. I suspected he already knew a great deal about Marlow before they met on the beach in Bermuda over spring break. Marlow was serious, unpretentious, rather dowdy, and very rich. Who would appeal to that kind of young woman more than an impecunious graduate student uninterested in wealth?

I moved past the last batch of lighted trees. The shouts were far away now. I walked softly. There were no flagstones here. The ground was humpy and I stepped carefully. I wouldn't use my flashlight until I reached the magnolia. I could see the dark mass of the tree against the velvet of the sky. The steady rumble of the surf masked the sound of my steps. I stopped twice, sensing movement somewhere near. I peered into the darkness, straining to see. The tree was now so near it seemed to fill the horizon. The onshore breeze rattled the huge glossy leaves.

"Jasmine?" The call was soft as the distant cry of a mourning dove. "It's Aaron. Hey, I've got a sandwich for you."

A branch creaked. Magnolia leaves rustled like the slap of bare feet on a boardwalk.

I shouted, "Jasmine, don't answer! Don't say anything." I flicked on the flashlight, swung it back and forth, stopped the beam at the base of the huge tree, held it on a crouching figure. Aaron flung up his hand to shield his eyes in a face suddenly distorted by rage.

I clicked off the light, moved sideways, stumbled. Even as I fell, I was scrambling to get up. But Aaron had a flashlight, too, and now I was pinned in its glare, the hard white beam dazzling my eyes. I heard the thud of his feet and knew he was hurtling toward me; my knee flamed in agony.

I rolled over onto my elbow, screamed, "Jasmine, get down, run, get to the hotel.

Aaron killed your mom. Run —"

The yelp of pain and crash of bodies was so near.

"I got him, Grandma, I got —"

I turned on my light. Neal and Aaron were a writhing mass of arms and legs. Grunts of effort, hoarse and desperate, came from their throats.

Oh, Neal, Neal . . . I tried to get up, sank back, knew I had to help. My knee throbbed. I pulled myself across the ground toward Neal and Aaron.

Jasmine called for Marlow, her voice high and frightened. "Marlow, come, please, please . . ." She ran past me and I knew she was on her way to safety. There were other calls now, too, loud shouts, coming nearer and nearer.

Aaron was on top of Neal. He lifted his flashlight, the beam slicing crazily through the night sky. ". . . kill you, you . . ."

Neal heaved, tossing Aaron to the side. Aaron rolled away, came to his feet in a crouch. Neal scrambled up, took two steps, tackled Aaron and they thudded heavily to the ground just as Chief Inspector Foster arrived. Foster pulled them apart.

Aaron blinked in the brightness of Foster's flashlight. He lunged away but police officers swarmed around him. They pinned

Aaron's arms behind him, hustled him away.

I had a last glimpse of Aaron's face, suffused with rage, eyes glittering, mouth twisted. How had I ever thought him handsome?

Neal, breathing heavily, blood staining one cheek, his left arm crooked in pain, knelt beside me.

"Neal . . ." I'd wrenched my knee in my fall and I knew I'd need help getting up. But I would never have gotten up if Neal had not come. I looked at him in wonder. "If you hadn't come . . ." One old life would have ended and one so very young.

Neal swiped at the blood dripping from the cut beneath his eye. His words came in bursts as he drew breath into strained lungs. "I was coming back up the beach . . . I saw Aaron. He didn't have his flashlight on." Another gulp of air. "He was supposed to be checking the caves. I knew he couldn't even have got to them yet. And there he was at the top of the concrete walk . . . looking around like he didn't want anybody to see him. That seemed damn strange to me, so I followed him."

And saved two lives.

twenty four

Rain slatted against the huge panes on the second floor of the airport terminal, obscuring the faraway line of palms, turning the day a misty green. Our flight was scheduled to leave in a little less than an hour. I was uncertain what I should do. No one wants to confront anguish. Most of us will walk an extra mile to avoid sadness and despair. Yet, I felt I had to speak. I know enough about sorrow and guilt to understand that even a hapless effort is better than none and I wanted desperately to ease the agony devouring Lloyd and Marlow. I glanced at the clock. The minute hand moved forward. Now. Or never.

Our group was no longer divided, though on this misty day everyone seemed separate and alone in a far reach of the waiting area. Marlow and Jasmine sat together, Marlow holding her little sister's hand. Marlow's face might have been sculpted from marble, pale and heavy. Dark sunglasses emphasized the ice-white of her face. I knew she was hiding the tortured red of eyes that had cried until there were no more tears.

Jasmine clutched her bear. His blue turtleneck matched hers. Jasmine's hair was neatly brushed and she wore a blue ribbon. I knew Marlow had gone to that extra effort. Jasmine would be well cared for. Steve Jennings held up the *Wall Street Journal*. I noticed that he wasn't moving the pages. Diana and Neal sat on either side of their father. Diana smoothed back her red-gold hair with a trembling hand. She bent forward, spoke. Lloyd stared at her dully, then shook his head. His ruddy face looked old and crumpled. Neal shoved a hand through his short dark hair and shot a worried look at his sister. The bandage beneath his eye hid the jagged cut from his fight with Aaron.

The click of my cane — yes, the knee was going to be a bit of a problem for a while — seemed overloud in our quiet corner of the terminal. I stopped in front of Lloyd. He didn't look up.

"Lloyd, I'd appreciate a word with you." I spoke loudly enough that Steve Jennings lowered his newspaper to look at me curiously.

Lloyd lifted eyes that took a moment to focus. He rubbed his temple. "Henrie . . ." It was not an answer. It was scarcely a recognition of my presence.

"If you'll come this way." I spoke with kind firmness.

Lloyd blinked.

I was Emily's mother, the grandmother of his children. Lloyd was, always, a man of courtesy.

It took a moment for him to gather himself, to stand, and then we were walking slowly away, my cane clicking on the hard floor. He moved heavily, like an old, old man. We walked to the end of the corridor and stood in a window that looked out on the rain-washed runways.

He stared at me. "Sorry you got hurt." For an instant, there was a flash of light in his eyes. "Neal's a good boy. Brave."

"Yes. Thanks to Neal, Jasmine and I are here today."

Those were the wrong words. Lloyd's face sagged. Connor was not here, would never be with us again. But maybe they were the right words for what I had to say.

"Lloyd, Connor's dead —"

He tried to turn away.

I grabbed his arm, held tight. "It wasn't your fault. None of it was your fault. You —"

He hunched forward, anguish clogging the words in his throat. "If we hadn't come here — she didn't want to come back. I made her come and that's —"

"Lloyd." I kept my voice low, but my tone was harsh enough to capture him. "Listen to me. Connor would have died if the wedding had been in Atlanta. Or Dallas. Or Bangkok. Connor would have died," and I spaced these words like the blow of an ax against a tree trunk, "if there had never been a wedding. Once Aaron looked at all the money, once he thought about how much there would be if everything belonged to Marlow, Connor was facing sure death, one day or another, one place or another. Bermuda had nothing to do with her murder. And you had nothing to do with it."

For a moment I thought he hadn't listened, wouldn't understand, couldn't accept release. He stared at me, his green eyes dazed. And wondering. "Anywhere," he whispered.

"Anywhere, Lloyd, anywhere. Connor was the victim, but so were you and Marlow and Jasmine and all of us."

Lloyd hunched his head forward, jammed his hands into his pockets. "Anywhere . . ." He turned and walked away, head down, toward the window, stood there unmoving. I knew he was not seeing the runways.

I watched him for a moment. I knew he had heard. Now, if only his mind and heart had listened. I took a deep breath and walked slowly back to the others.

My knee hurt, but I glanced at the clock and moved a little faster. This was going to be harder, much harder. When I stopped in front of Marlow, Jasmine looked up. "Hi, Mrs. Collins."

Marlow's face lifted, that white, stony face with the eyes hidden behind dark glasses.

I reached out my hand. "Marlow, please come and walk with me for a moment. I need your help."

She wanted to refuse. Refusal was there in the bleak jut of her jaw, the wooden heaviness of her body. Her hand tightened on Jasmine's.

"Jasmine . . ." she whispered.

"Jasmine's fine." I gestured toward Steve Jennings, the paper once again held low. "Steve, you'll come sit with Jasmine, won't you?"

The big man pushed up from his chair. His lined, weary face softened as he looked at the little girl. "Sure. Jasmine and I can plan our next trip to Disney World. As soon as school's out . . ."

His deep voice rumbled and Jasmine's high tone rose excitedly.

"About last night . . ." I looked determinedly at Marlow. She had to respond. If it were not for me and for Neal . . .

Marlow glanced at Jasmine, put a finger to her lips. She was on her feet.

I took her arm and turned us away from the others.

"I don't want to go far. I don't know when I'll ever feel that I can leave Jasmine." Her hands came together in a tight grip. "She could have died. She would have died. And it's all my —"

"No." We were at the far end of the waiting room, no one seated for row upon row of chairs. "Her danger was not your fault. Your mother's murder was not your fault. You were fooled, Marlow, deceived by a smiling young man with a handsome face and an evil heart. Right now you are desperately un-happy. You blame yourself. And if you are not careful, you will shut out the goodness in the world because you have been touched by evil. Marlow, I want to tell you about another young woman, many years ago, Henrietta O'Dwyer was her name . . ."

I talked to Marlow about my past, about the first man I loved and the mistakes I made. I told her things I've never revealed to anyone. I told her about the wrong man, who took advantage of me once again only a few years ago, and I told her about the right man who was good and honorable, the man I married.

"But how can you know?" It was a faint, stricken cry. "Aaron was so handsome. And he said he loved me. But I wondered sometimes. Mother liked him so much. And Jasmine. And yet sometimes, when we were alone, he'd be bitter about people who had money, and then I felt like I didn't know him at all. If only I'd walked away from him. If only . . ."

"Don't look back. You can't change yesterday. But tomorrow can shine. And you will know someday, Marlow. Look for goodness." I smiled at her. "You will find it."

She reached out, took my hands, drew me close, and kissed my cheek.

The loudspeaker sounded raucous and insistent, calling our flight.